THE 107TH STREET MURDER

L. D. BARNES

THE 107TH STREET MURDER

L. D. BARNES

Novel Barn Press

Chicago

The 107th Street Murder is a work wholly of the author's imagination. Any resemblance to actual persons living or dead is purely coincidental.

Published by Novel Barn Press

For information, contact:

www.novelbarnpress.com

Manufactured in the United States of America

Interior Design by: Emma Primavera

Cover Design by: Liz Demeter/Demeter Design

Publisher's Cataloging-In-Publication Data
(Prepared by The Donohue Group, Inc.)

Names: Barnes, L. D., 1953- author.
Title: The 107th Street murder / L.D. Barnes.
Other Titles: One Hundred Seventh Street murder | One Hundred And Seventh Street murder
Description: Chicago, IL : Novel Barn Press, [2018]
Identifiers: ISBN 9781732534803
Subjects: LCSH: Murder--Investigation--Illinois--Chicago--Fiction. | German American women--Illinois--Chicago--Fiction. | African American detectives--Illinois--Chicago--Fiction. | Chicago (Ill.)--Ethnic relations--20th century--Fiction. | LCGFT: Detective and mystery fiction.
Classification: LCC PS3602.A775639 A12 2018 | DDC 813/.6--dc23

ISBN: 978-1-7325348-0-3

Dedication

To my husband, retired Chicago Police Officer Frank R. Barnes, whose thirty-four years on the job provided me with the luxury of writing the perspective of a female cop without being one.

To Grace Kuikman and Mark Boone, my editors, who cheerfully strolled through my manuscript and helped me mature it into this novel.

To Chris, Martha, Cher, Linda, Nancy Gwen and the members of FLOW (For Love of Writing) who have listened to the bits and pieces and waited for the whole thing.

To Scott Smith and the Beverly Arts Alliance for The Frunchroom, the opportunity to read a chapter and then podcast it at https://thefrunch-room.com/2018/04/15/podcast-volume-8-write-your-way-out-edition-plus-show-notes/.

To Rick O'Dell of Smooth Jazz Chicago, who played the song that inspired this novel after it had faded from the airways, reminding me that it was a story worth telling.

Thanks to you all.

Monday, 16 Oct. 1978, 14:15

The Angel of Mount Trashmore

"My arm is killing me," Vito sighed, rubbing his bicep tenderly in the tight space of the garbage truck's cab. "One of them cans must've been heavier than it looked. And I need to take a leak bad."

A mischievous smile crept across the beefy wind-burned face of driver John Kelly as the truck bounced and jerked down the highway. A multi-car pile-up on the Steel Bridge turned the Calumet Expressway into a parking lot in both directions.

"You're getting old like me, my boy," John chuckled. "Tap yer foot, and the feeling'll go away. Most of them are false alarms."

If they hadn't been surrounded by charter buses loaded with little old ladies, and he hadn't been stuck between with his crew mates John and Joey, Vito would've hopped out of the cab on to the shoulder and relieved himself. But he couldn't. He'd have to wait until they reached their slot at the dump. Mercifully, John eased the truck out of the lane onto the shoulder to move past the clogged traffic.

"Here we go," John said proudly on exiting. "When you get home, an aspirin washed down by a cold brew will cure ya quick."

"John, you know Vito don't drink no more," chided Joey. "He's a Christian."

Joey admired Vito for going cold turkey for the Lord. It was something he couldn't have done, not even for Jesus.

"Well, chase it down with lemonade," John retorted as

they turned down the deserted stretch of Stony Island Avenue. "You'll feel better in the morning, either way."

The stench of methane, sulfur and rot, propelled by a strong breeze from Lake Michigan, exacerbated Vito's urge to pee. John mashed the clutch hard, down-shifted one gear, and floored it. The truck bounced along the six-story-high grass-covered banks that defined the eastern perimeter of the dump. Who'd have thought 'Ole Blue' was still capable of seventy-five miles an hour with a full load?

A yelling match outside the pit boss's shack blocked the entrance to the site. With several trucks idling behind him, one driver protested loudly. The boss wanted him to use one of the new holes at the back of Mount Trashmore, which meant a longer drive. The driver wanted to dump his load closer to the front, so he could finish quickly. Going to the back took extra time, which the traffic jam on the expressway had robbed him of.

Vito's crossed himself as the curse words flew. It expunged the sin yet did nothing to relieve the pressure in his bladder. With each cross, he prayed for the argument to end. Finally, his prayers were finally answered. The first truck belched a puff of smoke, heading fast down the new path, tires sending clods of dirt flying. "Go, go, go," yelled the pit boss, waving them down the same path.

At the edge of the new hole, Joey scrambled out of the cab, leaving the door open for Vito. Joey sprinted into position on John's side of the truck to guide it back to the very lip of the hole. Vito rushed to the edge. As the whine of the trucks' hydraulic lifts filled the air, Vito was able to relieve himself, eyes cast skyward in thanksgiving.

When Vito returned his eyes to earth, he saw her tumble, head-over-heels, into the pit. Banging his fist on the side of the truck, he screamed for John to stop. Stunned, he rubbed his eyes as if to erase the horror of the image that they beheld. Looking down, Vito hoped she'd unfold her wings and fly up.

But she didn't. There, doll-like and unreal, she lay amid the garbage, still as a dead butterfly.

Joey ran to join Vito as John lumbered out of the truck. Standing together, the trio took in the red plaid shirt and rust-colored stretch pants on her motionless body, her damp white blond hair covering her face. Vito buried his chin hard into this chest, pressed his eyes tight shut, and crossed himself repeatedly, his lips moving in a frenzied litany of silent prayer.

"Vito, VITO!" John shouted, shaking him by the shoulders. "Where'd she come from?"

"Our *truck*," Vito howled, opening his eyes wide. "Oh, dear God, she was in the back of our truck!"

Wrenching himself from John's grasp, Vito's knees hit the ground hard as he fell to pray.

"She's an angel!" he exclaimed with tears running down his face. "Don't you see? *A heavenly angel!* God sent us an angel and we put her in the back of the truck and killed her. Oh, dear Jesus, sweet Christ Almighty, forgive us!

Standing together, John took off his hat while Joey squatted, trying to get a better look.

Joey whispered to John. "Is she dead?"

"Get down to the office and call for help."

Joey took off running down the pathway.

Surrounded by a knot of whispering men, John wrung his hat in his hands. Feeling more helpless than ever, he strained to spot some movement or to hear a sound from the woman below.

"Lady, we've got help coming for ya," he called out.

Vito rocked back and forth mumbling over and over, "Forgive us, Lord. Please Lord, forgive us."

Monday, 16 Oct. 1978, 15:15

Catching the Job

Detective Rachael Culpepper walked back from the sky-blue Formica dinette table. Flanked by odd-sized filing cabinets, the tiny table with shiny chrome curved legs stood out against the assortment of gray, tan, black, and brown mismatched office furniture. The clear glass pot of Mr. Coffee was tinted amber by constant use.

Her newest partner, darkly handsome, curly-haired Tony Breese, was tethered to his desk by the mangled cord of the old Dick Tracy-style black PAX phone they shared. Calls received on the PAX phone could come from anywhere within the department. The system connected every police station and office together in a private secured network. If something happened to the regular phones, PAX kept communications flowing, which could be a blessing or a curse.

Tony scooted his desk chair across his patch of linoleum tile as he listened, depositing old case files in the bottom drawer of his desk. To Rachael, it didn't sound good. After several flat "uh-huhs," he moved the mouthpiece away from his face to address her quizzical look.

"Hey, Culpepper, what kind of shoes you wearing?"

"Loafers, Breese," she said, raising an eyebrow, "Why?"

Raising a finger to signal that he would explain shortly, he went back to listening intently and scribbling furiously. Asking about her shoes bothered Rachael. They'd only been partners for two full pay periods, so it wasn't easy to guess what was swirling around beneath his dark curly hair. Sure, his green eyes and deep voice made Detective Breese irresistible to the civilian ladies; however, contrary to departmental gossip, he and Rachael were all business. Tony didn't seem to be the kind of partner who'd be matchmaking for her, not even with someone within the department. Whatever it was, at this hour, it wouldn't be good.

"Communications Center," he said, holding his palm over the mouthpiece during a break.

"Okay," she said, yet it didn't satisfy her curiosity. Sipping her coffee, she sat back in the creaky snuff-colored leatherette chair behind her desk, watching him take notes. When he began the verbal back-and-forth confirming the information, the question about her shoes bothered her more. Working plain clothes had taken away the surety of black uniform oxfords, but it probably meant nothing. It reminded her of when she'd been transferred to Vice over PAX, where the mere thought of the blood red patent leather platform heels she'd worn while on "hooker detail" made her feet tingle.

In the span of one shift, she'd left her comfort zone of being a uniformed officer to a neon bright Donna Summer clone walking an invisible dog trying to curtail the caravan of unsatisfied husbands headed for Rush Street. Those who didn't have time to troll for willing women in the singles bars cruised the industrial areas behind Merchandise Mart for a quick fix from their marital boredom. The Chicago Police Department's job was to ensure that residents of Chicago's Gold Coast were able to walk at night without being harassed.

With her long, strong legs sheathed in gold lamé tights, Rachael attracted lots of Johns. The added inches from the cheap red platform shoes she'd bought put her at eye level with drivers in pick-ups, but made her nearly fold herself in half to talk to the ones in regular cars.

The Johns didn't care about Rachael's ungainly walk in the red shoes, her bargain basement wig, or how much lipstick she plied on as protection against the night air. They wanted time with the big fuzzy blonde whore. Instead, they got arrested.

In the first week, they were so successful that the bosses were ecstatic with the improved stats. The chief told the mayor, who chose to trumpet it to deflect the press from other civic problems. Rachael's fellow officers were worried that it would limit her effectiveness as a lure for their hunting, but horny men don't watch the newscasts. The caravan continued unabated.

Everybody was happy except Rachael. No one else in her family had ever gone undercover as a decoy. Her grandfather Tierney drove a paddy wagon, wading into bar fights in his day. Her father Danny walked the beat down Halsted Street on the West Side; even her older brother Aiden spent plenty of street time in a squadrol before becoming a police chief for a college town in Indiana. They never had to play decoy dress up.

According to her sergeant, the world of crime was changing. Everyone should "go with the flow." The department had put women on the street a few years ago, so Rachael had to do a good job and not complain. She did have to admit that she was the only one in her family with the figure for it. She'd bought the cheap red shoes because her Dad said "only chippies wore red shoes." Still, the assignment made her feel like the girl in the fairy tale who couldn't stop dancing once she put on the cursed shoes; out there, night after night, walking and chewing wads of gum.

The sergeant decided the backup team would do all the arresting, including the paperwork. Rachael thought her job would have been performed more efficiently by hiring an actual hooker, but the state's attorney wouldn't allow it. She wondered how the real pros did it night after night without going stark raving mad.

One night, the backup team's undercover car broke an axle on its way into the alley. Seeing cops hop out to make the arrest, the helpful John decided to grab Rachael and then flee. The pummeling she gave him resulted in multiple facial hematomas, cracked ribs, and a charge of assaulting an officer.

In the fracas, her heel caught in the thumbhole of a manhole, twisting her ankle. When the ER nurse pulled the shoe off, Rachael gleefully tossed both of the red monstrosities atop a trash can while being rolled to x-ray. When she hobbled back down the hall barefoot, discharged with a bandaged ankle and a crutch, she noticed the shoes had disappeared.

After medical leave, she was transferred to a South Side district. Triumphantly, she buried the box of rumpled metallic tights, funky patterned tube tops, and the fuzzy wig behind the hot water heater in her basement. She really hoped that this call wasn't going to make her pull them out of their hiding place.

"You're not going to like this, but..." Tony's voice trailed off as he reached for the regular phone handset. "We've caught a new murder at Mount Trashmore in Hegewisch."

"Mount Trashmore? You mean the city dump?" she asked.

"Yep. I ruined my best pair of Florsheims over there a while ago. Hope you got a pair of rubber boots in your locker. Believe me, you're gonna need 'em."

Rachael shot him a dirty look. Tony didn't own a pair of Florsheims. In the short time they'd worked together, everything she'd seen on his feet were so much better, shoes with names you couldn't pronounce without an Italian accent.

Tony pushed a file folder with the scribbled incident report number across the desk, then dialed as quickly as the old rotary phone let him. Rachael knew this assignment would get them out of the confines of the office where they'd spent most of the afternoon catching up on paperwork. It was funneled to them by Sergeant Burke because he knew the oldest of their cases solved itself by street justice while their other murders went stone cold.

Tony's crooked his neck, pinning the phone to his shoulder. Waiting for the call to connect, he gulped down his leftover black coffee. His eyes sparkled as he broke into a big smile upon hearing the voice of his girlfriend, Cynthia Broadacre.

"Hey baby," he lowered his commanding voice into a sexy purr. "You busy?"

He listened intently, adjusting his gun in his tan shoulder holster. While she told him of the plans for their evening, he put a couple of fresh pens along with a new yellow legal pad into his blue vinyl folder emblazoned with a large white Chicago Police Department star. He breathed a deep sigh, then shared the bad news.

"Aw, darling, sounds mighty good, especially the wine and the homemade French onion soup. But as much as I hate to say it, we've caught a new murder."

Straightening up to his full six feet, he stretched all the kinks and curls out of the phone cord. Still listening, he deftly sprayed breath freshener into his mouth and adjusted the knot of the gray-on-gray silk tie.

Rachael gathered her equipment and started a new murder book. She didn't listen to Tony's conversation. It was the typical exchange between cops and their lovers. She'd done the same thing many, many times, putting things on hold, bargaining for future time, promising it'd be better once she got through this one hot job.

Tonight, she didn't have to make that call. Her date phoned earlier in the morning to cancel while she and Tony chased a worthless lead. The message, on the back of a piece of chopped up arrest report paper simply stated "not available tonight. Will call later." Cop shorthand for a longer message someone didn't have the time or desire to write out. Rachael crumpled it up and tossed it into the circular file under her desk.

"Oh yeah, baby," Tony purred into the phone. "You know what I *need*."

Rachael recorded a status beside their names on the white-board near the office door. Resting in the crook of her arm was a metal clipboard box. A remnant of a failed love affair. She'd seen the metal box sitting on a shelf at the lumberyard while she waited for Dan the Roofer to load his truck on their third date. Intended for contractors who gave job estimates, the aluminum box now carried an assortment of departmental forms, business cards, pens, and a pair of extra handcuffs.

Tony switched the phone to his other ear. He turned his back to Rachael's desk, sitting on the edge of metal surface, giving Cynthia a little more time but not allowing himself to get too comfortable.

"Cynthia, darling, you know I'd love to talk longer, but the sooner I get to this case, the sooner I'll be able to call you to say I'm on my way, if you'll wait up for me."

Tony made a mock kiss into the phone. Rachael smiled, turning to face him only when she heard the jangle of car keys.

"You gonna pick up anything in the locker room, Rach?" he asked, now hurrying to leave.

"Nope, I think I'll be okay in these shoes, what about you?"

He stopped to glance at his feet, then wrinkled his nose and huffed. "I hope they don't get ruined."

Rachael looked at them. The leather was dyed such dark oxblood that they were nearly purple, stitched with gathers perfectly pinched by skilled hands. His clothes weren't cheap. For a detective, he dressed many notches above his paygrade, but being single with a lot of girlfriends might explain it. Rachael was more worried about his perfectly pressed navy blue merino wool trousers than his shoes, but she didn't say so. She'd knew polyester pants were the best choice for plain clothes work. Most stains scrubbed out with Lysol concentrate before you washed them.

Heading out the door, Rachael sighed. Other cops in the office nodded at them in sympathy, knowing from their walk that they weren't slipping out early, but headed out to work a new case. No one liked catching a fresh job close to the end of the shift. As their black car headed out of the parking lot, Tony gave her the details of the case he got from the

Communication Center desk.

"What we have is a twenty-something dead white female with no face," he said in a matter-of-fact tone.

"Damn, does it mean we have to dig through the trash looking for her head?" asked Rachael.

"Nope, not this time," he said triumphantly as he barreled through the last intersection and hit the ramp connecting to the Calumet Expressway. "We're lucky. This one wasn't decapitated. The murderer was kind enough to only cut her up so no one would recognize her."

"How'd they find her?"

"The garbage truck helper was taking a leak when she tumbled out with the rest of the stuff. Good thing he had a full bladder, or she might never have been found."

Rachael looked out the car window wondering why someone went after her face. Was it who she knew or what she knew? Or a message for someone else? Hopefully, they'd be able to tell once they saw her.

April 1977

A Lover's Spat

"Damn it, Lee," Dillon said, his dark eyes focused on her, his black curls bobbing around his shaking head. "It's, it's... all made up; it's bullshit."

"How can you say that?"

Dillon looked at her, hoping she'd read what was in his heart, but her face was stone cold. She had a craw full of complaints to serve up like the heaping plastic basket of French fries sitting between them.

"Cause I ain't done nothin'," he countered.

"Oh yeah?" she said with her head cocked to the side.

"Lee, nothin' happened!"

"You're always flirting...."

"Yeah? Miss Hanging-at-the-Garage?"

Tears welled up in her eyes. Dillon stabbed her in her most tender place, the love of her late father's garage. To her, it was a shrine, the place she'd spent the happiest times of her childhood. From the moment she knew how to cross the street alone, she'd gone there to be with her dad. They'd play tic-tac-toe on old newspaper, or she'd read to him from library books. She'd hand him tools. Even now, after his death, she still saw him in the shadows, smelled him in the grease and oil, touched him in the fading, florid Germanic script on the yellowing service cards the guys didn't have the heart to throw out.

"You kidding me? Those guys are your cousins. I'm there because I love the place. If the garage was your Mom's beauty shop, I wouldn't care if you hung out."

"Ha! If I hung out at her shop, ya'd swear I was screwing

the beauticians *and* the blue-haired grannies."

With a pleading smile, Dillon stretched his leg across the space under the table, thinking he'd defuse her anger with a touch.

"But Lee, baby," he purred, rubbing her shin with his foot.

Touching her only made it worse. How could he be so dense? No wonder he was two years older than the other seniors graduating high school. He sat back, opened his arms in a gesture of surrender and asked the fatal question.

"Okay, who the hell am I 'posed to be screwing?"

"Gwen Ann Dawson."

"Ya believe that stupid bitch?"

"I believe what I see," Lee straightened up. "Her money order to the prom committee with your name on it."

"What're you talking about? I ain't taking Gwen Ann's ugly ass to prom."

She stared at him with arms across her chest.

"There's no white orchid at Steuber's Greenhouse paid for by you?"

"Hell No! Purple carnations are all I can afford."

Behind her eyes, the heat of anger was building into tears.

"Evergreen Plaza has a burgundy tux on hold – for you!"

"Like hell they do!"

"The guy lied when I called?"

"Yeah, Gwen Ann paid those four-eyed wimps to lie. She probably gave 'em hand jobs." He settled back in the booth, satisfied with his answer.

Next, Lee decided to tackle the bigger accusation flung at her in the gym locker room in front of the entire class of senior girls.

"Why did Betty Parker see you at Ford City Mall in a dress shop with a brunette?"

"Don't you get it? That cow and her herd will be sitting at home prom night. They want you sitting home too, crying like them."

"Still doesn't explain it," she said with a tilt of her head.

"If ya didn't see me," he said sitting back in the booth, "what does it matter?"

She tensed her jaw at his lack of defense, rage simmering below the boil-over point.

"It matters to me what other people say about you," Lee said with a raised eyebrow.

"I can't believe ya let them bitches get to ya."

He didn't want to tell her he was shopping for her gift, and that the brunette was the store clerk.

"Ya know I'm a friendly guy. I was killing time at the mall, so what?"

"So what?" she spat out. "Why don't you go tell Gwen Ann? Why don't you tell Betty to get her nose out of our business?"

"'Cause it don't matter. Let 'em flap their gums. Nobody believes what they say."

Someone put money in the jukebox. He reached his open hands to the center of the table, imploring her to give him hers. She drew a deep breath but didn't move. He should have started talking again, but he let the lyrics of a song about unfaithfulness twist up in her head. Instead of hearing a man blaming other people for a breakup, she took it as reinforcement of Dillon's bad acts. It stoked her fury as they sat silent.

When the song ended, she stared at him, tears flowing. Then, speaking softly through sniffs, she laid out her pain.

"What I see ... is ... you think I'm crazy. You don't care ... what hurts me. You ... want to spend your time ... drinking beer ... working on cars ... and screwing anybody with a pussy."

"Lee, baby, I care 'bout ya ..."

The twisted lyrics reverberated in her head with every word he spoke.

"Baby, I can't believe you're letting jealous bitches get to ya."

She started talking, low at first, her rage building to a crescendo.

"You don't have time to do overtime to pay for prom stuff, but you have time to hang out at the mall? You have money for that heap-o'-shit car of yours, but I'm supposed to be grateful for carnations? I ask you to do something that doesn't cost money, you can't do it. Not even for one night. You can't leave your daddy's sacred wallet on a chain outa your pocket, not even for me. All you can say is 'doesn't matter'!"

Lee dissolved into a sobbing mess. Taking discarded napkins from the table, she tried to dry her eyes, but only succeeded in smearing ketchup on her cheeks. Watching her, he pulled a couple of clean napkins from the dispenser, pushing them gently into her hands as she sniffed and gurgled.

"Lee, baby, gimme a break. We've got time to do those things next week. Besides, I'm here with *you* now when I should be working...."

"I don't think ... you wanna ... go to the prom."

"I do," he said softly. "But you can't keep accusing me. Ya can't believe what you hear. Why do you listen to those bitches?"

"Because I love you, but I don't really know if you love me."

"You don't know?" he asked, "I spend every waking moment with ya; I do everything I can for *you*."

"But you never say it unless I say it first."

"Jesus fucking Christ," he scoffed, "Is that what this is all about?"

"And you never defend me if someone is talking about me."

"If that's all it takes for ya to doubt me," he sat back and folded his hands, "then we don't need to be together."

She couldn't believe what he had just said to her. She flung a handful of ketchup-covered French fries in his face as her elbow knocked a plate off the table, shattering loudly on the floor.

He lunged across the table. His open hand connected with her cheek, leaving a crimson outline under her eye.

"Damn you!" she screamed. "I hate you!"

He should have pulled her to him, hugged her back to her senses. Instead, he flung an empty plastic tumbler at her. She ducked. When it hit the back of the wooden booth, it sounded like a gunshot.

People leaned around the high backs of their booths to see what was happening. They saw a black clad figure standing with arms outstretched, trying to stop someone from leaving the last booth. In a split second, a girl crawled out from under the table. As she headed to the door, she straightened up trying to salvage a shred of dignity.

"COME BACK HERE!" Dillon screamed, standing beside the booth, "Ya left ya stupid fucking purse!"

She didn't stop, but at the door, a large group of guys made it impossible for her to escape. With fists balled up at her sides, she stomped her foot.

"Hey, let the lady out," shouted one of the guys, "She's having a bad night."

They chuckled as they playfully jostled each other, pretending to make a path for her. Dillon made his way through the restaurant, catching up to her.

"Nice. A whole bunch of prom dates for ya," he hissed low. "What'd ya do? Advertise in the paper?"

One guy grabbed the door, holding his arm out to stop anyone from entering.

Lee couldn't believe Dillon to be so heartless. Before she could say another word, he threw the purse at her. She grabbed it midair. Her self-appointed bodyguards roared their approval. Dillon's eyes went wild with loathing.

"Don't call me," he hissed, pointing his finger at her like a gun. "Leave me the fuck alone. I've had it. We're over."

Everyone stood frozen in place, except Dillon. He stomped to his truck.

"You okay, Miss?" asked one mockingly.

She ignored him, fishing for car keys in her purse.

"I don't know what you did to him," called another guy from the group, "but whatever it was, will you do it to me?"

"Fuck off," she hissed.

As they moved away chatting and laughing, Lee felt the owner of the restaurant tap her on the shoulder.

"I hate to bother you Miss, but your boyfriend didn't pay the check, and I'm going to have to add two bucks more for the broken dishes."

Fighting back tears, she flopped the purse on a table to search for her wallet. Outside, Dillon jammed the key in the ignition of his red Chevy Luv truck. Slamming into reverse, he floored it, sending a shower of gravel from his wheels, nearly ramming another car.

"Keep the change," she muttered to the older man as she handed him a ten.

Dillon saw Lee move through the door, but he sped out of the lot before she could reach his open window.

Monday, 16 Oct. 1978, 15:30

Crime Scene

Tony parked the black Crown Victoria near the ambulance that responded to the call when the pit boss thought the victim might still be alive. Parked next to them was a car with municipal plates belonging to the crime lab. The garbage trucks were parked around the edge of the pit, their crews watching. It's not every day that you see a dead blonde tumble out of a garbage truck to lie among the waste of eggshells, orange rinds, banana peels, rotting meat, and soiled baby diapers.

"Jeeze, I was worried about my shoes. This looks like we need coveralls! That evidence tech is standing knee deep in the trash," Tony slammed the car door.

Rachael shrugged, "I'll go. You've got a date later. I know you don't want to smell like a garbage can."

"Culpepper, that's mighty nice of you." He mockingly punched her upper arm. "But I can't have these guys thinking I'm a priss. We'll both go together. I've got clean clothes in my locker back at the station."

While Tony talked with one of the firemen, Rachael's mind again flashed to Dan the Roofer. The firemen had secured two long ladders to the side of the pit—the same kind of ladders Dan always had strapped to his truck.

"You want to go first?" asked Tony.

"Yeah, I love ladders."

"Yeah, me too," grunted Tony. "That's why I didn't join the fire department."

They descended carefully and waded through mounds

of refuse, avoiding broken bottles, jagged can lids, and clots of rotting food. They came to a stop near Phillip Carlyle, Evidence Technician.

"Howdy Phil," said Rachael, watching him rise from a squat. "What we got here?"

Rachael didn't have the heart to tell tall, lanky Carlyle dressed in his russet rubber apron, white shirt, and hospital gloves, that he reminded her of the horror actor Boris Karlov. Ear length fawn-colored hair topped off Carlyle's mad scientist look, despite a handsome face and bright blue eyes.

"Sorry to bring you out this close to the end of the shift, but it's a doozy."

"Great. Just what we need," remarked Tony, peeling a scrap of damp newspaper off his pant leg.

"Female, twenty to twenty-five... definitely a dump job," he grimaced at the gaffe. "Uh, no pun intended."

Doubling over, he took off the sheet covering her. The fully clothed girl was lying in a position so natural that she looked like she'd stretch and say "hello."

Tossing the sheet aside, Carlyle walked in a wide arc to the front of the victim. Tony and Rachael followed in his footsteps. He squatted carefully, so as not to disturb anything the victim was lying on. The body had fallen in a relatively clear spot with only a thin layer of garbage underneath her. Rachael made notes while Tony squatted beside Carlyle, looking and listening.

"She had everything going for her to be found," said Carlyle. "The helper taking a leak, this being a new section of the dump where she didn't have piles of garbage bags to sink into, and her bright-colored clothes. If she were in black, gray, or white, she probably wouldn't have been noticed."

He was right. All around them there were hundreds of black and white plastic bags. She was lying on fanned-out papers in an oversized red plaid flannel shirt and rust-colored pants, making her stand out against the landscape of bagged trash. The dark chestnut suede boots seemed new, without salt residue or water stains. She wore a wide, black lace scarf tied in her white blonde hair. A big black belt encircled her waist, cinching the man's shirt into a tunic. Several strands of clunky multi-colored wooden beads were looped around her neck and glittery plastic bangles encircled each arm.

"Olivia Newton Dead here should have a purse," said Tony, gesturing his exasperation with both hands. "Where the hell is her purse?"

"Not everyone carries a purse, Tony," Rachael chided him.

"Trust me, even the ones who don't have a thing to tote, carry those whopping big bags. It's part of the uniform; they don't leave home without them. Besides, she doesn't have any pockets."

"We didn't find a purse anywhere near her," said Carlyle, "I wish we had... I think this is going to be a tough one. I hope you haven't had dinner yet."

He used a long wooden rod to move the victim's thick blonde hair showing them her badly mutilated face.

"From the amount of cutting, I'd say she was unconscious or drugged when it happened. No one conscious could tolerate this much slashing without defending themselves, even from something as sharp as a razor or scalpel," said Carlyle. He inched the rod under her forearm to raise her wrist, moving the hand slightly, revealing an unblemished palm.

"See? No defensive wounds. Her hand is clean as a whistle. The other one is balled into a fist, but there are no scratches on it. We'll know more after I get her on my table."

"Were the pants that way when you found her?" asked Rachael, trying to rule out sexual assault.

"Yep, they were undisturbed at the top. Neat and smooth all the way down."

Carlyle used the wooden rod to push up one side of the flannel shirt, revealing a smooth even waistline of the stretchy fabric. If she'd been raped, no guy would pull the pants up or make them neat.

"Did you check for a cut between the legs? Those tights are hard to peel down, but easy to cut," said Tony.

"Yeah, I peeked. Didn't see a rip, cut, razor slash, or tear. Unusual, yeah?" Carlyle stood up again, putting the wooden rod in the crook of his arm. "I'll bag her hands to see if there's any debris under her nails from a struggle, but I don't think I'll find any."

"What do you think was the time of death?" Rachael asked, still looking at the job the murderer did on the girl's face.

"Over 24 hours most likely. Her liver temp was cold when I got here."

"Too bad we don't know the cause of death," said Tony, "It'd give us more to go on."

"Too much blood for me to make a guess. But I'm sure it wasn't natural. She doesn't look like a heart attack or stroke victim. I'll know more when I get her cleaned up back at the morgue."

"Thanks, Phil," said Rachael.

Tony and Rachael started visually combing the area, hoping to find something belonging to the victim. Nothing lying nearby screamed dead girl, yet Tony bagged up a few things close to her and turned them over to Carlyle for analysis. Disposable cigarette lighters, a broken lipstick case, a few stray bottles, and, best of all, several used condoms. If this stuff didn't match up with anything, it'd be okay; but it might pay off later.

"Ready," shouted the Carlyle to the firemen above, heading for the ladder.

They lowered down a body bag on the aluminum-framed stretcher. Two paramedics climbed down to help. Carlyle and the firemen worked together, preparing the victim for her move to the morgue as Tony and Rachael climbed up out of the pit.

With the detectives out of the pit, the firemen moved the

two ladders together. Using them as a ramp, they pulled the stretcher up using the winch on their truck.

Rachael was relieved to be out the trash pit. Smelling the damp earth as she climbed out gave her the sensation that she was crawling out of a grave instead of a landfill. She didn't like the feeling.

It was time to talk to the garbage truck driver and the helpers. Tony took Vito—the one who saw the victim first—near their unmarked car. Rachael approached John Kelly, the driver. Joey leaned against the front bumper of the old truck, smoking nervously. The noise of the fire engine's winches and the ambulance's running motor was enough to ensure confidentiality even though they were only a few feet apart.

John had a trucker's tan from the end of the t-shirt sleeve worn under overalls to his wrist. A well-chewed stogie hung from the corner of his mouth to ward off the bad smells. Before she asked him anything, he nervously started talking.

"Mornin, ma'am. I'm John Kelly, driver of Ol' Blue here. We're outta the 19th Ward," he said, twisting his knit cap to relieve his anxiety. "The 107th Street yard, you know the one, cross the highway? The lads and I had no idea she was in there, none at all."

"Mr. Kelly, I need to ask you a few things. I'm Detective Culpepper from 91st and Cottage."

"A course, a course, ma'am, anything I can do 'ta help," he said, pulling a wash-faded blue and white bandana from his back pocket, shaking the wrinkles out of it with a snap.

Rachael looked down at her notebook to give Kelly a chance to wipe his face with it, especially around the damp edges of his cloudy gray eyes.

"Where were you working today, Mr. Kelly?"

"Me and the boys were doing Western to California, 103rd to 111th."

She hoped that Tony was getting the same story she was so they could let these guys go home without dragging them to the station for a long night of interrogation.

"You don't think they ignored her, do you?"

"Oh no, ma'am. Not Vito," John blustered. "Religious as the Pope he is. He turned Apostolic, Evangelical, or somethin' of the sort. Trust me, he knows dead when he sees it. He prays for everything we find dead. Dogs, cats, raccoons, rabbits, ya name it, he prays o'er it. For her, he'd of turned back to being Catholic to say a solemn novena. Woulda made me and Joey say it, too."

"You don't think Joey saw her either?" she asked.

"I'm sure he didn't. Hell's bell's, ma'am, if'n we had, we'd a piled her in the cab and gone straight to Little Company Hospital with her! Ol' Blue got a bit of speed in her yet."

His voice was choking up, but he covered it with a cough.

Rachael gave him a moment.

"Why do you think they missed her?" asked Rachael, pen poised. "A few too many nips this morning?"

"Oh no, ma'am. Joey's in AA now. Got a bunch of sober chips, that one. Vito, he quit cold turkey the very day he found Jesus."

Rachael nodded as John twisted his hat together with his bandana. When he saw she was finished writing, he spoke again.

"The way I'm thinking is someone piled lots of stuff on top of her, mind ya. To hide her. The boys are good at staging cans. Vito pulls 'em out, and Joey shakes 'em down. This time of the year there's lots of extra things lying about. Cardboard boxes, branches, wood, bags of leaves and the like. We break the crap up, toss it on top. We're supposed to write warnings and then citations, but them things can ruin a man's Christmas, if you get what I mean."

Rachael knew city workers got tips.

"And the weight didn't tip them off?"

"No ma'am," he said shaking his head sadly, "Ya don't notice weight 'til your muscles get tired and seize up on ya, near the end of the route. Joey and Vito sling together. I'd bet she was some where's near 107th, because we did the alley twixt Western and Artesian first. The boys were fresh. I drove straight outta the yard, right to Western, then south. I like to do a nice square, I do. But it coulda been Maplewood, down by the tracks. Lots of shenanigans go on in those weed thickets; they do."

Thanking him, she took down his home address and phone number, knowing he was not a person of interest, but hoping he might have more to tell later. She gave him one of her business cards printed on gray cardstock with a blue skyline running along the bottom with an embossed police logo floating above it like the sun. He climbed up into the truck to wait.

Joey moved to the edge of the pit. As Rachael walked over, she saw him trying to release the tension by playing with something in his hand. She figured it might be his AA chip. As she tapped him on his shoulder he moved back a step before turning in her direction.

"Can I ask you a few questions?"

"Yes ma'am, anything you want to know ma'am."

"Where did she come from?"

"No idea," he said sadly, sniffing back tears.

"Have you ever seen her before?"

"No ma'am, I sure haven't. I live over in Pullman. Ain't nobody there with long white hair like that. Not even the grannies."

"I see," said Rachael, trying to determine if he was pretending to be frazzled, or if this incident had really shaken him. He started talking like John.

"Ma'am, I wish I'd seen her. I wish we'd known about her before we got here. We might have been able to save her. I wish ..." his voice trailed off into a sniffle. She gave him a few seconds to recover.

"The crime lab guy said she'd been dead for a long time.

You couldn't've helped her. But you can help me. Give me your phone and address. Okay?"

Joey nodded, concentrating his gaze on a tiny black rock in a sea of gray gravel. When he finished, he stooped down, picked it up and put it in his pocket. Rachael made the notation by his name: "likes mementos."

Vito was a yes/no interview for Tony. The pit boss gathered all the other men together. He asked if anyone saw her before she fell into the pit. When no one raised a hand, he looked to Rachael. She gave the pit boss her card, telling him to release the crews. To her surprise, the pit boss stuck two fingers in his mouth, whistled loud, and waved his index finger in the air, signaling everyone to finish up and leave.

All the men stood silently as Phil and the ladders came out of the hole. Vito watched closely as the firemen tended to the stretcher. Vito crossed himself over and over as the impromptu pallbearers walked slowly over to the ambulance with solemn efficiency. They placed the stretcher inside gently, closing the doors softly, returning silently to their truck.

Everyone dispersed quietly. Climbing into their trucks, they dumped the remainder of the garbage into the pit. Vito was the last one to scramble up into the cab. Watching the lumbering garbage trucks make their way slowly down the gravel path, Tony tossed Rachael the keys. Following the ambulance, Rachael's car was the last vehicle in the procession.

April 1977

Dillon's Ire

Dillon's taillights disappeared from Lee's view in the darkness of the Lithuanian cemetery and the last farm in Chicago's city limits. He seethed. When did Lee become an airheaded bimbo? She'd been his soul mate. What had changed her? As kids, they'd stolen out of their houses to climb leafy trees and dream of their future together. This wasn't part of those dreams.

At eleven, they "borrowed" the keys to Dillon's father's car, teaching themselves to drive, cruising down alleys at night to avoid parents or police. At twelve, they filched beers from grownups and hid them in the cool basement to drink on the sloping embankment of the railroad tracks. They'd pilfered cigarettes from their mother's purses, using the walk to the comic book store to smoke and then walk back home to erase the smell from their clothes and hair.

They'd lost their virginities to each other, laughing at the awkwardness, surprised about the pain, washing the bloodstained, semen-coated sheets in the bathroom sink before anyone could discover their naughty deed.

In high school, when the tragedies struck, they comforted one another. At the end of freshman year, Dillon's father died in a construction accident. The company paid a large settlement. In her grief, Dillon's mother turned from her children to booze and gambling, quickly burning through most of the money.

Lee's father died the following year, his heart attack giving them no warning, leaving her and her mother instantly in debt with no insurance and no family to help them. Sorrow and circumstances brought Lee and her mother closer, but it wasn't so for Dillon and his mother. He hated being ruled by her, hated her drinking.

So Lee and Dillon fell in together, dulling their pain with sex. But the more Lee brought up her grief for her father, the more she reminded Dillon of his mother crying in her drinks. He began to pull away, leaving her alone. He sank deep into a place she couldn't reach. It was dangerous territory.

Dillon drove, getting more and more pissed off. As soon as he was beginning to escape the abyss of his own sorrows, some ugly bitch had decided to make trouble for him, to accuse him of cheating on Lee. How could Lee be so stupid? Asking him to wear a sissy blue tux with a matching shirt full of ruffles instead of the all-black one he wanted?

His anger made him miss the turn for home. The lights of McCann's Funeral Home's parking lot reminded him that he didn't blubber and blow through money like his mom did to keep her grief at bay. He acted. He beat the shit out anyone who pissed him off, and a few who didn't. He worked tearing cars apart, putting them back together. He was a man of action, like his dad. He stomped the accelerator hard, running the yellow light at 107th Street instead of trying to stop, not caring about the cop who usually sat in the White Hen Pantry parking lot, drinking coffee, waiting to write speeding tickets.

Why'd Lee need him to leave his dad's trucker's wallet out of his pocket for the prom? She, of all people, should understand that it was his only connection to the man he adored? Didn't she know it was an insult to buy him a flimsy leather square barely big enough to hold a driver's license and a condom? She wanted him to be up to date. Why wasn't the long silver chain attached to the trucker's wallet good enough? He would polish it until it gleamed, and it'd be the only thing anyone saw. He bet any of those other girls wouldn't give him shit about it. They'd be happy to have him in all black with the silver chain flashing on his thigh. They'd be thrilled to go to the prom with him. All he had to do was ask and they'd go, no matter what he wore. Lee'd see when he showed up with another girl on his arm and the chain hanging from his pocket. He'd show her.

The trees of Talley's Corner absorbed the loud engine hum as he barreled through the green light at 103rd. Since his dad died, he'd beat the fuck out of any weak asshole, especially those pampered bastards at the Brother Rice campus flashing past. Rice Boys wore sissified uniforms, with ties. Dillon had his own uniform, all black, leather jacket, jeans, shirt, and boots. It gave him an aura of strength and viciousness. He wore it everywhere. Why couldn't Lee see he needed a black tux with a black shirt as his armor? Why'd she want him in baby blue like a punk for all to see? Why did she, of all people, want to make a fool of him?

Deep into his pain, he narrowly missed colliding with an ambulance running on 99th Street, headed to the ER of the hospital where Lee worked. He hadn't heard the sirens or seen the lights.

Passing apartments full of little old Oak Lawn ladies reminded him of the gray headed sex headshrinker on TV, Doctor Ruby or Ruth, who said that you marry your mother, only a younger version. He was going to prove her wrong. He was going to run from anything reminding him of his mother and her drunken sadness, like he was running the light at 95th. Anyone. Even Lee. Pulaski Road curved, preventing him from seeing the line of coal cars. But when the road straightened, those cars looked like doors blocking the 87th street crossing. They were stopped for who knew what reason. If he sat there, forced to be still, he'd pull off sun visors, snap off the rear-view mirror, or throw anything out the windows that wasn't bolted down. The only thing left for him to do was to hook a U-turn and go to Bleekers Bowl to throw a few balls down the lanes with the rest of the insomniacs.

Monday, 16 Oct. 1978, 17:12

Prelims

"This one's going to be easy," Tony said, watching the cars speed past them on the Calumet Expressway.

"Yeah? What makes you think so?" asked Rachael.

"We got fingers and teeth. That's all the crime lab boys ever need," he said casually. "By morning, they'll have an ID, we'll find the boyfriend, and we're done."

"Oh, you like the boyfriend for this one, even without signs of sexual activity?"

"You're the one saying there wasn't intercourse," Tony mused. "Me, I think he got him one last shot, willingly of course, after which, she put herself back together to go home. While driving her home, he broke it off. They fought in the car. Next thing you know, he's killed her. Probably stabbed her in the temple, accidentally, of course, with a screwdriver or pen or something. Had to do the face carving to cover up the cause. Panic set in, he dumped her in a can on his way home, covered her up, and there you have it. Motive, opportunity, semen, and death."

"Wow, case closed in three sentences. Nice." She maneuvered to the northbound Stony Island exit ramp. "So, we notify the family, they give us a name, we do a quick background check, a tidy arrest, and on to the next case?"

"That's what I'm hoping, Rach. I've got some time-due built up and there's a lady with plans for me."

"Ah ha, taking your sister to Milwaukee for the weekend, *again*?" She teased.

He laughed, knowing as soon as they hit the station, he

was going to make his phone call, sign out, and head for the comforting arms of Cynthia. She'd be very pleased he wasn't showing up at two o'clock in the morning, like he'd predicted. He could taste the chilled Sangria on her warm lips.

"Miss Cynthia Broadacre will be accompanying me on a deluxe two-day stay at the Essex Motel on Michigan Avenue overlooking Grant Park in beautiful downtown Chicago, thank you."

"I see," said Rachael, knowing damn well Tony never frequented the Essex—he was more the Drake or the Blackstone type. "Very nice, Monty Hall. What's behind door number two?"

"Wouldn't you like to know?" he replied mischievously.

Rachael decided this line of inquiry had come to its natural end. They drove along in silence. Tony's attention wandered to a bus lumbering towards the 103rd Street CTA garage lot, heading for its overnight berth. He wondered what manner of crimes had been committed along the bus route. With a slight sigh, he mumbled "job security." Rachael didn't even ask what or why.

"You know, Rach, my friend, Denise McGruder comes from a big family. Seven older brothers, three of whom are unmarried."

"Thanks, but no thanks," replied Rachael, "I'm not in the mood for a fix up. My last two ended badly. I don't think you'd appreciate having to attend a McGruder family funeral because of me."

"What a load of bull. You weren't the cause of the roofing guy kissing the ass end of a cement truck doing 60 miles an hour. Besides, the other guy you were dating was an idiot to go so long before having his stomach taken care of. You can't blame yourself. He didn't know he had intestinal cancer."

"Who knew?" muttered Rachael with a deep sigh.

Tony knew he'd crossed the line, so he shut up and let her concentrate on the traffic. People-watching on this Indian summer night was very easy. The sudden heat brought people out to the Fun Town amusement park on Stony Island Avenue and 95th Street. The parking lot backup was blocking the northbound lanes of Stony, creating a traffic jam, complete with honking horns and testy shouts. Tony contemplated walking up to the intersection to direct traffic while Rachael eased their car through the jam, but without a uniform, flashlight, or a whistle, it'd only cause more shouting from the civilians. Finally, Rachael managed to inch over.

The smell of hot dogs and fresh popcorn wafted through the air. Through the gaps between the cars, Tony saw people milling about carrying cotton candy, ice cream bars, and over-iced sodas. Squeals and laughs filled the air, drawing his eyes to the neon lights on the rides. Along the fence separating the park from the traffic, young lovers lingered, holding gaudy stuffed toys, some talking, some flirting, and others kissing.

"Man, oh man," exclaimed Tony. "Our victim could've been there last night, eating corn dogs and smooching. Now, she is on her way to the morgue. Ain't love grand?"

Rachael glanced in the direction of the amusement park, seeing all the sweethearts gathered along the fence. It wasn't the sight she was in the mood to see.

When the light changed, Rachel floored it, taking the turn like she was going on a 10-1 "officer needs help" call. Tony braced himself for the rest of the ride.

She didn't break the silence when she pulled into the station parking lot. She knew Tony meant to make her feel better about her love life, but she wasn't ready for unsolicited advice. All she wanted to do was the initial work-up and get home before midnight.

Heading into the old 11th District station that the department had converted into detectives' space, Tony was stopped by a couple of off-duty cops fishing to see if he wanted to join them at the unit's favorite watering hole, but he asked for a rain check with a telling wink.

Rachael wanted a break before this case became her life's focus. She felt that it wasn't going to be as quick as Tony wanted or as simple as she wished. She dug into the desk drawer for the report forms.

"We do the preliminary and go home?" she asked rhetorically.

"Yeah, unless you want to go door-to-door in Beverly asking if anyone stuffed a dead blonde girl in their garbage can?"

"Bad idea," Rachael said. "They always go off into other things, never saying what you want to hear."

Tony plunged into the paperwork, knowing nothing he'd say was going to make Rachael feel any better.

April 1977

The Favor

They munched on potato chips while sipping warm sodas. Hopping the fence was easy. So was sitting on the concrete bench intended for bus riders outside Morgan Park High School's athletic field. What had been hard was hiding the snacks in their blue cotton gym suits.

"Come on, Cara," Lee begged. "Do it? For me? You like going to dances."

"Lee, he's your boyfriend," she exclaimed. "You'll be mad at me."

"Nope," said Lee, shaking her head, "he's not my boyfriend anymore. I'm mad at him. Besides, we broke up."

"Broke up?" asked Cara. "Over what?"

"Stupid prom stuff."

"He'll get over it," said Cara, nodding her head full of red curls twisted into a sloppy bun. "You two'll be dancing to Foreigner while I'm sitting around looking stupid."

"Oh no, you won't," Lee said, blue eyes sparkling. "I'll ask Mikey. If Dillion bolts, we'll have Mikey to take us home. Besides, Dillon's rented a Lincoln he can't get his money back on. His mother's pestering him for pictures to put up in her beauty shop. Plus, Mikey'll be happy to go. He hasn't asked anyone yet."

"You're so sneaky," squealed Cara, "But shouldn't you see if you guys can get back together?"

"Ha," Lee huffed, swinging her long white ponytail over her shoulder. "I wouldn't go with him if he begged me. He hurt my feelings. He needs to know how it feels. That's where you come in. He'll think you want him because he's the best-looking guy in the class. He won't figure we're plotting."

"What if he finds out?" asked Cara.

"Nothing. This isn't the kind of thing that pushes his buttons. If you spill something on his car's metal flake paint job, then you've got trouble," giggled Lee.

"You think he'll go for it? He barely knows me," said Cara.

"He'll go for it," said Lee knowingly, "He'll like you coming on to him. He ain't got a lot of cash, but he's got a lot of ego. He won't be able to resist."

"Okay," Cara agreed with a big smile. "I'll do it."

Tuesday, 17 Oct. 1978, 05:30

Getting Dumped

A good night's sleep followed by a hot steaming cup of coffee was exactly what Rachael needed. She felt like conquering the world; probably even solving a case or two with no background info at all.

The phone's ringing annoyed her. Either Tony had an idea, or he needed a ride to work. She hoped it was the former, because she wanted to be alone listening to Larry Lujack and Tommy Edwards. If Tony rode shotgun, he'd cramp her style, stifling her ability to laugh at the silliness of Animal Stories.

She grabbed the handset on the third ring. It was the familiar voice of her boyfriend, Blake. His timing was terrible. She'd have to cut the conversation short to get to work on time.

"Hey Blake, how are you?"

"I heard your message last night."

"Okay," Rachael said, failing to pick up his tone. "What's up?"

"I'm calling to tell you that I'm not playing your game anymore. I won't be put on a shelf and dusted off when it suits you."

"Blake, you knew what kind of job I had when we met. I told you my hours were erratic at best. I thought you understood."

"What I understand is you run all over town. I call your office, and all they tell me is you're 'out on the street.' Don't you ever get *any* of my messages?"

"I get all of them, but I can't always to get back to you right away. I'm running down leads, trying to get murderers off the streets. We go where...."

"Oh, I know where you go. Benny saw you last week down in Mother's of all places! The biggest pick up joint in town. I'm supposed to believe you were running down a lead there?"

"Yeah, Blake, we were. One of the bartenders was related to our victim. We went to talk to him."

"You're trying to play me for a fool. Benny's not the only one who's seen you."

Rachael wanted to ask what Benny was doing in Mother's. She wanted to know why Benny conveniently left out the fact it was a Wednesday afternoon, not the Friday night flirt fest, but instead, she listened. It was obvious Blake had made up his mind to break it off.

Rachael wondered how she had misjudged him so completely. Was it because he'd lock up every night at nine thirty? Or because his biggest problems were if the produce truck was late, or the freezers went on the blink or, God forbid, one of his cashiers miscounted her till? What did he know about Rachael's world, where rape, robbery, and foul murders had no schedule?

"You know how to cancel me at the drop of a hat, or should I say the sound of a zipper?"

"Wait a minute, Blake. I don't have to justify myself to you."

"Good, because it's over with us, Rachael. I'll leave your stuff on your porch. I hope you find someone who can put up with your alleged 'work.'"

When the line went dead, her anger flashed. She could make Blake's life miserable. She still had her ticket book. He always parked in the dead-end alleyway behind his store; she might forget it was private property. Or, from a pay phone, she could call his car in stolen.

She pulled her jacket off the back of a chair, heading out the door. It was a new day, and there were criminals to catch.

May 1977

Prom Night

Snuggled up against Dillon, Cara O'Toole's excitement was palpable.

"Did you see the dress Phyliss was wearing? Looks like her mother was at the sewing machine again. I know it's a Vogue Oscar de la Renta pattern from four years ago. I bet she made a short one for Phyliss's grammar school graduation and kept it in reserve." She giggled.

Dillon could hardly make his turns because she was so close and wouldn't allow him elbow room. He grunted "yeah" again.

"Heather shouldn't have worn yellow. It's a pretty floral print, but too many ruffles. Made her look like a Chihuahua in a tutu. That's why I didn't pick a Laura Ashley dress. They're too fluffy."

Dillon grunted again. Cara kept rattling on, but not about what she really *wanted* to discuss. She knew he didn't want to hear anything about Lee, or the dress she wore. It was a knockout, a form-fitted plum-colored lace halter. The fabric was so dark it looked black, topped by a gauzy navy blue capelet, obviously from another dress. It's something Lee wouldn't have added if she'd gone to the prom with Dillon. It made Cara's coral sleeveless chiffon look juvenile, even after she'd fought her mother to get it because she thought it made her look grown up. Gunne Sax dresses had nothing on Fredricks of Hollywood.

During the prom, the couples had plenty of opportunity to see what the other one was feeling. Mikey was very uncomfortable; Dillon and Lee glared at each other, leaving Cara the only one who was having a good time. She was in her own world, a fairy princess dancing on her castle's parapet, oblivious to the storm about to blow her into the moat of despair.

Dillon's hands felt red hot on her back when they danced. Cara didn't know it, but he almost popped his cork on the dance floor. He was in a fever, inflamed by her closeness and his anger at Lee. With Cara in his arms, pressing against him from head to foot, smelling of cinnamon and roses, all he could do was rock from side to side. His hardon was excruciating.

"Hey, look," he'd swung Cara around, "there's no line at the photographer."

He dragged her across the dance floor, marching to the backdrop before the slow song was over. Once the photo was taken, Dillon whispered in her ear.

"Cara, it's time to go."

She skipped off to the ladies room while he waited by the exit door. He watched the line to the photographer begin to snake towards the coat room. Remembering that they'd checked Cara's velvet wrap, he redeemed it before she came back. Draping it over her shoulders, they left to perform a dance of unforeseen dangers.

Dillon scouted out a good place to park the car he'd rented —the burgundy 1978 Lincoln Continental. Tonight, there were no cheap hotel rooms available. They were booked up far in advance because it was prom night for so many schools across Chicago. He wished he hadn't cancelled his reservation at the Highway Inn in Markham when he broke up with Lee. He thought about the kids from the North Side who traveled to the no-tell-motels south of Midway Airport to shed their virginity on sheets their mothers wouldn't find. Dillon knew anything north of Midway was too expensive, even with Cara offering to help foot the bill.

He drove down the hill off Vincennes Avenue in Blue

Island, to where one side was a high freight train embankment and the other had three houses spaced at a distance from each other. One was a frame with age-yellowed newspaper covering its windows; another was a cottage set back on the lot, with foil covering the windows; and the third, a long, low shoebox-shaped house with thick drapes.

Dillon expected the preliminaries of kissing and petting, which Lee insisted upon before putting out for him. She called it romance. While they tongue kissed, he'd get to rub her tits or stroke her thighs, but he had to follow a fine line. No fingering her snatch, no trying to push her head down to kiss his thing, and no pulling up her skirt to hop right in. He really didn't mind because it always built up the tension. The extra waiting made him explode like a bomb.

He was ready for some major league begging and explaining with Cara, but surprisingly, after two French kisses, she pulled away from him. With a big smile and a giggle, she climbed over the front seat without him saying a word.

"Hey, where ya going?"

He reached out to stop her, to show her he was romantic, but Cara thought he was encouraging her by caressing her legs and ass as she wiggled through the opening. Why'd he want to stay in the front seat? Where else could he make love to her like he'd promised except the back seat? She wanted him to make her a woman like Lee. Cara desperately wanted to be "grown up" before she graduated. It was difficult being "sweet sixteen" as a senior. The double promotions were great on paper, but when you hit the real world of high school, they didn't mean a thing. Being the youngest in the class made her yearn for the things the older girls had—the knowledge, the sophistication that only came from being "made a woman." When those girls wore "virgin" pins on their clothes, everyone knew it was a joke. When Cara wore one, they nodded in sympathy.

Dillon slipped himself out of the fly of his tux trousers,

careful not to scrape his delicate foreskin on the teeth of the zipper. Cara had stuffed her lace panties into her fancy sequined clutch purse like he'd asked her before leaving the dance. She braced herself with one foot on the floor of the car. They were in sync, running on one high emotion, mutual horniness.

Hitting the seat with his knees, Dillon positioned himself between her legs. Playfully pushing up the front of her frothy lace skirt, he saw her velvety thatch of rust-colored pubic hair. She blushed because he was looking intently at something she hadn't thought he'd gaze at. She didn't imagine he'd look at it like that. It made her feel powerful, like she was one of those naked women in her father's *Penthouse* magazine. When he reached out to run his fingers in her hairs, it tickled, made her wiggle. The tree limbs full of new leaves waving across the streetlight made dappled patterns on the skin of her creamy thighs. He stretched to kiss her again, she propped herself up on her elbows to meet his lips. Three kisses were all he could bear. Holding himself off her with one arm, he rubbed himself against her opening. She didn't know what to think, the sensation was intense and confusing.

She seemed slick enough so he didn't need to spit on himself to slide in. Guiding himself with his hand, he marveled at the feel of her. She was his second virgin. She was so snug he couldn't contain himself.

She tensed. The stretching sensation between her legs was a shock. She gasped loudly. The books she'd read didn't say it was going to feel like an Indian sunburn was being done to her insides. He continued to push steadily. Books made losing virginity sound romantic. It was much more uncomfortable than anything she had imagined.

He stopped moving, pulling back, letting her breathe easy for a few moments. She thought it must have hurt him too because he shivered and shook. She kissed his neck as he rested atop of her, unaware of the damage he'd done.

Leaning forward, he kissed her deeply, smelling her, tasting her mouth. In the narrow space of the back seat, there was no place to scramble away. She was enjoying the feel of him, his lustful ardor. The heavy petting was good, but never this good. Her face was damp from their sweat and his kisses.

"We've done it, right?" Cara asked hopefully, not wanting him to know she wasn't thrilled with the feeling.

"Not really." He looked up from between her breasts. "Let me push one more time, okay?"

She wanted to tell him no, but somehow it had to get better. In the books, it always was better the second time. Cara ran her fingers through his thick black hair giving herself time to think. This might be her last chance before going to the all-girl college she picked out for herself, thinking it'd be easier to concentrate without boys around because she wanted to graduate in three years instead of four.

"Okay, but if it doesn't work this time, we have to stop. It's hurting a lot."

He nodded, stroked her cheek, but he knew he was going to break it this time, no matter what. And then he was going to screw her good and proper.

"Open your legs some more, okay?"

He pecked her on the cheek. Centering himself, he pushed hard with a grunt. She screamed.

The books didn't say it'd bring tears to her eyes. In the books, it was a little pop and then everything was fine. So fine, she'd want him grunting and shoving himself in her. But all she wanted was to get him off to let her run away from the pain.

Now that he was past her newly broken hymen, Dillon stopped pushing. She fitted to him tightly. His whole body felt her, like sunshine on his skin. His primal urges took over. His breath become gasps, as he hunched himself fast and faster. All control of his body left him. The heaving contractions of her pain made her belly squeeze him. Her twisting and squirming made him shiver from the inside out. He scooped her butt into his hand, adjusting her into the crease at the bottom of his belly. Now, their bodies were locked together, their fate sealed.

He'd promised to pull out at the crucial moment, but it wasn't to be. She was doing something to him he couldn't understand while she was sobbing.

Then, it happened. She felt something run the length of her spine. She heard a primeval noise, low and rumbling, then building into the crescendo of a high pitch before it stopped. It was a noise she'd never heard before. She lost her breath for a moment, then she slipped into a dark velvet place where every inch of her tingled. When the darkness faded, she remembered the sound. She hoped it only happened in her mind; she didn't want him to think she was some kind of animal.

But the noise manifested itself in several different ways. They both added to the sound, they harmonized their sensations into a cantata of lust. It was the death knell of their collective youth, the howl of human creation.

The feeling ran deep into Dillon's belly, making him nauseous. It dragged semen from him, sapping every ounce of his strength. He lay over her, deep inside her, powerless, unable to pull out or move. It happened as nature intended, against all their hopes and plans.

When he recovered, he saw she was semi-conscious. He shifted his butt, making his penis slip out of her. Bracing with his arm and one leg on the floor of the car, he took most of his weight off her, hoping it'd help her breathe. Her eyelids fluttered open and she smiled.

He was relieved; all he had to do was tell a little white lie. He used a garage rag from the floor to wipe her blood off the seat, keeping it off her dress. He wouldn't have to pay extra when he took the car back. He used the same rag to wipe himself before his rumpled-around-his-knees tux pants got stained. He kissed her gently. Cara kissed him back. Perhaps he wouldn't have to tell the lie right now. After all, she was new to this. He kissed her over and over, keeping her flat on the seat. When her kisses began to inflame him again, he stopped. They didn't have the time for a second round.

"We better get up front and go home. I don't want your dad grounding you."

She smiled, grazing his cheek with a kiss as he slipped to the floor of the car untangling himself from her. Sitting side by side, they made plans.

"I want to do this again. Like tomorrow night," she said. "Can we?"

"Sure. I figure we don't have to stay at the senior class barbeque because my folks are going to some shindig at the Martinique. I can call my brother to check when they've left; then we can go to my room and do it in a real bed. My bed. He won't tell. He'll have his girl with him down in the rec room. He likes to screw her on the pool table."

Cara smiled feeling very adult, very womanly. Now, she knew what it was like. She knew what the older women were giggling about with their girlfriends. Now, she knew why they stopped before saying too much. Like members of a sorority, they all understood the delicious mystery.

She was happy she'd given her virginity to Dillon; happy that Lee had dumped him. Happy that he wanted her again. And next week, when one of the older girls went to the doctor, she'd get Cara a packet of birth control pills to make her safe. Then she'd spring for a hotel room to celebrate. She'd lie to her parents and say she was going to a pajama party.

Dillon crawled over the front seat first, settling into the driver's side. Holding his hand out to help her, she didn't notice that fluid had drained from her as she wiggled through. Only a small part splashed on her inner thigh. Some landed in the layers of lace bunched around her like a ballerina's tutu. But most of it remained inside her, silently active.

Tuesday, 17 Oct. 1978, 06:56

A Prank for Rachael

When Rachael got to the office, a large pink bakery box from Blake's store was sitting on her desk. He was being spiteful, making someone drive six miles across town instead of leaving it on her doorstep.

Rachael put the box in her lap, turning her back to open it. Although she might have been angered by the breakup, Blake's looks were mediocre, his company boring, and the sex unremarkable. She was going to throw it in the trash, but when she saw what he'd included in the box, a better response presented itself.

"Hey Culpepper," shouted Homer Burnett from across the room, "you gonna stare at 'em or share 'em?"

"Share 'em Burnett," she said over her shoulder, "but a girl's gotta pick out her favorites first."

She snickered softy as the group of co-workers began to move toward the coffee pot on the little table. Rachael was going to be the darling of the squad room, even if the damn donuts were hard as houses bricks.

Atop the donuts was a nasty note that he didn't even sign. Rachael quickly crumpled it up, shoving it in her pocket without another glance.

Rachael watched as guys plucked donuts out of the box, spreading powdered sugar into the sun streaked air.

The box held Trojan condoms. In Blake's world of estrogen and canned goods, the box of condoms was a huge insult, tantamount to shouting she was a whore from the top of the Sear's Tower. In her world of testosterone and death, they were a badge of honor.

"What you need isn't *one* boyfriend, but a whole herd of boyfriends."

Rachael shot an annoyed look at Tony, "Yeah, Blake was too straight-laced to date a cop. Maybe a crossing guard or a meter maid, but not a cop. He needs someone with regular hours. Remember last week? Down on Rush Street, questioning the staff in Mother's?"

"Benny tattled on us to your boyfriend?" exclaimed Tony, frowning. "Now that's one low-life son of a bitch!"

"Yep, but you know what? Benny did me a favor. Let's get back to work."

June 1977

Graduation Day

Cara was ecstatic. She'd received an acceptance letter from the one "seven sisters college" she really wanted. Now all she had to do was walk across the stage and get her diploma. Stepping out of the shower, she wrapped a towel around her hair and danced across the thick rose-colored shag carpet to her bed. The black-faced digital clock and matching rack stereo system were the only things in the room that weren't white French provincial. A light breeze wafted through the window, fluttering the Irish lace curtains. Lying naked on the thick beach towel spread atop her yellow satin bedspread was deliciously sinful.

With the door locked, she rubbed lotion on her legs, tangling her toes in the folds of gauzy lace hanging from the canopy frame to the edges of the double bed. With the leftover lotion on her palms, she brushed her breasts. To her amazement, her nipples were super sensitive.

Pulling the bolster pillow from her chaise lounge, she lay with her eyes closed, pretending it was Dillon, her mind skipping from present to future. She was thrilled her parents let her choose Vassar in upstate New York, even though her father had strongly recommended Saint Xavier on 103rd Street. He pleaded for Marist Catholic College in the same city as Vassar, but Mother protested a Catholic education, so Vassar it was. Cara knew she was walking on campus with only half of the school motto "Purity and Wisdom" intact. They'd teach her the wisdom part. The purity part needed work now that she'd lost her virginity. Being away from home with no true friends, it wouldn't be so hard to pretend. With no boys around it meant that it'd be easy not fall into having premarital sex again.

She was sad she couldn't talk Dillon into attending Duchess Community College across the Hudson River from Vassar, but his heart was set on Coyne Technical Institute down on Paulina and the Eisenhower Expressway. It was as far as he was able to stretch himself or his finances.

Lee wouldn't go to college at all. Cara thought living across the tracks in Mount Greenwood was supposed to be cheap, so why didn't Lee and her mother have money to send her to college? According to Lee, she couldn't even afford to take classes at Daley or Loop Junior College. She had to wait a whole year to start because she needed to work full time to help her mother keep their home and pay the bills.

As Cara slipped into remembering the feel of Dillon's weight on her, the pull of his hands around her waist, the taste of his lips, a noise jolted her.

"Cara," Mrs. O'Toole called, jiggling the doorknob, "What in God's name are ye doing with the door locked? Have you not showered yet?"

"I have Mother," Cara shouted, "I'm doing my hair right now. I'll be down in a few minutes, okay?"

"Well, hurry yer'self up. Your father is itching to leave to get a decent parking space."

Cara's pillow lover would have to wait. Moving to her vanity, she combed her damp hair into two thick, curly ponytails. Hanging on the door were her peach dress and dark green graduation gown. The new bra seemed snugger than when she bought it a week ago, but her period was due any day. The imported pantyhose pinched her waist. She should've stuck with her regular brand, but these were so pretty she couldn't resist. Mother always said women paid a price to be beautiful.

The Diane Von Furstenberg wrap dress flattered her, yet

she couldn't understand why the inside tie seemed short. She hardly made a shoelace bow with it. She must have gotten the only irregular in the entire store. Slipping on her Gucci sandals, Cara wondered how she'd loved the look of them so much that she'd bought them too narrow. In a couple of days, this would all be behind her.

Timothy O'Toole knocked softly on his daughter's bedroom door. He'd been waiting for this day for four years, and he wasn't going to miss sharing any of it.

"Aren't you ready yet?" he asked, "Your mother's trying to drown me with coffee."

Cara swung the door open with a big smile. "How do I look, Daddy?"

Cara was radiant from head to toe. Her hair was thicker and shinier than ever, her crimson curls cascading beneath the mortarboard. Her skin was as pink as the inside of a conch shell. She wasn't a baby any more. She was fully grown. He'd have to tell her not to come to his fire station anymore; she was too good looking to be around the pack of wolves he worked with.

"You look wonderful," he said, blinking his eyes to clear his vision. "Truly, wonderful. Your grandmother would be so proud."

"And when you hear my speech, you'll be even prouder," she said, wondering why "prouder" sounded wrong. Everything in the world had changed for her, and now the number that represented her age was simply that, a representation. She felt more grown up and more alive than ever, and she liked it.

Timothy O'Toole crooked his arm and offered it to his darling daughter. She took it with a smile as they headed down the staircase. At the bottom stood her mother. Teagan O'Toole took a moment to fuss over Cara's appearance, to straighten the mortarboard over the mass of curls, to hide the zipper pull on the gown, and to square her shoulders. Now, her daughter was picture perfect.

"Ah, there you are. The graduate. Pretty a picture as ever there were," she said, blinking back tears.

Teagan had graduated from University without the benefit of family marking her achievement. She'd done it on her own, after her tragedy. But today was different. Today was Cara's day, and nothing would ruin it, not even the drunken louts from the fire station who called themselves Cara's "firey godfathers."

The ceremony went off without a hitch. Even the weather cooperated. In the audience, the O'Tooles sat next to a woman who had obviously come alone. In a sea of uncles, aunts, grandparents, and cousins, she sat quietly, not exchanging a nod or a whisper with anyone.

Teagan O'Toole was intrigued. The woman looked familiar, but she couldn't place her. From the clothes, one could tell that she didn't lunch at Beverly Country Club. She wondered if she even belonged on the east side of Western Avenue. The suit was decent but dated. No doubt it had hung in a closet, waiting for just such an occasion. The blouse she wore was wilted, the collar impervious to spray starch. The shoes were care-worn low flats with clip-on bows.

As the principal started on the M's, the lone woman's attention was fastened on the stage. She moved to the edge of her seat, waiting as families clapped, and friends cheered and whistled. Her child was the first "N" in the bunch. They mispronounced the name "Leivald," but she clapped unrestrainedly. Fortunately, the last name was simple enough. Watching her only daughter take the prized diploma and shake the principal's hand sent her into a cheering frenzy. The only ones to join her were a couple of the other graduates. Timothy thought it sad that the girl had such a small circle of friends, but he was happy when he saw that Cara was one of those clapping for the blonde girl on the stage.

Teagan O'Toole glared at the woman with contempt.

How could she lower herself like an over excited teenager? But her husband thought it commendable that the mother applauded for an entire family. Ann Nabb noticed neither of them. She was too happy for her only child after all the struggles they'd endured in the last three years. Even the year that Lee had to be held back after the death of her father was behind them now.

When the O's were being announced, Teagan pulled out an embroidered lace hanky to absorb her tears. Dabbing eyes was what sophisticated women did to express their joy, but Timothy made enough noise for them both. Scattered throughout the crowd were several of Cara's Dutch uncles, a few real cousins, plus part of the engine company from the 76th and Pulaski Fire station. Finally, when they called out Cara O'Toole, the cheering section erupted. Raucous whistling, stomping, and shouting followed Cara as she walked briskly across the stage to receive her diploma. Teagan sat straight backed, sniffling with the dignity of a queen.

Before long, with all the graduates back in their places, the class was announced, and caps were tossed in the air. The ceremony was over. The audience streamed down the aisles, but the O'Tooles and Mrs. Nabb waited for their daughters to make their way through the crowd. Teagan stiffened when she recognized Lee approaching. She didn't approve of Lee and Cara as friends. She had considered Lee to be a bad influence. She was poor, trashy, and two years older than Cara. To Teagan, it didn't matter that Lee had been held back because of the loss of her father and a birthdate that fell after the September kindergarten enrollment cutoff date.

Cara slid herself under her father's arm.

"Mom, Dad, guess what? You were sitting right next to Lee's mother. Mrs. Nabb, this is my father, Timothy O'Toole, and my mother, Teagan."

With Lee in her embrace and a huge smile on her face, Ann Nabb turned toward the couple.

"Pleased to meet you both," she said. "And on such a happy occasion."

"Haven't we met before?" Timothy O'Toole asked. "You look so familiar."

Teagan flashed a look at her husband. Even if he did know this woman, why would he try to become reacquainted at this moment?

"Aren't you Lieutenant O'Toole?" she asked, "I've seen you accompany victims to the ER at Christ Hospital where I work."

"Why yes!" he exclaimed, shooting out his hand. "I'm sorry I didn't realize it sooner— especially with our girls being friends and all. Forgive me."

"Of course," Mrs. Nabb replied.

"Where are you ladies headed next?" he asked.

"We're off to Snackville Junction," beamed Lee's mother.

Mrs. O'Toole strained to maintain a poker face at the mention of the tiny restaurant nestled next to the neighborhood dry cleaners. How could they possibly consider it a suitable place for a graduation celebration? A lunch counter where the food was brought to you on a model train?

"We've got a table at the country club," Mr. O'Toole said. "I insist you join us. These girls have earned it. Besides, I don't think Snackville Junction serves pink champagne," he said with a wink.

Teagan hadn't uttered a word during the entire exchange. Both girls hugged Mr. O'Toole and headed down the aisle toward the parking lot. Mrs. O'Toole followed them at a stately pace, clutching her black leather handbag to her body as though it were a shield. Mrs. Nabb quickly gathered a few rumpled programs from the chairs, stashing them in her purse rushing to keep pace with the group.

"I hope they have a nice tuna club sandwich," she said.

Nice tuna sandwich, indeed, Teagan thought, *The club has chefs, not fry cooks.*

Mrs. O'Toole marched across the warm asphalt of the parking lot, toward the open doors of her husband's car. She took her place on the passenger side of the front seat, forcefully pulling the door out of her husband's hand to close it. The girls piled into the back seat of the O'Tooles' car. He deflected her rudeness by speaking directly to Mrs. Nabb.

"Why don't you sit in back with the girls, Mrs. Nabb," he said pointing towards the open door with a bright smile, "and when we're done, I'll bring you back to your car."

"Why, thank you, Lieutenant O'Toole!"

Dillon Whelan observed the scene while surrounded by his loud adoring family. Having both his girlfriends whisked away angered him. It wasn't the way he had planned it, but at least it kept him from having to decide whom to kiss.

Tuesday, 17 Oct. 1978, 11:42

A Positive Identification

"I looked through those bags of trash from the pit early this morning," Tony sighed. "I found zilch. It was all kitchen scraps."

"Do you think you got stuff from DiCola's or the Maple Tree Inn?" Rachael asked.

"Both," he replied. "There were industrial-sized cans mixed in the trash."

"How did you keep the debris off your clothes going through it?" she asked.

"My veterinarian friend gave me those gloves that reach all the way up to your shoulders."

The phone on Tony's desk rang. The crime lab produced an ID for the victim. He wrote the name on the tab of a manila file folder. Rachael recorded the name on her yellow pad. Now, Tony could stop referring to the victim as "Olivia Newton Dead."

With a sweep of the Law Enforcement Agency Data System, Department of Motor Vehicles, and the National Crime Information Center, they were closer to notifying the next of kin. Rachael headed for the bank of terminals, her half-drained coffee cup in hand.

She grumbled about being the one who always had to turn on the computers. The men didn't like typing, so they left them off for as long as they could. Waiting for the machines to boot up, she topped off her fourth cup of the day. Tony joined her.

"Why are you smiling Breese?" she asked. He was way too happy for the day after catching a new murder.

“It was a wonderful night. Cynthia outdid herself. Toast triangles dotted with shrimp smeared with black jelly.”

“Did the black jelly have salty little bubbles in it?”

“It did,” he smiled impishly.

“Shrimp toast with caviar,” she stated flatly, knowing he was dumbing it down to tease her.

She knew Tony was no stranger to fancy foods, good wines, or exotic women. His family was very high brow, from old money involved with Morse code and the telegraph when it was the new high-tech invention. All his relatives lived in mansions along the lakeshore from Winnetka to Waukesha. He’d been raised a gourmand. Why he became a Chicago cop was the mystery, explained perhaps by his mixed racial background, which like hers, gave him a different perspective on everything.

“Dinner was filet mignon with potatoes and gravy.” He smiled adding, “Breakfast was good, too.”

“Nice,” said Rachael, remembering her evening of reheated Kentucky Fried Chicken and Napoleon, her cat’s, half can of Friskies tuna.

A flash from the DMV’s monitor caught Rachael’s attention. Tony poured another cup of coffee, strolled over to the computer, and announced a hit.

“We’ve got a hit on a driver’s license. Lievald Nabb, South Whipple near 108th. Damn. She just turned 20.

“‘Lievald.’ What an odd name. I wonder what’s the origin.” Tony said, as he slid into the chair next to Rachael.

“A reversion to Gaelic roots? The name of some mythological heroine?” Rachael asked. “After all, 108th and Whipple is an Irish neighborhood. Wonder if they called her ‘Liv,’ or ‘Lee,’ or ‘Val?’”

“She’s the tragic heroine,” Tony said solemnly. “The crime lab says death by blunt force trauma to the back of the skull. Crunched like an egg. Whoever it was, they were enraged. No skin or blood under her nails, not a drop of semen or any sign of intercourse either. Funniest thing, they found a linen hanky in her fist. They're gonna see if there's any residue on it."

Another monitor showed nothing in the NCIC database, so the victim didn't have a criminal background. The LEADS screen showed "fingerprints on file" citing Christ Hospital as the source.

"If she hadn't worked for the hospital, we wouldn't have gotten the positive ID," sighed Tony.

"You think she's been reported missing?" Rachael asked.

"Someone's got to be going crazy by now. Crime Lab said she'd been dead 24 hours or more when she fell out of the garbage truck. That's plenty of time to realize she hadn't made it home for dinner. I'll call the 22nd District to see if they know something the computers don't. The desk sergeant could be waiting before he put it in the system."

Tony returned to his desk while Rachael used the computer to dig deeper. She overheard Tony ending a call that went nowhere.

Rachael wheeled around in the chair, letting the computers behind her do their work. Tony gave her a thumb's down as he moved past her to go to the screen behind her.

"There's a hit on a juvie record," he said looking over her shoulder.

Sure enough, there was a Nabb who'd been out joy riding, but it was a fifteen-year-old boy from the far North Side. When the other machine search came up empty, Rachael decided to hit the special address listings phone books to see if there were family members residing at the address. One name appeared, an "Albrecht Nabb."

"We've a match on phone and address," Rachael said glancing at the clock. "Ready to hit the streets?"

"This is what I hate," Tony said, "telling someone that their loved one's killed and that we don't know who did it. I wish we could wait until we caught the bastard, give 'em someone to blame right away."

Rachael knew Tony didn't like blindsiding families with bad news any more than she did. Without a missing persons report, the family was blithely living their lives, waiting for their daughter Lievald. Now Tony and Rachael had to break the news to them and live through the nightmare with them.

"Let's hope they have some idea of who'd do this," Rachael said. "The saving grace is that we don't have to show them the body right away. Without the fingerprints the case would've gone cold before we even started."

"This might be very interesting. Hastings, the medical examiner, confirmed what the crime lab technician had speculated: No sexual assault, no drugs or alcohol in her system. She'd eaten a couple of hot dogs, partially digested, of course. It wasn't a wine-and-dine killing. And she was about nine weeks pregnant with her first baby."

"You thinking young wife? Albrecht, the husband the killer? We can have lunch right after we book him."

"Could be as simple as that," said Tony. "If we book him into the 22nd District, I'll buy you lunch at The Maple Tree on Western. You like Cajun food, yeah?"

"Maybe I want Chinese," Rachael said. "Think we can come up with a reason to take him all the way to 11th and State? We could eat upstairs at Guey Sam's in Chinatown and then shoot some pool downstairs at the Golden Dragon Pool Hall."

"We can't do it," Tony announced with a smug smile. "I've got a hot date tonight...."

"Cynthia again?"

"Cynthia won't be free until next week after her business trip. Tonight, it's with beautiful, bodacious Bethany."

"Then we better get this over and done as quickly as possible," Rachael giggled. "So as not to interfere with your hot date. In and out in about twenty minutes, ya think?"

"We can stretch it out longer if necessary." Tony turned south on Kedzie Avenue. "I don't need more than an hour to get ready."

"Okay. Case closed in six and a half hours. I can dig it," Rachael replied,

"If we close this one too soon, Sarge will put us on a new one and screw up my date…."

On both sides of the street, the Cape Cod frames were lined up like soldiers, block after block. It was typical of the post-war ideal. The American Dream, each white house uniformly alike, yet over time, many with individual touches rendering them unique but not so much so that they stood out.

Rachael wondered which one of them housed their victim and which one her killer. Rachael observed the residents going about their day, caught between the grit of the city and their fondest dreams and wondered who'd be devastated by the news.

They turned on 107th, bearing toward the railroad tracks. The neighborhood gradually morphed from regimented neat single-family dwellings to eclectic blocks of 1950s modern, to old hand-built cottages, to asphalt-sided frames, and Sears Roebuck catalog kit houses. They located the address, but Tony circled the block, counting the number of doors from its end.

The two continued to drive around the block, looking to see if any detail however minute screamed out at them but nothing did. Tony drove to the end again, and then made a sweep of the alley. He counted the gates and garages until they reached the back of the residence. All the garbage cans were accounted for. Two 55-gallon drums, painted radiator silver, were stenciled neatly with the address and were filled with ordinary bagged trash. Tony wrinkled his nose as he pulled small bags of trash from the Nabb household can and tossed them in the trunk. He and Rachael would sift through them at the station parking lot, hoping for clues. They parked the car and walked around the little house before going to the door.

July 1977

A Surprise Revelation

The bedroom door was closed. That was not like Cara to close it early in the morning. She usually dressed in the bathroom, but trying to get into her shorts, she had to lie on the bed today. She was more bloated than ever before her period. She knew it was coming and coming hard because she'd missed it last month. This one was going to be a doozy, probably lasting a week or more.

She pulled up one elastic panty girdle over her belly. Looking in the mirror, it helped flatten out the bulge that was forming around her navel. She needed something more if she was going to get into the new shorts she bought at Carson's for the picnic. White shows every little bump.

Cara reached into the dresser for another one. She lay down on the bed and struggled to get it in place on top of the first one. The mirror told her that she was nearly where she needed to be, but it also was a sign that she needed to go shopping to replace most of her underwear. The pretty new sheer nylon bras from Lily of France shrunk after one washing, making her breasts push out of the top and sides. The fabric of the pink one must have thinned in the wash because her nipples showed through more than ever. She wouldn't buy that color again.She reached for the third and last girdle she owned when she heard a knock on the door.

"Just a minute," she said, but her mother barged into the room before the third panty girdle could be tossed under the pillow.

"Cara, what's the holdup? We're expected at the picnic.

Your father's waiting in the parlor."

"I'll be ready in a minute, Mother," Cara said hiding the girdle behind her back. "I've got to pull on my shorts."

Her mother saw that she was hiding something, and, raising her eyebrows, lowered her voice. "Give that to me," she demanded.

Cara handed her the thick panty.

"What on earth are you doing?" She pointed at the latex panty girdle Cara was wearing."It's hot as the devil's armpit. I told ya, you've been eating too much lately. Shorts and girdles never mix. Put on a sundress."

Cara stood in place, immovable under her mother's sweltering gaze.

"Get on with it, shuck out of that girdle before you sweat yourself sick. It's over 82 degrees outside. You'll be fainting from heat stroke if you wear that thing."

"Okay, Mother," Cara said, hoping that she'd be given privacy to do it. As she stripped off the double layer of latex, Teagan crossed the room, going to the dresser. Dropping the pink panty girdle in the drawer, she plucked out a plain nylon panty to match the color of Cara's dress. Cara was still frozen in place when her mother's eyes scanned her semi-nude body.

Cara's breasts were doubled in size, spilling out of her new bra. The areolas, which should have been hidden by the pink of Cara's bra, had darkened to nut brown, staring at her like the eyes of an animal trapped in a hedge. Worst of all, running down Cara's stomach was a faint line of color accentuating a slight bump radiating around her navel. Teagan was transfixed; the panty slipped from her hand, fluttering to the floor.

"God's death!" moaned Teagan. "Oh, Cara, what have you done? What have you done?"

Cara had no answer. She had no idea what her mother was talking about. She sank down on the bed and felt her mother's firm hands grip her thin shoulders, shaking her.

"Who did this to you, Cara? Tell me who it was. Who?"

"I don't know what you're talking about, Mother. *I* put the extra girdle on."

"Not the girdle, lass. I want to know his name."

"Whose name?" Cara answered puzzled.

"The boy that did this to you! Tell me which little bastard was it? You tell me. Now!"

"I don't know what you're talking about…."

Teagan O'Toole's mind raced to situation after situation, trying to remember a time when Cara behaved strangely—out of character—when she might have come home disheveled. She tried to figure out how she could have missed some sign. Cara blubbered, shocked at the way her mother was treating her. Teagan could stand it no longer. She would get it out of her if it was the last thing she ever did.

"Tell me who it was, Cara. I won't let him get away with ruining you. Tell me, you hear? Tell me!" She screamed over and over, in such a shrill voice that it frightened Cara to her core.

Cara stared blankly at her mother. The screams brought her husband from the back of the first floor, up the stairs two at a time. She watched him gently grab her mother's wrists, calling her name slightly above a whisper, attempting to calm her down. Freed from her mother's grasp, Cara scrambled to the middle of the bed and pulled on her panties, crouching in a defensive position, protecting herself from anticipated blows from a woman she no longer knew.

Teagan ranted at her husband Timothy, spewing a flood of Gaelic words and curses he did not understand. He countered each phrase, demanding to know what was going on. Finally, she stopped, took a deep breath, pointed at their cowering daughter, breaking the news in a hoarse whisper.

"Some bastard has ruined our daughter."

"What makes you say that?" Timothy asked.

"Ah Timmy, take a look…."

After a moment of uncomfortable silence, Timothy eased

down next to Cara, draping his arm around her slumped shoulders. Mustering all the calm he could, he asked her gently, "Cara, baby, did someone mess with you?"

"No Papa," she whispered, wondering how her mother knew she'd had sex. She'd been so careful to hide it. Cara buried her face in his upper arm, wishing this moment away.

Timothy O'Toole stared at his wife, tears streaming down her twisted face. He'd never seen her like that—in the throes of a breakdown.

"If she says no," he asked his wife slowly, trying to defuse the situation, "what makes you think something has happened?"

"Stand her up," Teagan ordered sadly. "Have a close hard look at her. Look at her like she's a person going to the Emergency Room in your damned ambulance, not your daughter."

Cara sat still, not wanting to have her father inspect her like she was at the doctor's office. It was bad enough that her mother had revealed that she'd lost her virginity, to him—her father.

"Teagan, honey, there's nothing wrong with her that a little time in the gym won't cure. She's eaten too much at all those parties and picnics. She'll work it off before she leaves for Vassar," said Timothy.

Teagan looked askance at her husband, a look that conveyed her disbelief at his naiveté."God's death, man," she spat. "Look at her! Her nipples are dark as mud. There's a line on her belly. She's not bloated. She's showing the signs. Just as I'm standing here, she's pregnant."

Cara jumped to her feet. "I am not!" she yelled indignantly.

"You're going to stand there and tell me your hymen hasn't been broken?"

Cara drew herself up to her full height and replied with a flat, unconvincing "Yes."

"This is a conversation for the two of you," her mother said to Cara's father. "I'll be downstairs in the parlor. You can come and fetch me when you're done with Virgin Mary."

Once Teagan was gone, Cara ran to her father's arms panic stricken, sobs rattling her fragile frame.

"So... Cara honey… who did this to you?" he asked gently. Cara sobbed uncontrollably.

"I'm not upset with you, baby. Your mother will come around. It may be a shock, but we'll do whatever we have to. Understand? Whatever is right for *you*, okay?"

Cara had no idea what her father was talking about. She was mortified to tell her father that she'd had sex at the prom. How would he ever trust her again? How'd he still love her? She sucked the snot back up into her nostrils and, with a big breath, calmed her jumping heart.

"You say the word, and I'll break him into pieces. You don't have to be afraid. School is out, and no one will be the wiser. You tell me who, and I'll kill him for raping you."

She glared at him wide-eyed. Rape was something you read about in the paper; it didn't happen in Beverly.

"You're safe baby. Just point him out, and I'll take care of it for you."

"I wasn't raped," she said in a whisper, burying her head as tight into his chest as she could.

"What?" he asked, putting his hand under her chin to move her eyes up to his. "Don't worry, he can't hurt you again. Tell me his name. It's okay. I promise, sweetheart, I'm not mad at you."

Cara's mouth was dry, but she slowly repeated her simple statement, looking straight into her father's sympathetic eyes.

"I… wasn't… raped, Daddy."

A relieved smile spread across his face. He pulled a blue bandana out of his jean pocket and dabbed at her eyes. He wanted it all to be a big mistake, a misunderstanding that they'd laugh about over the potato salad and barbecue.

"And your mother is wrong. You're not pregnant."

"I'm not," she said adamantly. "But I'm not a virgin anymore, either. I'm not a bad girl. I only did it three times."

Timothy O'Toole sat on the bed stunned. His baby girl experimenting with sex without talking to him first?

"I know it was wrong, but everyone was talking about it. So us girls drove out to Hinsdale and Joseph got 'em out of the machine."

"Got what out of a machine?" he asked.

"Rubbers, daddy" she said proudly. "They have a machine in the men's room of the Hinsdale Oasis on the Tollway. That's where all the boys go to get them. We got on the Tri-State at 95th, and drove to the Oasis. While Joseph was in the restroom, us girls got a soda at the counter. We were back in Beverly in no time."

The frown on her father's face was not reassuring.

"Honest, daddy," she said trying to make him feel better. "I bought three, and I used all three. And I don't have any intention to buy anymore until I get home from college. Sex is okay, but it's not like I thought it would be."

"Stand up Cara," he said.

"We were careful, Daddy. We did everything to stay safe. Everybody knows you can't get pregnant the first time, but he wore a rubber anyway. The second time, we stood up to do it, and the last time I was on my period."

Timothy O'Toole was stunned at her admission. He was beginning to believe his wife's accusation. After all, Cara did have a faint, dark line running from her navel to the top of her panties. Softly palpating her abdomen, he detected a small hard spot around her navel. He wrapped his arm around her, rocking her gently.

"Cara honey, condoms aren't foolproof. You mother could be right, but we'll go to the doctor Monday, to find out. Get dressed. We'll go to the picnic and not say a word, okay?"

"Sure Daddy." Hugging him tightly, she burrowed her

head into his chest, savoring the bittersweet moment. Tim O'Toole bit his lip, tamping down the conflicting emotions as he stroked her hair.

Tuesday, 17 Oct. 1978, 13:57

The Notification

Rachael and Tony parked in front of the small cottage set near the back of a narrow lot. It might have been a coach house converted into a cottage with a dormered roof. The house was dwarfed by a giant oak tree's overhanging branches. The walk was littered with acorns.

"Let's hope Albrecht is home," Tony said.

Rachael nodded. She steeled herself for what she knew would be coming next. Nobody enjoyed notifications, but they were the first step in solving a case.

The brown wooden screen door lacked a doorbell on its frame so they resorted to knocking on the window. After a while, a sleepy-looking woman opened the weather-beaten inside door. She was visibly upset, pulling the sash to her terrycloth robe tight around her, poised to chew them out.

"Can't you people see the 'no solicitors' sign on the window? I'm not interested in Bible study. I work nights."

"We're sorry ma'am," Rachael answered, fishing inside her jacket for the chain holding the plastic sleeve that held her badge around her neck. "We're not from a church. I'm Detective Culpepper, and this is Detective Breese. We're police. Is a Mr. Albrecht Nabb home?"

The woman glared at Rachael as if she had two heads. She pulled her lips into her mouth, biting them. Then, stiffening her spine, she pulled her head up to deliver a bitter message.

"Mr. Albrecht Nabb has been deceased for three years. If this is something about his old business, you'll have to go to the garage on Kedzie and talk with the new owners. My husband ran a clean and honest shop. I don't have any of the records or paperwork here."

"I'm sorry to hear that, ma'am." Rachael said.

Tony decided to jump in at that point, hoping he could charm his way into the woman's confidence.

"Could we come in for a moment or two? It has nothing to do with the garage."

Rachael inched sideways, yielding more of the doorway to him.

Mrs. Nabb blinked. "Sure," she relented, unlatching the screen door. "But only for a few minutes. I've got to get back to sleep before my shift tonight. I think you both can appreciate that."

"We sure can," Tony said, giving Rachael a knowing look as the woman turned away from the door.

"What's this all about?" Mrs. Nabb asked.

She perched on the edge of the seat of a tattered plaid recliner. Tony and Rachael occupied the matching love seat. Tony put his notebook on the smoked glass top of the blond colored wood coffee table to read from it.

"Do you know a young lady by the name of Lievald Nabb?" he asked point blank.

"What has Lee done?" she asked with the weariness of a mother who'd reached the end of her rope. "Do I have to bail her out?"

"Is Lee your daughter, ma'am?" he asked gently, leaning forward.

"Yes, and sometimes she is a handful—especially since her father's been dead. She likes to play pranks with her friends, but she's never been arrested before. What did she do?"

"She hasn't done anything to be arrested," Tony replied. "May I ask when was the last time you saw her?"

"We pass like ships in the night. I've been on third shift, and she's been on seconds for a while. We both work at the hospital. I saw her day before yesterday when I was coming on, but I heard her upstairs when I got home this morning. What is this all about?"

Tony looked her straight in her eyes.

"I'm very sorry, Mrs. Nabb. We're here to inform you that your daughter has been found dead."

The woman stared at Tony, her face frozen in shock. She shook her head from side to side in denial, mouthing the word "NO" over and over again. She tried to form words, but her voice wouldn't cooperate. Tony held her hand, giving her something to cling to. After an awkward silence, she finally found her voice, and it was barely above a whisper.

"That can't be. You're mistaken," she said. "I heard her stirring around upstairs this morning. She's up there sleeping right now. Come see for yourselves…."

She snatched her hand from Tony, crossing the tiny living room floor before either of them could stop her. She bolted up the narrow staircase two steps at a time, her robe fluttering behind her.

"Lee! Lee! Lee!" she yelled out as Tony and Rachael pursued her up the stairs.

She pushed open the closed door with both hands. Directly opposite was a half-open window. Two squirrels had gained entry. Seeing humans, they scampered across the clothes-littered floor, hopping out the window onto the steep pitched gable.

Mrs. Nabb ran to the bed, and tore off the bunched-up covers, revealing an empty bead. She crumpled to her knees in a spasm of pitiable sobbing. She hugged the comforter to her breast, rocking back and forth.

"No, NO, NOOOOO!" she cried over and over again. "Not my Lee! Oh God, not my Lee!"

The two waited, hovering close, quietly giving her time to compose herself on her own accord. Soon, she stopped sobbing and stood up.

"I've got to clean this room up. Lee keeps it in such a mess, always on the run, never time enough to get herself organized."

She went to grab a sheet from the bed when Rachael stopped her.

"Mrs. Nabb, you have to leave everything like it is. We'll help you clean up, but not until forensics takes a good look. There might be a clue here. Do you understand?"

She blinked, yet wouldn't let go of the comforter. Tony and Rachael had seen this before. They hoped there was nothing on the linen pertinent to the case. Rachael guided the poor woman back through the door and watched Tony take his handkerchief to gently close the open window, hoping the squirrels hadn't ingested any evidence. He stood in the middle of the bedroom surveying his surroundings. Once the women were downstairs, he descended and stepped out the front door to radio for the crime lab. Mrs. Nabb lay on the arm of the love seat, crying into the fabric, muffling her anguish as Rachael watched.

"Why, why, why didn't I know she was gone?" she cried. "What kind of mother am I? How couldn't I know that she wasn't home? How? Oh my God, how did I not *know*?"

"Did she leave the window open often?" Rachael asked trying to pry information out of her without inflicting more pain.

"All the time. She liked the fresh air." Mrs. Nabb smiled wanly as she looked up at Rachael. "She left it open even on the coldest days...."

Mrs. Nabb stared blankly at Rachael, the reality finally dawning that her child was dead. Her face was contorted in grief, and her shoulders shuddered as she lapsed back into heart-rending wails. Rachael allowed her free rein to release her emotions as Tony came back in from the radio call.

Mrs. Nabb couldn't stem the flow of tears as her breath caught in her throat, like a baby whimpering.

"I heard her up there, I tell you!"

She folded her hands imploring the detectives. "You got it all wrong. It's all a mistake. She's gone out and didn't wake me. It's a mistake.... "

"What's her hair color?" Rachael asked as gently as possible.

"She's white blonde like her father." Mrs. Nabb pointed to a picture atop the television in the corner of the room. Tony ambled over to take a look.

"Did she have a car?" Rachael asked, hoping perhaps that Mrs. Nabb was right, that the girl had left the house without her knowing it. But she knew that fingerprints don't lie.

"She has a little green sports car. It should be parked out front."

Seizing on this shred of hope, Mrs. Nabb sprang from the love seat, to the front room window. Placing her palms on the center of the pane, she perked up when she saw that the car was missing. Turning back to the detectives, her face was blanched white.

"It's not there. I didn't notice it wasn't there. I didn't even notice...."

She collapsed to her knees in the middle of the living room, mute.

Tony squatted next to her, patting her back gently, trying his best to console her, imploring her not to be hard on herself. It was Rachael's opportunity to scribble down a few notes.

Mrs. Nabb cried until her voice was hoarse. Rachael glanced at her watch; it had only taken forty-five minutes to ruin this woman's day, possibly her entire life.

"Is there someone we can call for you, Mrs. Nabb? Someone to come and stay with you when we leave?" Tony asked.

She stared at him, blinked back tears, and shook her head no.

"All gone. All gone," she said.

Tony repeated the question, but Mrs. Nabb was more in control of her faculties than Tony and Rachael had imagined.

"No one. There is no one left; there is no one now that Lee is gone."

Rachael had witnessed so many sad scenes that she was concerned that she had become hardened, inured to outpourings of grief, but the pathos of Mrs. Nabb's loss proved that she hadn't. Tony spoke, breaking the silence.

"We're going to get the person who did this, Mrs. Nabb. Rachael and I've found quite a few killers in our time on the force. But the guys from the crime lab are coming to take a look at Lee's room. They'll need to dust for prints and perform a few other tests."

"You tell them to look real good because I want you to find him. He's lucky my husband is dead. He'd be hunting for the bastard who did this to our baby!"

She pounded her fists into the tops of her thighs with enough force to cause bruises. Then, on a dime, her mind snapped back to the reality of the situation, and she began to demand answers from them.

"Was my baby raped?" she asked, grabbing Tony by the arm.

"No ma'am, she wasn't raped," he said.

"She was a virgin. She told me herself. She didn't spread her legs like some of the girls she ran around with. Lee was a good girl. A good Lutheran girl."

Rachael stared at Tony with raised eyebrows, knowing that he'd withhold the fact about the pregnancy. Under the circumstances, that revelation wouldn't help matters at all. It would only inflame them.

"May I see her? Will you take me to her?" she asked pathetically.

"We want to wait with you until the crime lab arrives. Once they finish up in her room, dust the doors for fingerprints, then we can go," Tony answered gently.

Mrs. Nabb nodded her head. She'd worked long enough in a hospital to know that what she'd experience at the medical examiner's office was irreversible.

"Would you like something to drink, Mrs. Nabb?" Rachael asked.

"I could use a cup of coffee," she said, standing up. "Please. Call me Ann," she said.

"I'm Tony, and she's Rachael," Tony reciprocated.

As Mrs. Nabb and Tony went to the kitchen for coffee, Rachael went to look at Lee's photo on the wall. She was a pretty girl with shocking blue eyes, platinum white hair, and a slightly chipped front tooth. She was smiling broadly, holding a trophy aloft. Rachael thought it sad that she wouldn't be the subject of more pictures. She looked around the living room, hoping to find Lee's personal phone book or some other possession to allow them to enter into her world without having to ask her mother.

On the table was a stack of business cards. All were from automotive places—a specialty tire firm in Blue Island, a couple of junk yards, a tow truck company, auto parts stores, and the MG Club of Chicago. Some had phone numbers scribbled on their backs in a woman's neat handwriting; others showed cryptic notes. Sitting down to quickly copy the information on her pad, Rachael replaced the cards just as Tony and Ann reentered the living room. Tony nodded his head, a hint that Rachael should distract Mrs. Nabb while he recorded what he'd gleaned from the conversation with her in the kitchen.

"Ann, this is wonderful coffee," Rachael complimented her. "What brand is it?"

"Nothing fancy. It's Jewel's generic brand. The trick is to add a pinch of salt to the grounds. It gives it a kick, don't you think?"

"It certainly does," Rachael said, diluting the saltiness with an extra spoon of sugar.

"What do you do at the hospital?" Rachael asked, keeping

Mrs. Nabb talking about herself.

"I'm a ward clerk. I'm usually on the Ped's, but I float too. I need the extra money. Things have been tough since Albrecht passed."

"Were these business cards from Mr. Nabb's garage?"

"Oh no. Lee is quite the mechanic herself. She's putting every extra dime she has into that little struggle buggy of hers. Calls it a classic and says it will put her through college once she gets it restored to mint condition. I think it'll put her in the poorhouse. Every time she gets one thing fixed, something else breaks. But she loves that little car."

It wasn't lost on Rachael that Mrs. Nabb referred to her daughter in the present tense as though she were still alive.

"Do you think you should call someone at the hospital?"

She stared at Rachael, blinking her eyes as if she were unaware of the reason behind Tony's and Rachael's visit.

Something snapped her back to reality, and she responded.

"Karen. The nursing supervisor. I need to call Karen."

She reached for the phone and dialed slowly, waiting after each spin of the rotary dial as if she didn't have it committed to memory.

Rachael scanned the room while Tony went back in the kitchen and stood by the sink to look out the window. Had Lee been abducted before being killed, she could've been dragged through the neighboring yard without being heard. If the killer knew about her habit of keeping her bedroom window open, it was a possibility.

"Karen, I'm sorry, but I can't come to work tonight. I hope I'm not leaving you in the lurch." Mrs. Nabb sounded robotic. She was going through the motions, bearing up well until the inevitable question got asked. Then she lost it.

"No, not sick time. I don't need sick time. I feel fine. I'm not sick," she said, struggling not to answer the question, trying to hold out without uttering the word.

"Karen, it's Lee, she won't be coming in, either. She's not

sick. Nobody's sick. Oh my God, how I wish she was only sick, Karen. She's dead, Karen. My baby is dead."

Ann dropped the phone, sobbing loudly.

Rachael picked up the receiver. "Hello, I'm Detective Culpepper, Chicago Police Department," Rachael identified herself. "We're investigating the death of her daughter, Lee."

The woman on the other end of the line was stunned by the news.

"Yes, ma'am, we have a positive ID on Lievald Nabb. Could you kindly notify her supervisor? We'll be contacting the personnel department later. I'm afraid I can't provide you with any further information at this time," Rachael explained. "If her supervisor has any questions, they can reach me or my partner, Detective Breese at 744-3510. Leave a message with the Detective Division if we're out on the street," she said before hanging up.

Tony came back into the living room just as the crime lab van pulled up.

Tony admitted forensics and escorted them up the stairs to the bedroom. Rachael opened with the standard questions as one of the technicians dusted the front door.

Before long, Rachael had an image of a girl who had planned to be a partner in her father's auto repair business, but he died before her dream was realized. She resorted to working for the hospital doing data entry to help her mother make ends meet after his death. Both women were barely able to keep their heads above water. Ann Nabb worked every extra shift the hospital offered. She was exhausted. Rachael pressed Mrs. Nabb to identify someone to stay with her after they left because of her fragile state of mind.

The technicians performed their routine quietly, efficiently, and quickly. Tony came down the stairs with the forensics expert, following him to the van. In the meantime, Rachael asked Mrs. Nabb if she was ready to get dressed.

"Dressed? Oh. I need more than a robe and nightgown,

don't I?"

The light that had brightened her dull eyes while reminiscing about her daughter had been extinguished. She stood up, but the realization was too much for her, and her knees buckled. Rachael helped her to the staircase.

"You know, this isn't something I'd ever considered. I thought Lee would be the one to do this for me. You never imagine having to bury your child."

At the bedroom door, Mrs. Nabb stopped, leaning her body against the door's frame. Drawing in a deep breath, she braced herself and straightened up.

"I don't have to get dressed up, do I?"

"Put on whatever you'll be comfortable in, Ann," Rachael said.

Rachael went back into the kitchen to wait for her to get dressed. About ten minutes later, Mrs. Nabb emerged in a pair of stone washed jeans and a white pullover sweater.

"I'm as ready as I'm ever going to be," she said biting her lips. "Should I follow you in my car?"

"We'll drive you there, Ann. It's the least we can do," Rachael said.

They stopped at her front door. On the wall hung a wooden plaque in the shape of a big skeleton key. Mrs. Nabb removed a set of keys and locked the door behind her.

Tuesday, 17 Oct. 1978, 14:27

The Cook County Morgue

Tony drove more cautiously than usual with Rachael and Mrs. Nabb in the back seat. Cruising the streets like a patrolman surveilling his beat, he eschewed the expressways, driving below the speed limit most of the way to the Cook County Morgue.

He realized that Mrs. Nabb needed time to adjust to the reality of losing her only daughter. Knowing her delicate state of mind, Rachael kept gently prodding to uncover a relative or close neighbor as support for her after the identification of the body. The detectives knew that reactions to a sudden death differed widely, but no matter how they manifested themselves, the survivors needed the comfort and support of family and friends. It was a concern because Rachael and Tony would need to hit the bricks seeking the killer before the trail could go cold, and as insensitive as it may have sounded, they couldn't extend their handholding beyond what they deemed necessary.

Fortunately, while waiting for a stop light to change, Mrs. Nabb suddenly remembered the phone number of a cousin who lived behind Beverly Woods Restaurant. Rachael wrote it down. She thought it'd be better to call from the waiting area at the coroner's office.

Suddenly, out of the blue, Mrs. Nabb exclaimed, "I bet Lee's with her friend Cara and the twins!"

"Tell me about this friend Cara," Rachael said.

"Cara O'Toole's her best friend." Mrs. Nabb covered her mouth like a naughty schoolgirl. "Silly me… she's Cara

Whelan now. Got married last summer, to one of Lee's old boyfriends, but to me she'll always be an O'Toole. I guess it's because I thought Lee and Dillon would marry. After him and Lee broke up during senior year, Cara moved in. At first, I thought she was trying to patch them up, but one thing led to another, and, over the summer, they got married. And you should see those babies. They're adorable. Born on Valentine's Day. Lee helps with them all the time."

Rachael made a mental note of this. She hoped Tony had done the same.

As they rode west into the waning afternoon, Mrs. Nabb fished in her purse, searching for a packet of pictures held together by a wide rubber band. Under utility bills, work schedules on folded green paper, cash register receipts, and assorted tubes of makeup, she found it. She shuffled the stack of Polaroids, thickly backed studio shots, and curled drugstore prints in her lap like a deck of cards. Through the rearview mirror, Tony saw her press a dog-eared photo into Rachael's hand.

"Detective, aren't they little darlings?" she asked. "That's my Lee holding them. She loves those babies as if they were her own. Spends every spare minute over there, helping out."

"They're very cute," said Rachael. "Do you have a photo of Lee by herself?"

"I bet Lee's over there right now, changing diapers or playing with those babies…

If I remembered Cara's phone number, we could stop at a pay phone and check."

"It's better to be sure, Mrs. Nabb," said Tony from the front seat.

"Well, okay, if you think that's best, Detective."

She returned to the pictures on her lap, flipping to find one to satisfy Rachael's request.

Proceeding north on Kedzie Avenue, Tony eased over the railroad tracks that bordered the Evergreen Park City Hall/

Police Station complex north of 95th Street. He was hoping that Mrs. Nabb's attention would be occupied as they drove past the long expanse of grassy cemetery stretching to 87th Street. Fortunately, she didn't look up. While passing the stretch of shops and neat 1950s homes of Ashburn Park, Mrs. Nabb found the one she was seeking. Gazing at it fondly, her eyes welled up.

"I know I've a better one at home, but this is as close as I can get from this bunch." She smiled proudly as she gave it to Rachael.

"That's Lee and her dad, standing in front of our business; his garage was over on Kedzie near 108th."

The resemblance between father and daughter in the deep thoughtful blue eyes, straight noses, and full lips was striking. Her straight hair spilled over her shoulders, nearly touching the waist of her khaki shorts.

Albrecht's wash-faded blue coveralls were stained with oil and grease, yet apparently it didn't repulse Lee. He pulled her in close with a thickly muscled arm.

Rachael held the photo up high. In moments like this, she wished their cars had a regular radio in the back seat instead of the noise of active police work as it streamed out of the front speakers. Tony turned it down as low as possible, but it still distracted.

"She might be over at the garage right now, under a car, helping one of the guys we sold the place to. She's their carburetor expert. She's got one spread out all over her desk," said Mrs. Nabb, a mixture of pride and hope in her voice. "She's working on somebody's English car, a Spitfire, Jaguar, or something. When she was six, Al gave her one as a practical joke. He thought it would keep her busy while he worked on a car, but the joke was on him. She took it apart, cleaned it, and put it back together good as new."

Caught by the long traffic light under the viaduct that is the back door to the Norfolk-Southern railyard, the air took on a faint sugary smell. It grew stronger as they passed through the three-way intersection of 79th, Kedzie, and Columbus. As they started climbing the high railyard overpass, Tony smiled at the tall, pudding yellow-brick Nabisco factory, where Oreos were baking, the aroma floating on the air, a small pleasure that Mrs. Nabb, now reduced to tears, was oblivious to.

By the time they reached the southern edge of Marquette Park, she had composed herself. Rachael handed her more tissues. As Tony turned east on Marquette Boulevard, she observed the facades of the brick three-flat apartment buildings that lined the thoroughfare.

"How I miss my Albrecht," she sniffled, "so very much. When we first got married, we had an apartment on this stretch overlooking the park. It was nice. Being on the second floor was like living in the trees. That's why we named her 'Liebwald,' German for 'lovely forest,' but the nurse misspelled it. We didn't change it because Al said it made it impossible to translate. We'd be the only ones who knew what it meant. He worked at the railyard, and I worked at Holy Cross Hospital. We saved up enough money to buy the gas station in cash. At first, he rode his bike back and forth, but when winter came, he'd found this little house by the tracks to rent. Business was good; when Lee started walking, we went to the bank and got a loan to buy it."

She handed Rachael another photo, a faded one of Mrs. Nabb as a young woman holding a baby in front of one of the dark brown brick porches identical to the ones they were passing.

"He was a good man, a hard-working man. He didn't mean to leave me and Lee in debt. He was born in Germany; his family came here after World War I. He was a small child, but the accent stuck. With his bright blonde hair and blue eyes, there was no mistaking where he came from."

Tony eased into the left turn lane at the corner of California where Holy Cross Hospital dominated the landscape. Seeking to avoid car dealer row on Western Avenue, Tony took Rachael back through her childhood neighborhood: She was a Gage Park girl; her parents still lived there.

"In '74 when the oil prices went crazy, Albrecht's business suffered. People paid for their gas, most of the time, but it was hard to keep up with the prices. In the morning the price was one thing, and by the afternoon, you were in the hole to the oil company because your income wouldn't cover the cost of your next shipment. Thinking it was temporary, he borrowed from the bank, using the house as collateral. Then those crazy guys started their shenanigans calling themselves Nazis, marching in the park, causing trouble. Customers stopped coming in for repair work. They sprayed 'Nazi Go Home' on the garage. My husband wasn't a Nazi; he was a corporal in the U.S. Army in World War II, translating German into English, for goodness sake."

Tony glanced at her through the rearview mirror as she talked.

"We were together twenty-nine years when he died of a massive heart attack. I blame it on those jerks in the Nazi Party. His heart was fine before all the stress they caused. He wasn't sick a day in his life before he dropped dead in his chair at the garage."

When Tony made a right on 55th Street, she went quiet. All the way to the boulevard, no one spoke, but when they passed the pumping station on Western, the one with the Chicago city symbol in a bed of flowers that were still blooming despite the time of year, Mrs. Nabb opened up again.

"I wish I had the time to grow flowers like those. All I seem to do is work. I work any extra shift I can get for the extra money. We managed to pay off most of the second mortgage with the money we got from selling the business, but we still owe on the house. Lee really stepped up, choosing not to go to the pricey college that offered her a scholarship. Even with her getting a full ride, I'd have lost the house trying to keep it up on my salary alone. And there were expenses we couldn't cover no matter what we did. Books, fees, room, and board, it adds up fast. Lee and I will be able to stop working extra shifts in about six months. Then she can start living her life again. She'll be able to start Daley College—you know—the one at Ford City. They have an x-ray technician program that will have her set for life. She'll never have to worry about a job, 'cause there are always folks who need x-rays."

The words "she can start living her life again" struck Rachael as acutely ironic. Ann Nabb was still holding on to the hope the body found wasn't her daughter's. She was determined to see with her own eyes that it was an awful mistake so that she could tell the detectives, "I told you so."

Tony jogged east onto Ogden Avenue, passing the barrel company that still made wooden barrels, stacking them on the wide sidewalk at the corner. Going only a few blocks on old Route 66, the mother road built in 1926, before coast-to-coast interstate highways, Tony made the last turn onto Winchester Street, weaving between the trucks making deliveries to the Cook County Hospital and the patients looking for free parking spaces for their appointments in the vast network of clinics at the Medical Center. He used a little known alley to cross from a loading dock to the driveway that ran between the back of the hospital and the County Morgue.

Maneuvering into a parking space designated for Chicago police vehicles only, Tony glanced in the mirror. Rachael's eyes were on Mrs. Nabb as she pulled herself together, straightening her sweater. Without a word, he opened the door for her. Tony took hold of her forearm as she stepped out of the car.

The detectives were familiar with the observation area. The small rooms lined both sides of a long hallway, each with a picture window covered by industrial-sized Venetian blinds, a wooden bench bolted firmly to the back wall, a few folding chairs, and one hospital tissue box on the ledge. The tile floor was polished to a high gloss, but the walls needed a new coat of institutional green paint. A cloudy, over-erased chalkboard showed "Nabb" in Room Number 9, not far from the entrance to the hall.

Once Mrs. Nabb was seated, Tony went to the attendant's desk to get the process moving. It gave Rachael time to prepare the poor woman for what was to happen next.

"Ann, they're going to open the blinds soon. When you're ready, I want you to stand up to take a look. It won't be easy because there was a lot of damage to her face. But I'll be right here behind you."

Ann Nabb looked quizzically at Rachael, trying to grasp this new information about her daughter. Damage had been done to Lee's face? She nodded her head as Rachael continued.

"Now Ann, if she has any kind of birthmark—any mole or tattoo, please tell me. They'll show it to you first, so you won't have to view the body in its entirety."

Mrs. Nabb turned wide-eyed to Rachael, grabbing both her hands. "It can't be *my* Lee. But, you tell them to show me her right hip. She has a strawberry mark that looks like an upside down crescent moon."

"I'll tell them." Rachael slipped her hands free and stood up as Mrs. Nabb turned her attention to Tony sitting next to her.

"It won't be my baby. I know it. She's with one of her girlfriends somewhere and forgot to call. Then you can take me home, where I can wait for her to show up."

"Sure, Mrs. Nabb," Tony said sympathetically, lacking the heart to crush her hopes. In his experience, he knew that one quick glance through the glass would do. "When you're finished, all you have to do is sit down," he told her.

Rachael quietly talked into the intercom on the wall. The technician took some time to arrange the sheets to expose the right leg of the body only. Then a buzzer sounded, signaling that they were ready to raise the blinds.

Mrs. Nabb took her place before the glass, and the detectives stood on either side of her, ready to catch her should she faint. Rachael and Tony had seen people sink to the floor without a sound.

The sight of the uncovered leg with a pink patchy "C"-shaped birthmark destroyed the last shred of hope that the poor woman had clung to. Her breath escaped her throat in a piercing scream that echoed throughout the corridor. She sank back onto the bench, limp and defeated.

"It's her! It's my baby. My darling Lee."

Hearing the clank of the lowered blinds, she gathered herself, and uttered a request that startled the detectives in its resoluteness.

"I want to see her face!" she demanded, grabbing at Tony's hands.

"I wouldn't advise that," he said softly, gently grasping her by the elbow.

"I have to see," she wailed, glaring at him. "I need to see what they did to my baby!"

"It's not easy to see," Rachael said trying to dissuade her. "It'll stay with you. You'll have trouble getting the image out of your head."

She turned to Rachael, as calm as the eye of a hurricane.

"I know," she said, "but I need to see. Tell them to show me. I must see."

Tony conveyed her request over the intercom. There was nothing Rachael could say to prepare Mrs. Nabb for the shock when the blinds were raised.

Ann Nabb steeled herself with a couple of deep breaths. With a quick tug at her sweater, she went back to the window to wait. The detectives stood behind her, ready for her to collapse. Rachael pressed the button for the attendant to raise the blinds again.

This time, Mrs. Nabb didn't make a sound. She stared at

the gruesome sight for what seemed an interminable duration before bending down to put her open hand against the glass, level with Lee's mutilated cheek as if to caress it. She turned to Tony.

"Is there anything I have to do before you take me home?" she asked.

"No ma'am. This was merely a formality. You can sign the release for the body at the funeral home, and they'll take care of all the necessary paperwork."

"I'm ready," she said.

They escorted her to the car. The ride back to the Nabb home transpired in complete silence.

Tuesday, 17 Oct. 1978, 15:46

Signs of an Escape Plan

Rachael sat in the back seat with Mrs. Nabb all the way from the morgue. Now, in front of her house, Ann Nabb looked at the small wooden structure as if she had never seen it before. Tony turned and looked over his arm stretched across the back of the seat. The poor woman was white as a sheet with tears running down her face. A few minutes passed. Tony was the first to break the silence.

"Mrs. Nabb, would you let us look in Lee's room?" he asked.

"Yes," she replied distractedly.

But she didn't move. Her tears had stopped, but her mind raced, searching for answers to her questions of who, what, and why. Trying to remember any little thing to help the detectives, her mind was blank. Rachael decided to see if it was time to make some headway. With a gentle pat on Mrs. Nabb's arm, she spoke.

"Ann, why don't you see if you can find your keys in your purse?"

Mrs. Nabb stared at her, trying not to blink. Tears gathered in the corners of her eyes, the slightest blink sending them down the same moist path as the others. She sniffed hard as she reached into her purse. Fishing deep, she found the hand-made macramé fob. It plunged her into despair.

"Lee made this for me," she croaked, "for my birthday."

She dropped the keys. Rachael retrieved them from the floor, letting her cry it out. In his peripheral vision, Tony spied a woman in an oversized blue sweatshirt with matching stirrup pants head for the car. He got out to meet her, keeping her at a short distance from the vehicle.

"Good morning ma'am," he said as he stopped her in her tracks.

"I'm Mrs. Fahy," she said, craning her neck to look inside the car. "I live next door to the Nabbs. Is everything okay?"

"She's had a bit of a shock."

He didn't sidestep her as the woman attempted again to look inside the car.

"Which side of her house do you live on, Mrs. Fahy?" he asked.

"I own the brick house to the right of Mrs. Nabb," she said. "And who might you be?"

"I'm Detective Tony Breese, ma'am," he replied.

He took a card from the inside breast pocket of his jacket. She inspected it, running a finger over the dark blue embossed skyline extending across the bottom of the card.

"You're not from the 22nd District?" she asked.

"No ma'am, we're not."

"What's Lee done *this* time? Steal a car? Rob a store? You here to take her in?"

He leaned close, inviting her to conspire with him. "Lee has been taken in before?" he asked.

"Not that I know of, but it wouldn't surprise me if she had. With her sneaking around at night, like nobody hears her. Climbing down the tree near her window, pushing her little car around the corner before she starts it up so she won't be discovered…." she whispered to Tony.

Tony gave her license to spill what she knew, whether factual or pure unsubstantiated gossip. In his line of work, no possible leads could be dismissed, no matter the questionable credibility of the source.

"Now, mind you, she has never been anything but good to me, but after her father died, Mrs. Nabb kinda let her run wild. It's not her fault, really. There was no life insurance, so they both had to work extra to make ends meet. Albrecht owned a garage over on Kedzie."

Tony glanced over his shoulder to see Rachael help Mrs. Nabb compose herself. He was grateful that she was able to distract her for so long, allowing his interrogation of Mrs. Fahy to run its course.

"Are you close to Mrs. Nabb?"

"I'd say so," she said.

"We used to sit and drink coffee together, trade dishes—neighbor stuff. But with her working all the time, she didn't have the time anymore. Now we talk only if I see her on her way to work."

"When she gets out the car and gets settled in the house, you might want to go over and spend a little time with her," Tony advised.

Without another word, she winked at him before scuttling off. Over her shoulder, she watched the two women make their way up the walk and into the house.

Inside, Mrs. Nabb dropped onto the couch in a state of stupor. Tony and Rachael sat next to her on either side. Moments later, the doorbell rang. It was Mrs. Fahy. Neighborhood gossips had their place in any investigation, but Rachael questioned whether it was too soon to bring her into it. Instead, she stepped outside and closed the door behind her.

"I'm Mrs. Fahy, Mrs. Nabb's friend," she introduced herself. "Your partner said I should come over when you got her settled down."

She pulled out the card Tony gave her to substantiate her claim.

"Mrs. Nabb is in a very delicate state right now," Rachael cautioned her.

"Your partner never said what was wrong."

"Please, take a seat on the step, and I'll explain," Rachael said.

Rachael stooped, extended her hands to Mrs. Fahy, and

looked into the woman's wide eyes.

"Mrs. Fahy, I'm sorry to say that Lee Nabb was found dead. We're just returning from the morgue, where Mrs. Nabb made a positive identification."

Mrs. Fahy crossed herself twice.

"Sweet Mother of God," she sighed. "That poor woman… What can I do to help?"

"You can stay with her for a while, until her cousin arrives. We need to look through Miss Nabb's room to see if there's any evidence that will help us solve the case."

"Why am I sitting here?" the woman chided herself. "Let me make a pot of coffee."

"That would be most appreciated," Rachael said. "Let's go inside. Mrs. Nabb should be settled down by now."

When Rachael opened the door, Ann Nabb was focusing at the tops of her shoes, oblivious to Mrs. Fahy's presence.

Mrs. Fahy moved to the kitchen quickly, starting a pot of coffee. Looking around as it brewed, she found an opened bag of cookies on the counter. She sat four mugs in a row on the sink before dumping the cookies onto a clean saucer. Seeing Mrs. Fahy approaching the coffee table, Mrs. Nabb burst into tears.

Mrs. Fahy took a place on the couch and the two women embraced. As they rocked back and forth, Mrs. Fahy cooing words of comfort, Tony skimmed the papers lying on the coffee table while Rachael scrutinized cards and notes attached to refrigerator magnets in the kitchen. Nothing stood out to either of them as a clue. When the coffee was ready, Rachael poured two cups and brought them to the living room.

Confident that Mrs. Fahy could handle things, the detectives climbed the stairs leading to the dormer bedroom that Leivald Nabb had occupied.

The two stepped into a palace of purple. The dormer's slanted walls were painted pale lavender. The overhead glass light fixture was painted on the inside to match. Mauve throw rugs were scattered between the door and a bed covered by boysenberry sheets. Dark purple curtains framed front and back windows, one pulled tight against the eastern exposure, the other thrown open, welcoming the western sun. The only departures in color were posters of Devo, Blondie, Led Zeppelin, and the Boomtown Rats.

"Oh my," Rachael said, scanning the room. "She had a party with paint and Rit Dye in here, didn't she?"

"We know she loved purple and punk rock," Tony said moving to the mirrored dresser also painted dark purple. "What other proclivities are you willing to reveal, Miss Leivald Nabb?"

Carefully sifting through each drawer, looking under the sparse collection of miscellaneous clothing, Tony saw that Miss Nabb hadn't hidden anything of consequence in her dresser. But something struck him as odd.

"Rachael, this dresser is nearly empty. Don't most girls her age have lots of socks and underwear?"

Rachael looked up from the desk, where she was sitting going through the drawers.

"There should be drawers full. She's working; she's gotta go somewhere every day. How many pair you got over there?"

"Four pair of socks, two pair of panties and a bag of potpourri," Tony said, holding up a plastic net bag.

"Definitely not enough," Rachael said, surveying the room. "I'm coming up empty over here too. There isn't a journal, a diary, or a datebook."

"I'll bet it's all in the missing purse!"

"Back to the purse, are we?" Rachael retorted.

Tony smiled.

Inspecting all the drawers, there was nothing. For a girl as attractive as Lee, there should have been love letters, tokens from dances, gift cards from flowers, or something.

"This bookcase is missing a few things, too. Not one photo album, yearbook, or scrapbook," said Tony, moving his finger over the titles on the standing volumes. "Only textbooks, cook books, and a kids' weekly encyclopedia from the A&P."

"There's not a photo up here, either. Not one. Mrs. Nabb had a packet of photos, photos hung on the living room walls, and on the fridge. This wasn't a photo-shy family. If Lee was as fond of her father as Mrs. Nabb had said, where's *his* picture?"

"Every photo she had, Lee was in it," Tony speculated. "You didn't see many solo pics of her in the stack, did you?"

"You're right, they were doubles, triples, or groups," Rachael said. "The only solo shot was her school picture."

From other cases they had worked, this was a big red flag. The room looked like a stage set, not like where a young working girl would live.

"Are you thinking what I'm thinking?" Rachael asked.

"If we didn't have a body, this would be a case of a runaway. There's not much of the stuff a young girl should have. No matter how poor they were, she'd have more clothes than this," Tony replied.

As Rachael watched, he pulled out each item in the closet for her to see. There was a pair of wool pants, a blue pleated skirt, a fancy ruffled blouse, a cocktail dress, and several men's dress shirts. In a house this small, there couldn't be many more places to store clothes. The closet should have been crammed.

Nor was an extra purse hanging on a hook. From the recent pictures, there should have been at least three of them stored somewhere. Even more telling was that there were no piles of dirty clothes, no shoes or jewelry. As messy as the room looked at first, Rachael realized that the squirrels had been playing on scatter rugs, and some clean sheets had fallen on the floor. A bag of potato chips tangled up inside them were what the squirrels had been feasting on. Underneath the bed was clean, free of dust bunnies. Nothing personal had been left behind, not even a box of tampons.

"Looks like Miss Lee Nabb was getting ready to book," Rachael agreed. "You think things went bad before or after she planned her escape?"

"I'm not sure," Tony said as he moved to the window overlooking the backyard. "Mrs. Fahy wasn't exaggerating. She said that Lee had been running wild since her daddy died, and Mrs. Nabb was unawares. Look how close the crook of that oak limb is to her window. Shimmying down it wouldn't make a sound."

Rachael stepped to his side. She saw the wide windowsill where, with one move, she could be sitting among the leaves hidden from view. The rest of the climb was an easy descent. The broad branch sloped to a wide low crotch, where the drop to the yard was less than two feet. With a hop over either of the short fences that bordered the property, she wouldn't have had to pass the first floor bedroom window.

As Tony took notes, Rachael stood looking at what Lee would've seen, had she managed to elude her killer.

Tuesday, 17 Oct. 1978, 16:30

Interrogation at the Garage

Rachael opened the passenger side door and slipped into the car. She began perusing the list of business cards she'd made in the Nabb living room. Tony jabbed the key into the ignition of the Crown Victoria, and before shifting into drive, he turned to Rachael.

"All we got is those damned business cards?" he asked. "Not much of a lead."

"Let's go to the garage Mr. Nabb used to own," she said, "See if anyone knows anything."

The drive to the garage should have been quick, but the two wanted to find out if there might have been clues in the neighborhood that might have been overlooked. Rachael had ruled out finances. The house was built on the cheap, no garage, front porch, or any other amenity that would make it marketable. It was strictly utilitarian. It sat on a lot that wasn't considered desirable because of its placement at the rear, a situation that made it difficult to secure a mortgage these days. Nestled between the homes of city workers, firefighters, and cops, Tony chuckled when he remembered what the realtors referred to as baby makers

"What?" asked Rachael, not seeing anything on the street to prompt a giggle. "Where?"

"Oh, nothing. Remembering how my Uncle Henry would've called these houses baby makers."

"Why? 'Cause it's nice and quiet back here?"

"Quiet now, but at night it comes alive in song—a mournful cry to lost innocence, purloined freedom, and increased responsibility."

"What does?" she asked.

"The lowly train horn."

"Beep, beep, train horn," she said, "What's the big deal?"

"Ah, Lassie, have you never pondered why ye have four brothers?" he teased her by dropping into his best Welsh brogue, "Did ye think 'twas romance after getting home from a rip-roaring shift of three to eleven, rousting drunks, writing tickets, and arresting felons that made your dad feel amorous?"

"Breese, I took it for granted we were all vacation babies, conceived on or near the waters of Lake Michigan, Lake Geneva, or Chain-O-Lakes. All our birthdays are in the late winter, early spring. Still don't see what the trains have got to do with it."

"Look how close to the tracks those houses are."

"Do you realize how loud those horns are?"

"Don't you get used to the noise and ignore it?"

"One late train is all you need to break your sleep." Then nine months later...."

"Yeah, yeah," interrupted Rachael. "Let's see what we can find out over in this garage."

The garage was an old gas station, built of cinderblocks, painted over and over until they had acquired a thick stucco skin of battleship gray. The wooden sign over the front of the office was the newest addition to the entire place. Tony parked on the street because the fenced-in corner lot was crowded with cars, parked everywhere the gas pumps used to be. The two bays were full, one car up on a rack, and one on the ground. As they walked up, Rachael counted three sets of feet, one on the concrete and two under a car. A radio blasted WLS competing with the whirling of the compressor as it powered the hoist. The first to notice them appeared stunned to see a man and a woman standing at the open door of the bay. It was obvious they weren't from the neighborhood. Wiping his hands with a gray towel, he approached them.

"Hi. What can I do for you?" the man said.

"I'm Detective Breese, and this is my partner, Detective Culpepper. Do you know where we might find the owner?"

"I'm one of the owners. How can I help you?"

Tony hadn't sized up this young guy with his slightly pimpled face, bright blue eyes and tousled black hair as a garage owner. He had folded the legs of his coverall into six-inch cuffs, but his chest and arms were well muscled, straining the denim fabric.

"I'm Mikey Shaw," he said. "Two of the others are here, but if you need us all, I'll have to call Mr. O'Toole and Dillon on their jobs."

"I believe three of you'll do just fine," Tony said. "Can we talk someplace quiet?" he asked.

"Yeah, sure, we can go into the office. Come on in. I'm used to the noise."

He pushed open the over-painted wooden door, holding it ajar with his arm, smiling at Rachael, nodding for her to go first.

The office was small, providing only room enough to stand before the big wooden desk that substituted for a counter. Two chairs were situated under the picture window next to the front door. Another door led to the spots where the pumps once stood. Behind the desk were color coded shelves. Two rows of big pink windshield wiper fluid bottles were on the bottom, green Quaker State motor oil occupied the middle, and red, yellow, and white cans of STP, brake and transmission fluids lined the top shelf. A dark wooden sign in black script hung in the middle with the slogan, "In God we Trust ~ All others pay cash." The paperwork on the desk's surface was well organized. A stack of mail and two invoices lay on the wide blotter pad next to a chipped White Sox mug full of pens and pencils.

Settling into the corner chair, Rachael pulled out her notepad.

Mikey entered before Tony, allowing him to sit behind the desk. When all were seated, Mikey poured a paper cup full of scorched coffee from an old percolator they kept in an open bottom desk drawer.

"Would you like some coffee?" he offered, extending the cup toward Rachael.

"Thank you," she said, leaning forward to reach the cup.

"We've got sugar and creamer too, if you want it."

"No thanks; black is fine," she replied.

With the notepad resting on her lap, she started the questions.

"Who owns this garage?"

Mikey's fresh face beamed. He was proud to be part owner and spokesman for the group.

"There's me," he smiled broadly, "my cousin Albee Meegan, my friends Jamie Duncan, Dillon Whelan, and his father-in-law, Timothy O'Toole. Dillon and Mr. O'Toole—they're the ones with day jobs—they won't be here until later, unless you need me to call them."

"That won't be necessary," Tony said. "I think we can get what we need from you guys."

"What's this about?" Mikey asked after a sip of coffee.

"We're here to ask about the former owner's daughter, Miss Leivald Nabb," Rachael said.

"Oh, you must be doing the background check on Lee for the carnival folks. She said they'd send someone around to talk to us," Mikey offered. "She's a great girl. A good worker, too. She can fix cars as good as any guy. We'll miss not having her around to help out."

Tony and Rachael both noted the word "carnival" on their pads.

"When was the last time you saw Lee?" Rachael asked.

"Thursday afternoon. She was in here to get some brake fluid for her MG," Mikey said. "She plans to leave it with us when she leaves for Florida; then I'm gonna drive it to her after she's settled."

"That's nice of you," said Tony.

"She's a sweetheart. We'd do anything for her. We used to work with her old man, helping him fix cars when we were in high school. He encouraged us to take auto shop and then go to junior college for business classes. He didn't pay us, but because of him, we didn't get into trouble, we learned a trade, and we now have a business of our own."

"You haven't heard from her since Thursday? No phone call or anything?" Tony asked.

"Nope. Sometimes the hospital gets busy, and she puts in overtime; then we don't see or hear from her for days."

"This past weekend, nobody saw her around the garage or in the neighborhood?" Rachael asked.

Mikey shook his head no.

"I wish I had," he said. "She's busy getting ready for Florida. Last week, she brought some stuff over here all packed up. Didn't want to upset her mom by leaving boxes around the house. It would remind Mrs. Nabb that she'll be alone for the next six months. Lee says they'll provide space for her in a trailer with two other girls, which will be cramped because she's used to being by herself. Look at those boxes. She says they're only the start. She's got summer clothes and lots of household stuff because she'll have a company apartment once she gets to Florida."

Rachael wanted to examine the contents of the boxes, but until they sprung the news of Lee's death, she'd have to wait.

"When did she say she was going to Florida?" Tony asked.

"She was vague about that," Mikey said, "but I know the carnival doesn't have many more dates in the neighborhood: St. Christopher's in Midlothian and St. Marks in Palos Heights. I don't think there is another after that. Lee said they'd be leaving after those two."

Mikey's smile turned into pursed lips. He wasn't pleased about her leaving, no matter how much he pretended that he was. The detectives noticed it. Rachael wondered if Lee had picked up on it too.

"We'd like to ask the other guys some questions," Tony said.

"Sure," Mikey said. He went out into the work bay, and in seconds, he was back at the door with the two mechanics trailing him. Both wore grimy coveralls and oily, stained gym shoes. Taller than Mikey, they gave new meaning to the phrase "Irish Twins," with about one inch of difference in height between them.

"Thanks for taking time out to answer a few questions, gentlemen," said Tony. "When was the last time you saw Lee Nabb?"

"I saw her Saturday night. She was at Bleekers, in the bar about 10:30. It must have been her lunch hour," Albee, the youngest looking one, said, as he casually wiped greasy hands on a garage towel.

"I haven't seen her since she dropped off a couple of them boxes here Friday morning," Jamie, the taller one with dark eyes, piped in. "Said she was on her way to do some more shopping, but she headed south, not north. Ford City was her favorite spot."

"And no one has seen her since?" Tony asked.

The three shook their heads no. Tony decided it was time to drop the bomb.

"I'm sorry to say that Lee Nabb's body was found Monday morning."

Mikey dropped into a chair, Jamie's mouth flew open, and Albee fell back against the door jamb, dropping the towel on the floor.

"You're shitting me," Mikey said. "You said you were here to check out her background for the carnival."

"We never said what we were here for," Rachael replied.

They stared at the detectives. Tears ran down Mikey's cheeks. Albee and Jamie were incredulous, at a loss to make sense of the news.

"Does her mother know yet?" asked Albee, looking remorseful. He didn't want to be the one to give bad news.

"She's been notified," answered Tony.

"Oh my God," Mikey repeated, rocking back and forth in the wooden swivel chair.

Observing the men's eyes register shock and pain, Tony and Rachael drew lines through each name on their notepads. They were in genuine shock. For the next few moments, they asked one-word questions for which they got straightforward answers from the detectives. Then, a tearful Mikey asked if he could go to see Mrs. Nabb. Rachael consented, but before he prepared to go, she asked permission to go through the boxes that he had called to her attention moments earlier. They gave her the go-ahead.

Rachael proceeded to open the boxes with a pen knife as Tony asked questions. She thought it odd that they were not marked indicating whom they belonged to or where they were being sent. Inside, there were no personal items, no clues that gave Rachael a useful lead. They constituted things that anyone would need to move to a new apartment or to start a new life. What they did tell her was that Lee was hiding something that she didn't want her mother to know. The detectives finished the interrogation and released the men to go back to work. Afterward, they headed back to the office to do background checks on the garage owners before calling it a day.

July 1977

Cara's Withdrawal Letter

Sitting at the white French provincial desk where she'd done homework during her school career took Cara back to the day when Daddy's big promotion to Lieutenant in the Chicago Fire Department made it possible for them to move to a big new house up on the hill.

She and Mother went shopping at John M. Smyth's furniture store on Michigan Avenue. They took the Rock Island train downtown, caught a cab through the traffic, and rode toward the lake. When they hit the broad pavement in front of the store, Cara bubbled with anticipation. Taking the elevator up to the fourth floor, a wonderland of children's bedroom furniture awaited. Everywhere she looked was a rainbow of colors. A bunk bed forest sheltered safari animal floor lamps next to an array of canopy beds to please every princess. She held her mother's hand, navigating each row, choosing pieces for her bedroom in the new house on Beverly's Longwood Drive.

Cara imitated her mother's Irish accent as they discussed the purchases with the salesman. When it was time to add a desk to the ensemble, none seemed right. On their way out, nestled in a corner of the first floor near the elevator, was a beautiful gold and white wooden desk with a matching white leather swivel chair. Cara ran to it and spun in the chair. Near the top of each curved leg was the face of a woman carved into the wood. The drawer pulls were brass butterflies, wings outspread, sipping nectar from bouquets of flowers. The middle drawer was festooned with a tangle of flowers and curlicued leaves. The feet of the desk were lions' paws. Teagan O'Toole paid more for the desk and chair than she had for all of the bedroom furniture combined. It was her investment in her daughter.

Cara knew that this would be the last time she'd sit to write anything at her treasured desk, for it wouldn't be going to their apartment. Everything there would be hand-me-downs from Dillon's family, bought from a second-hand store. Her mother forbade her from taking anything from home beyond clothes and shoes, promising to lock up the room and leave it locked until innocence would come back to reclaim it. Cara blotted tears with one of her mother's handkerchiefs as she wrote.

> Dear Admissions Officer,
>
> Please accept from me, Cara Briana O'Toole, this letter of withdrawal from the freshman class of 1978. Due to circumstances beyond my control, I will not be able to attend classes. I am sorry for such short notice. In addition, please release my dormitory reservation. I am aware I will forfeit my fee for the student union and my textbook deposit. I hope you will be able to fill my place without too much trouble.
>
> Sincerely,
> Cara B. O'Toole

Wednesday, 18 Oct. 1978, 10:10

An Act of Philanthropy

The Nabb kitchen table was littered with bank books, bills, brochures, and coffee cups. Mrs. Nabb slouched in the wooden chair, focusing on the oak tree's trunk through the window. The coffee in her cup was ice cold. She held it tightly, as if she depended on the action to hold herself together. It was bad enough to have to bury your only child without the support of a husband, but to find out there wasn't enough money to do it was even worse. Tears rolled down her cheeks, soaking the front of her pajamas.

Lee had lied to her the past year. She was so preoccupied with trying to keep her head above water that she hadn't even noticed. But the lies were coming home to roost, like the evil black birds that descended in the famous Hitchcock movie. She loved Lee with her whole heart, and in that love, she'd neglected to notice the little things, the lies and half-truths, but now she saw in the light of day how much damage those lies had done. They'd killed her child.

If she'd demanded that Lee tell her the truth and stop harboring secrets, maybe Lee would still be alive. If she'd been more vigilant about where Lee went, and who she went with, maybe she wouldn't be faced with the prospect of burying the second person she'd loved with all her might. Had she been a better money manager, sold the garage to a *real* investor instead of the boys who wanted to carry out Albrecht's legacy, Lee might've been mad at her, but mad was better than dead. And if she hadn't had to work so much, maybe Lee would've been alive this morning to drink cold coffee and share gossip about the girls in the office. But, she hadn't protested when she found Dillon hanging out under the tree in the yard. She hadn't said anything when Mikey insisted on driving her to work. She hadn't dragged her out of the garage office where it was unseemly for a girl to be hanging around those boys working on cars. She had failed. She hadn't done her job as a mother.

The ringing phone jarred her from her outbreak of self-recrimination. She pushed aside the glossy brochure featuring coffin models to set the coffee down.

"Good morning, Mrs. Nabb, this is Detective Culpepper," she heard the familiar voice over the line. "How're you doing today?"

"As well as I can," she replied in a resigned tone. Rachael sympathized with the woman who had gone through so much in the past couple of days.

"I'm calling to see if we might come back over to talk… That is, if you feel up to talking," she qualified the request.

"I need to make some calls… lots of them," Mrs. Nabb replied.

Rachael found it odd because Mrs. Nabb had said that most of her family was gone. Who would she be making these calls to? she wondered.

"You can say when, and we'll work around your schedule," Rachael said. It doesn't matter if it's early or late."

"It'll have to be late. I've gotta talk to the people at the bank, and then be at the funeral home by three o'clock."

"How's seven or eight P.M.?"

"Seven should be fine," she said, her words trailing off into a low sob. Rachael was patient, determined not to rush her. After a brief pause, Mrs. Nabb gathered herself enough to talk more.

"Detective," she sobbed. "They're telling me I have to burn up my baby…."

She lapsed into a hiccupping sob.

Rachael grimaced as she listened.

"They say… I have to… I have no choice but to cremate my baby."

She let loose a banshee wail that penetrated Rachael's tough exterior, piercing her to the core.

"Now, now, Mrs. Nabb, you don't have to if you don't want to. You can opt for a closed casket."

"There won't be any coffin…." She gulped down the bitter words.

"She quit her job. She didn't tell me. Now there's no insurance. No money for a casket. No money for anything," Mrs. Nabb revealed.

Rachael added another detail to her list that was growing. She hadn't told her mother that she'd quit? It might be another reason for her murder. Could it possibly be drug related? Motives were roiling around in her head.

"What time are you going to the bank?" she asked.

"As soon as I can get my clothes on," Mrs. Nabb said.

"We'll be there in a few minutes. Let us drive you, okay?"

"I don't want to get you in trouble. You've got other cases…."

"As I said, we need to ask you some more questions. We can talk as we drive."

"It's very kind of you. I'll be waiting for you out front."

"See you in a few minutes," said Rachael before returning the phone to its cradle.

"What's going on?" Tony asked.

"There's no insurance to bury the poor girl. Lee didn't tell her mother that she was no longer employed at the hospital. Now Mrs. Nabb needs a ride to the bank, so I figured it would be a good time to get some more answers."

Tony stared at Rachael, his mind spinning scenario after scenario. Rachael maneuvered the car through the early morning traffic heading west.

"Good thinking, Rach," Tony said. You got a bottle of Paul

Masson on ice coming."

As they turned down Western Avenue, Tony asked, "Why can't you get to 107th without ducking and dodging?"

"It's indicative of this case I guess, three steps forward, two steps sideways."

When they pulled up, Mrs. Nabb was waiting at the end of the walk clutching a purse. When Rachael got out of the car, Mrs. Nabb approached her, with tears brimming in her reddened eyes.

"Detective, my baby is dead, and all they can say is 'null and void.' She quit her job. She didn't tell me. She walked away. The insurance lapsed. The people at the insurance company won't help me. The hospital won't help me. All they keep saying is the insurance is 'null and void.' My baby is dead. I can't afford to bury her, and they keep saying 'null and void.'"

The buckle in her knees suggested a woman on the verge of collapse. Tony rushed to her, Rachael joining him to support the distraught woman. After a few moments, Rachael made an excuse to re-enter the house.

"May I use your bathroom?" she asked. Mrs. Nabb gave her the keys.

Once inside, Tony guided her to the couch, where the two waited for Rachael to return from the bathroom. When she rejoined them, Tony asked permission to use the telephone. Mrs. Nabb nodded yes, and he raised one finger before winking at Rachael as she consoled the crying woman.

"Do you have time for us this morning?" Tony asked over the phone. "I'm bringing you a new client."

After a pause, he replied, "Splendid. We'll be there soon. I'm bringing my latest partner, Rachael Culpepper, too."

Tony sat down on the other side of Mrs. Nabb.

"Mrs. Nabb, I know a credit union that handles hardship cases. They have time to see us this morning."

"Thanks, Detective, but I can cash out my Christmas

Club account, plus my savings, and then ask for five hundred dollars. The funeral home says that eight hundred will cover the cost of cremation."

Tony glanced at Rachael. A quick calculation meant that she had only two hundred in savings. Unless her credit was pristine, an unsecured loan would be impossible, even for a small amount.

"Mrs. Nabb, you're going to need twice as much for a decent funeral. Leave your savings where it is and the Christmas Club funds, too. My friend Mr. Pugh does this all the time, and he has excellent terms—better than the bank."

Rachael had never heard of a credit union making loans to non-members, but she was willing to give him the benefit of the doubt. If it wasn't on the up and up, Tony would never have her confidence again. She'd learned to protect her job by steering clear of any hint of impropriety.

Mrs. Nabb looked toward Rachael for direction. In her heart Rachael hoped she hadn't put herself on the hook for part of the funds to give Lee a nice ceremony because Tony was donating the bulk and she would be asked to take up the remainder.

Without any conversation, Tony crooked his arm, signaling to Mrs. Nabb to go. Together, they rose from the couch.

Instead of moving to the front door, Mrs. Nabb went upstairs to the bathroom.

In her absence, Rachael told Tony that he was wasting the time she needed to question her.

"Don't worry, we'll have plenty of travel time; we're heading to South Shore—far east on 79th Street. We can talk then."

"But with this taken off her shoulders, she's going to focus on the funeral, not on the questions."

"I can see that she doesn't have much more info for us. We will have to solve this one with outside folks, not with her."

Rachael pursed her lips, but she knew he was right. Her

mind turned back to the credit union.

"Is this guy on the up and up, Tony?"

"We haven't been partners long enough for you to know *everything* about me, but I have a soft spot for vulnerable victims. A guy I know runs a foundation that fronts as a credit union. He lends money to people in dire need, and if they can pay it back, they do. If not, he forgives the debt. No nasty phone calls, no collection agencies, none of that."

"How does he manage?"

"He represents a family of philanthropists who want to do good but don't want to be pestered by people who don't really need help. Pugh administers the foundation on their behalf."

"Really?" Rachael said with a raised eyebrow.

"Really. Pugh's a friend of mine. You'll see."

In the car, Tony overheard Mrs. Nabb planning the funeral aloud to Rachael, complete with a spray of white roses on the casket. He knew that when she went to the undertaker, she would give them a card from Mr. Pugh. They would call him, and he would give them an authorization for a generous sum to pay for the choices Mrs. Nabb would make. She would never be the wiser. One day, Tony would reveal to Rachael the family contributing to the foundation was his and that he had hired Mr. Pugh to distribute the money.

August 1977

Cara's Chamber of Horrors

At her mother's insistence, Cara packed three bags of clothes, a bag of shoes, and a box of toiletries. She wasn't able to wear them because of her expanding figure, but she took them anyway. Her dad drove her over in his big red pickup because Dillon was at work.

"I think Dillon could have gotten my things in his truck," she pouted, looking out the window as they drove along the tree-lined stretch of 107th Street that led to Western.

"He would've had to make two trips honey," her dad replied. "It was bad enough to have had to watch Mrs. O'Flynn, our housekeeper, cry, but I didn't think we should have made her go through that twice, do you?"

"You're right, Daddy. But now Dillon will never carry me over the threshold for the first time," she pouted.

"He needed to get back to work, sweetie," her father said. "You'll need every dollar he can make."

Cara knew her father was right. What her father didn't know was that Dillon had told Cara that the pretty clothes that he'd bought her for Vassar were a waste of money. All she'd need was a couple of muumuus to wear until the babies were a year old because she'd be stuck in her apartment even if she did get her figure back.

She never felt more confused. The last two weeks had been a roller coaster ride from hell. The trip to the doctor revealed not only that she was pregnant, which she'd thought impossible, but that she was having twins. How did one baby turn into two when there wasn't supposed to be one at all?

The wedding, for her, felt more like the inside of a tornado. Everything was rushed. The blood tests had to be taken, not at a doctor's office or in a hospital, but up a flight of creaky old wooden stairs of a converted factory outside the Loop because the results could be accelerated, cutting the waiting from three days to six hours. Getting the marriage license from the basement of City Hall dressed in a dove gray A-line dress that didn't hide her swollen belly was embarrassing, but taking the elevator ride up in the old stone-cold marble building to the Marriage Court was torturous. Everything was cold, hard, and fast.

They stood in front of a judge, his face as wrinkled as the black robe he wore, mumbling a ceremony he would deliver twenty times a day, before strangers paid to be witnesses. She didn't have a bouquet because Dillon forgot to get one. Her mother stayed home because she'd a headache, or so she claimed. She couldn't ask any of the girls from Morgan Park or Mother McCauley to be bridesmaids because they were vacationing in Europe, on the East Coast, or in Wisconsin before starting college. She wasn't sure if any of them would have said yes, considering what a shame it was. When she told Lee about the pregnancy and wedding, Lee stopped speaking to her. Cara only had her dad to lean on, but he wasn't happy about the turn of events. No one was happy. The tears coursing from Cara's eyes weren't tears of joy; they were the result of a deep simmering anger coupled with a feeling of shame that was almost too much for her to bear.

Turning right as the truck rumbled over the railroad tracks, Cara was shaken out of her silence by the apartment buildings only a few car widths away from the tracks.

"Why are you turning here, Daddy," she asked, "Shouldn't we be on the other side of the street, where the houses are?"

"Dillon said the address was 3005 W. 110th Place, apartment 9 on the second floor," he replied, straining to make out the weathered brass numbers affixed to the green wooden doors.

"This can't be right. He must have given you the wrong address," Cara said as she spied an older woman watching them from above, sitting in an aluminum lawn chair, smoking a cigarette and drinking an Old Style straight from the can.

Her father parked the truck between a dumpster and a concrete staircase framed by black wrought iron railings leading to the second floor. Pulling a receipt from behind his sun visor, he showed her the address and Dillon's signature. Cara's heart sank. It was the right place. When Dillon had told her he would get them a nice place, she'd trusted him, but this wasn't at all what she'd visualized. Weathered storm doors protected splintered green wooden doors that had faded from the sun and peeled from the rain pelting through the torn screens. Each door was flanked by two double-hung front room windows. A third window, presumably the bedroom one, established the width of each apartment. Cara's bedroom at home was larger. There was no way she would be able to live under such conditions: so close to the train tracks, much less among the kind of people like the woman sitting in the lawn chair on the narrow wrought-iron balcony.

The two, after bumping suitcases on the way to the end of the balcony, opened the door to what, for all practical purposes, was no better than a no-tell motel room . The freshly painted walls were DuPont latex white, from the vinyl tile floor to the popcorn plaster ceiling, a single coat smeared over thin sheets of drywall to give the apartment a facade of livability.

"I see Dillon picked up a few pieces of furniture," Cara's dad remarked as he sat one suitcase in the tiny closet hidden behind the open front door.

Dillon had rustled up a room of mismatched furniture: a faded green plaid couch with water rings on its wide wooden arms; a pressboard cocktail table only large enough to hold a can of beer next to a pair of feet; a grease-stained gold-striped tufted armchair that was taken straight out of someone's garage, and—worst of all—a worn puke green flowered nursing glider with a defective rail that creaked like an arthritic knee.

Along the back wall of the big room was the kitchen, furnished with a stove, sink, and refrigerator. When you turned around, you were facing a beat up 1950s Muntz console television centered at the front window. The gouged enameled-topped kitchen table was shoved against the side wall. It lacked chairs because Dillon had no intention of eating there: he preferred to eat his meals on the tin TV trays in corner of the living room.

Cara eased herself into the nursing chair, her assigned place in the center of this chamber of horrors. Her father put the rest of the suitcases in the bedroom, where a naked mattress with a blond wood headboard, a mismatched dresser without a mirror, and chest of drawers completed the second-hand ensemble.

Giving his daughter space to process the abrupt change in her circumstances that the shotgun marriage had wrought, Timothy O'Toole made trips to Venture Discount Store on 95th Street and the neighborhood A&P to pick up necessities that his daughter would need to set up housekeeping.

Cara sobbed as she sat in the rickety chair trying her best to adjust to her new life on the wrong side of the tracks in Mt. Greenwood.

Wednesday, 18 Oct. 1978, 14:05

Interview at Christ Hospital

On the closed-circuit monitor, Officer William Warren Murphy watched Tony and Rachael walk down the hallway. He observed their gait, analyzed their demeanor, and guessed that they were detectives before they reached the high counter that served as the hospital's guard post.

Standing a hair over six feet, the counter hid the paunch that was slowly overtaking the waistline where his Sam Browne belt used to be, but his broad shoulders and barrel chest were still intimidating, even with the snowy white crew cut. He wasn't a man you'd want to meet in a dark alley.

"How might I assist ya, officers?" he asked when Tony and Rachael approached the security desk near the back door, offering their badge cases for inspection.

"Afternoon, Officer. I'm Detective Tony Breese, and this is my partner Detective Rachael Culpepper. We're wondering if we could talk to you about one of the hospital employees, a Miss Leivald Nabb?"

Murphy examined the badges and IDs.

Punching the button on his radio, he barked, "On your way back yet, Al? I need ya at the desk."

"Leaving the ER now," came a disembodied voice.

"Soon as I get this post covered, we'll be able to talk," he said, opening the swing gate of the counter.

"Go into the office," he said, pointing to a small glass-walled room full of file cabinets, a rack of walky-talkies, a desk, and coffee pot. "Help yourselves to coffee, if you want," he said. "I won't be long."

Tony half-filled two Styrofoam cups and handed one to Rachael as he looked around. A whiteboard with a few scribbled notes. A cork bulletin board with notices about insurance meetings, blood drives, and free flu shots. A copy of yesterday's *Chicago Sun Times* lay on the desk but nothing more.

"Look at this room," Tony said, "not a doodle, not a phone number, nothing. They get their coffee here, put their stuff down, but they stay outside, either on the move or on the watch. What you bet they're all retired from CPD?"

"I wonder how many years he did before he came here." Rachael looked around the room.

"Probably a lot. Did you notice his size? Back in the day, the department hired him for his brawn alone."

"I can see him wading into a crowd, picking up a guy by the collar and tossing him into the wagon. I wonder if he knew my dad." Rachael wondered aloud.

Officer Murphy appeared at the doorway, mug in hand. He went to the chair behind the desk.

"What can I do for ya detectives?"

His face was serene. He had the kind of presence that invited confessions, and when he was working, he often got them with the twist of his head and a pat of his hand on an offender's arm. He certainly didn't show any wear and tear from his years on the job.

"We need some information about a Miss Leivald Nabb who works here."

Rearing back in the swivel chair, Murphy responded in a slight brogue.

"Yes, I know little Miss Nabb. Her mother too—the widow Nabb."

Murphy smiled at Rachael. She returned his smile.

"Can you tell me what her position was at the hospital?" Tony asked, pen poised to record the answer.

"Sure'n I can. She worked in the data processing department. Third watch 'round here, three to twelve, but her hours were erratic; she'd be here early or stay late. At first, we thought it was a function of her job, but over time we saw her spending her spare time here, beyond what her job needed."

Tony glanced at Rachael.

"Really?"

He waited for Murphy to fill in the details. Murphy revolved in the chair, pulling out the middle drawer of a white vertical filing cabinet. Flipping folders, he pulled out one crammed with papers. Wheeling back around, he plopped the folder on the desk and folded his hands over it.

"So, what's this investigation all about?" he asked.

Rachael stared him straight in the eye. "We're here because Leivald Nabb has been found dead."

Murphy sat back in the chair, crossing himself and closing his eyes to say a silent prayer.

"Saints preserve us. That's not what I thought would ever happen to that girl. Not at all."

He pushed the folder across the desk to Tony. Tony began leafing through it. As he read, Murphy shared his impressions of her.

"She was a bit of a firecracker, that one. Always moving fast. Almost pretty, with a chipped front tooth, but it didn't stop her from smiling freely, if you know what I mean. She was whip smart, but she ran with the wrong crowd, if'n you ask me. Always coming in through the back door, late to work, trying to save a few minutes on the time clock. She knew all the guards, all the transporters, all the food service workers. She grew up with them in Mount Greenwood; went to school with the young ones. The older ones knew her from her dad's garage on Kedzie. After he died a few years back, she'd punch out on time, but hang about till the wee hours. I thought she was waiting for her mother to finish up, but even if she pulled a double, Widow Nabb was always out of here around one A.M. It took me a while to catch on to Lee's shenanigans. You know, using the hospital as a trystin' ground. Stalling freight elevators up on the high floors late at night, necking in the stairways, slipping into and out of janitor's closets and the like. After a while, she graduated to using empty hospital rooms. I felt sorry for her; I did. When her dad died, it ripped the heart outta her. Went after young men with a vengeance. I took note of the times and places, in case something happened or anything went missing. You're welcome to look at them."

Tony leafed through the scraps of paper, the alarm logs, parking lot warnings, and the violation logs. "Active" was a good word for it; there were two or three per week for nearly two years. One name kept cropping up, Dillon Whelan.

"At first, I was thinking Whelan and Lee were in a scheme to steal equipment or supplies, but when I found out he was only after her, I didn't let up on my vigilance; I simply changed my attitude—especially when I found out the bugger was a married man with kids. I kept up with me sightings, plus any others I heard of from the guys. It's all in there."

"How'd you find out he was married?" Tony asked.

"Everybody knows everybody else's business. Some like to talk to anyone who'll listen, sometimes for nothing more than the price of a cup of coffee. Dana Dawkins, Lee's supervisor is a good woman. They spent a lot of time together in the computer center, where Lee would spill her guts. When she was trying to get sympathy one day, she blurted out that Dillon had gotten married. She thought Dana should be easier on her but Lee would leave Dana in the lurch when she'd go off to meet Whelan. It pissed Dana off that she was being used. Ya see, when I make my rounds, I always visit the Data Center, making sure everyone in there is all right. Way down a long lonely hallway, isolated behind the parking garage, 'tisn't a comforting place to be, late at night. Dana told me about the affair one of the times she'd come in to cover for Lee."

After a short pause, Murphy asked, "How'd it happen?"

"She was bashed in the head, and then stuffed in a garbage can. She tumbled out of the back of a garbage truck at the

Hegewisch dump. She'd been covered up, so they didn't see her when they did the pickup."

"Dear Lord. What a way to go," Murphy replied. He pursed his lips. "How's her mother holding up?"

"Not good." Rachael said.

"Was she raped?" Murphy asked.

"No."

"Where can I find Dana Dawkins?" Tony asked.

"Down this hallway, past the time clock, take the elevator to the first floor. Turn left and ask the cashier to let you in," smiled Murphy, pointing like he was directing traffic.

Tony rose from the chair. "Where would Detective Culpepper find Mr. McDowell's office? From this file, it seems he was close to her, too."

Murphy rose from his chair.

"The department is tucked way back in a far corner. It's not easy to find. I'll escort her."

Tony moved through the doorway, over his shoulder, telling Rachael to meet him in the lobby when she was done.

The bio-medical department was at the end of several hallways that twisted and turned. Murphy stopped in the middle of one of them and patted Rachael's hand.

"There you go, lassie. Good luck with the investigation. When you catch Lee's killer, call me; I want to know who it is."

"Will do," said Rachael. "Thanks for all your help."

Wednesday, 18 Oct. 1978, 14:23

Interrogation in the Biomed Department

The first thing Rachael noticed about him was his eyes—deep green, catlike. His light brown eyebrows, blending into the tanned skin of his forehead, made them seem bigger than they really were. The florescent light overhead highlighted a mop of sandy brown hair, lending the illusion of him being surrounded by a halo.

Richard McDowell towered above the long high counter that he stood behind. His arms suggested that he was an athlete, though she couldn't divine which sport. Even a hospital scrub top he wore couldn't conceal his well-defined chest.

Twisting his head to catch Rachael's eye, he smiled. She nodded. She was here to investigate a murder, not feed her libido. Yet, this man exuded raw sexuality with his every motion, every look.

She approached the end of the counter, waiting for the young volunteer wearing the coral-colored smock to leave.

As the girl bounced past her and out the door, Rachael turned to introduce herself.

"Hello."

"Sorry about that. What can I do for you?"

She showed him her badge.

"If this is about the parking tickets I got before I moved to Alsip, I have a cancelled check to prove I paid them," he explained.

Rachael put her hand up.

"I'm not here about any tickets, warrants, or a summons. I'm working a case connected to the hospital, Mr. McDowell.

Officer Murphy said you know the hospital staff because they rely on you to fix their equipment. Is that correct?"

"It is," he smiled.

"I'm hoping you can give me some information on Mrs. Nabb and her daughter," Rachael said, placing her aluminum case pad on the counter to take notes, "When was the last time you saw Leivald Nabb?"

"Leivald? Is Leivald the mother or the daughter?" he asked. "I know them both, but I don't know either of them by that name."

"Leivald is the daughter," Rachael replied.

"Makes sense. I call the mother Mrs. Nabb, and well, Lee is always Lee. She doesn't go by her full name. Now I can see why."

"How well did you know Lee?"

"Fairly well. Nice girl. Mechanically inclined. She only brings me the worst of her problems; the simple things she fixes herself," he laughed. "But as good as she is, a couple times a week she's down here. It's her keyboard. I fish out all kinds of tiny nuts, screws, and washers that fall out of her pockets to slip under the keys. She's a wizard with carburetors, or so I hear."

"I see," Rachael said.

"When was the last time you saw her?"

"Let me think," he said thoughtfully. "A while ago. At her going away party."

"Tell me about it," said Rachael, making a note about the disconnect between what McDowell said and what Lee's mother said when she talked to the nursing supervisor. She firmly believed that Lee had been working.

"Some of us got together to say goodbye to her at Eric the Red's over on 111th near Kedzie. It was payday, a Friday night, but I haven't seen her since. She said she was leaving with the carnival. She'd quit here because it was almost time for them to leave Illinois for winter work in Georgia, South

Carolina, and Florida. Lee said they were offering more money than the hospital, plus the chance for her to travel."

"Did she say what she would be doing at the carnival?" Rachael asked, thinking most of the carnival work was menial labor and not very high paying.

"She planned to work as a cashier until they reached the winter grounds where the main office is; then they were going to have her run their computer system for them. They were modernizing operations."

"Do you recall the date of the party?" Rachael asked.

He flipped through a ledger on the counter filled with handwritten notations in pale blue ink. He bent himself in half, running his fingers up and down the columns, intently seeking some entry that would jog his memory. Tapping the counter hard a few times, he glanced at Rachael with a huge smile.

"How could I forget? It was Friday the thirteenth! We were teasing her about it being a bad luck day. We drank some beer, told some jokes and before we knew it, it was the fourteenth. The bad luck was gone. She liked it, even said she planned it that way. But I knew better. She seldom planned anything."

Rachael noted the date. "Was her mother at the party?"

"No. As a matter of fact, her mother was working. And, strange to say, her boyfriend didn't show up, either."

"What boyfriend?" asked Rachael.

"Her high school sweetheart. The one she sneaks in here after hours. They make up and break up every few months. He's most likely why she's becoming a carny. He's probably leaving, too. I never got to know much about him, just what she told me while I was working on her machines. I know he works in the railyard as a loader, but she never said which yard." McDowell answered.

"Do you know his name?"

"Yeah, it's Dillon something, I never knew his last name, sorry."

Rachael moved on to the next question on her list.

"Lee get into any trouble that you know of?"

"Officer Murphy had a few issues with her, but they were minor."

"What kind of issues?"

"The usual kind he has with the youngsters here. Lovers Lane antics. Necking in the parking lot, kissing in the stairwells, that kind of thing. Officer Murphy's forgot how good young love feels. You see, the transport boys chase the candy stripers, the new interns stave off the smell of death by making love to student nurses in the overnight rooms, everyone including the janitors use their closets for more than supplies—if you know what I mean. New parents conceive their next baby before they even get home. This place is a regular Peyton Place, if you know where to look."

"Really? Sex in a hospital?" Rachael asked.

"Clearly, you don't watch daytime TV," he said. "Ever see 'General Hospital'? Except here, things are much more heated."

"You think that there was anyone at the hospital who might have wanted to hurt her?"

"Naw, no enemies. Lee knows everybody in the Data Center, but she hung out with Bette Wilson and Phyllis White. They were like the Three Musketeers. They ate lunch together. She's close to a couple of the girls in housekeeping—Paula Fahy and Dorothy Sands. She was under their cars fixing things all the time. There's also a couple of the candy stripers that she was friendly with, but I don't remember which ones offhand. They all went to high school together at Morgan Park. Lee brought one of her friends from the carnival to the party, too. I think her name is Carla or Darla, but I didn't get to talk to her much. I'm sure she'll be easy to find. She's a midget."

Rachael had written down all the names.

"May I ask what this is all about?" he asked, finally.

"I'm investigating the murder of Lee Nabb."

She watched his body language for any unconscious clues

that might betray him as a person of interest. His smile disappeared, his eyes widening from the shock of the revelation. He folded over as if he'd been punched in the gut, reaching for the edge of the counter to steady himself.

"Oh no, that poor girl. So young," he sighed. "Her poor mother."

After a pause, he straightened up to peer into Rachael's eyes.

"Are you at liberty to say anything more about it? I mean, you know, like how she died?"

"No. Not now. The medical examiner's office is working on their analysis now. We'll know more later."

"I see," he said solemnly. "It's not something I should know about. Actually, she was a good kid. Always smiling."

An older woman in a full set of scrubs, came through the doorway. She stopped near the edge of the counter, waiting her turn. Under her arm was a fax machine that needed repairing. Rachael took it as her cue to leave. Leaning over the counter, she lowered her voice to add one last thing.

"I'd appreciate it if you kept this to yourself. The grapevine buzz might interfere with our work."

"I understand," he whispered back. "My lips are sealed."

Returning to her professional posture, she ended the interview.

"Thanks," she said. "Be sure to contact me if you remember anything. Anything at all."

He picked up the card from the counter top and put it in the top scrub pocket.

"I will," he said, extending his large hand.

Rachael shook it, then began to retrace her steps, heading for the elevator to find the lobby where she and Tony had agreed to meet. She hoped that he had finished interviewing Dana Dawkins. They could compare notes before they headed to the 22nd District station on Monterey Avenue to search for files on the names they gathered from Murphy and to get a copy of Lee's juvenile arrest report.

Wednesday, 18 Oct. 1978, 14:45

Dana's Dropped Clue

Tony sized up the woman standing in the hallway waiting for him. Dana Dawkins was in her late twenties, with a bubble of short curly dark hair framing her oval face. Her sparkling hazel eyes were accented by thick brows and feathery lashes. Her slightly upturned nose and full lips gave her a carefree beauty.

She was the picture of a professional woman in her dark brown tweed blazer and yellow cashmere turtleneck sweater, yet from the waist down, she dressed like a waitress with black uniform shoes peeking out from under a pair of black polyester pants.

"Let's go into my office," she said with a lilting southern accent. "Officer Murphy called to say that you needed my help."

Murphy was right. Her office was a devil to find. The unmarked door she was holding open led you behind the locked cashier's cages, after which you had to pass through the entire length of the accounting office, to another door with a state-of-the-art coded push button lock. They didn't get many visitors. It was the curse and the beauty of the computer center—the machines and records, along with Dana and her crew, were protected from prying eyes. Unless you knew to go back there and had the combination to two keypad locks, you'd never encounter them.

The main room was noisy and cold. All her workers wore sweaters or sweatshirts with thick wintery jeans. Some sported homemade fingerless gloves for warmth. A six-foot-tall, seven-foot-long dark gray metal box with rows of quickly flashing colored lights dominated one wall. From a slot in its side, a strip of oversized adding machine paper emerged, falling into a large metal box on the floor. Dana's workers translated the coded tapes into patient charges. On the other wall stood four different computers, each flashing their lights in a rhythm all their own. A four-by-six-foot rolling blackboard with the hospital's floor plans painted on it sat behind a large worktable. In the middle of the room sat six noisy keypunch machines flanked by small desks, making an L-shaped workstation for each of the college students. They barely glanced up when Dana ushered Tony past them, making for the door of her inner sanctum. Once inside, her desk was situated in front of a giant picture window that was blocked by the cinder block wall of the hospital's parking garage.

Tony noticed that the window was made of thick bulletproof Lexan plastic to foil a break-in. A t-shaped wire FM antenna had been taped high up the pane before it was attached to a radio that filled the room with the soft strains of WLS, one of the only stations strong enough to be picked up.

Dana removed her jacket as she motioned for Tony to sit across from her, her serious demeanor soon tempered by a hint of a smile.

"It's more private in here," she said. "Can I offer you a cup of coffee?" She pointed to a pot on a table behind her that was stacked with bundles of rolled-up papers, computer printouts, and medical books.

"Black please," he said politely as she filled his cup. He exchanged his card for the Styrofoam cup she gave him. "I'll try not to take up much of your busy day," he said.

"Take all the time you need," she said. "I don't get many visitors back here, but I'll certainly try to be helpful. And please, call me Dana."

"Dana," he smiled, pausing briefly before he dropped his

bombshell. "I'm here to investigate the murder of Leivald Nabb."

Dana sat stock still. She stared at Tony, unable to grasp the news he'd just delivered. "Sweet Jesus" and "Dear Lord" was all she could say.

Tears slipped from her eyes. She pulled tissues from a box in her middle desk drawer and patted her cheeks as Tony watched and waited. He crossed her off the list of suspects. Her surprised response was too genuine to feign.

Straightening herself in her chair after discarding the third or fourth wad of tissues, she pulled down the front of her sweater and sighed deeply, attempting to restore her professional demeanor.

"I sincerely hope I can help with y'all's investigation," she said. "I feel so bad about this. I tried hard to keep Lee out of trouble."

"What kind of trouble?" Tony asked.

"Running loose, mostly. The guards kept catching her 'round the hospital, making out, being downright naughty. She had one steady boyfriend, but I suspected she was dating more than one at a time."

"Do you have names for any of these guys?" Tony inquired.

Dana pursed her lips and shook her head. "Only the main one, Dillon something. I don't know his last name. We were able to keep her away from the local letch, Doctor "Feel-Good" Allen in ER and Peter "The Wolf" Randall from pharmacy, but I guess it didn't do much good."

She glanced down at the desk, biting her lower lip to keep it from quivering. She sighed slowly, holding back tears. Tony let her compose herself.

"I talked to that girl like she was my little sister. Talked myself blue in the face. Sorry to say, but the names of those boys were the last thing I thought about. Gosh, I figured it was her wild oats time, she'd get over it. But I knew the only chance I'd have to influence her was if I didn't get too preachy about it."

Dana was at war with her emotions. She wanted to cry because it hurt to know that Lee was dead, but it also hurt to know that she didn't have information to help the detective.

"Do you know of anyone she might have confided in about sowing her 'wild oats'? Another girl, perhaps?"

"No. She's a loner. She'd hang out with us when we went out of the hospital for lunch, but most of the time she was with her friend Cara."

"Why did you get involved with her?"

"Because Murphy in security told me he was going to pitch a fit with personnel because she was using hospital property too often as a hotel. He didn't say anything about the boy, but if he reported her, she'd be fired out from under me. Do you have any idea how hard it is to get good keyers? Lee's the fastest; she can…." Dana stopped suddenly and corrected herself.

"I meant to say she could do a stack of ER reports in no time flat. She and her mom needed money. I know they were under a mountain of debt. Every penny they got they needed to get by. Lee was making decent money, and I tried to give her overtime every chance I could, but it did no good. She wouldn't show up."

Tony made a note: money problems. He also wrote "no boy names" followed by a big question mark.

"How did you know about her mother?"

"Don't let the size of this building fool you. Big as this hospital is, it's really a small town. The gossip moves in circles, like ripples in a pond. Food service and the transporters hang together 'cause they all grew up together. The lab techs cluster up with the Asian nurses. Every guard, like Murphy, is a retired Chicago or Oak Lawn cop. Most of the janitors are black.

"The housekeepers are local Bohemian women. They get

their daughters hired whenever there's an opening, so those girls talk to my girls. The x-ray techs and pharmacists stay locked behind their doors. They don't know much, unless it happens underneath their noses. The interns and med students stick together because of their long hours, frequent naps, and shared poverty. Put down a half-eaten donut, and you'll get a flock of them, poor things. The on-call doctors are at home and the attendings are sequestered in their lounges. No communication there. Back here, we deal with the money, billing, payroll, and purchasing. If there's a dollar sign attached to it, we know about it."

Tony nodded and kept writing. She was full of information, but none of it seemed of value. Yet, you never knew what might point you in the right direction unless you asked questions.

"Tell me. In this 'small town,' who else might be of help in this investigation?"

"I'd say the night nursing supervisor or the bio-med techs, cause they see a lot of things while they move about. Trips to the lab, getting supplies, fixing equipment, and installing stuff. Lee had a lot of contact with them. She'd deliver the census reports to Ruth Colfax, but on the weekends it rotates through Rose Delgado, Vivian Weeks, or Dorothy Walls. They might have seen something, but I don't think Lee confided in any of them. They know her mother too well for her to trust them like she trusted me."

Dana continued talking as Tony wrote the names down.

"Except for Lee, the kids who work for me are students from Daley College or Moraine Valley."

"Why only those two schools?" asked Tony.

"The families who can afford St. Xavier, DePaul, or Loyola won't let them work. They spend too much money to have them distracted from their studies. But this is a real sweet job for a student. Good pay, steady hours, and if you work fast, there's quite a bit of time to study. Even if they finish up the work early, I don't make them go home 'cause you never know when the ER will heat up and swamp you with admissions. If it does, you have to rework the census and get it to the night supervisor."

Tony's notepad was filling up, but there wasn't a single promising lead. While Lee wasn't a bad girl, she had a few questionable habits. She wasn't a rich girl, so money wasn't the motive. It just didn't add up. Looking up from the pad, Tony took the interrogation in another direction.

"Did anyone other than Murphy complain?" he asked. "Anyone from the other departments?"

"Now that you mention it, Mr. James from housekeeping asked me about her. I'll bet she was sneaking around in the basement, too. I hope she wasn't stealing. You'd be surprised at what employees take from hospitals."

Tony noted the name, put "stolen items" behind it, jotting the word "drugs" next to the name Randall. Looking at Dana's face, she brought up Lee's other indiscretions.

"Lee shirked her commitments. I realize that everyone has problems at times, but Lee's came *too* often. I'd make a schedule, with everyone working one Sunday a month instead of two or three. They had to do the shift alone and wait for the next person to hand it over. At first it worked well; everybody liked having only one person here because Sunday is usually quiet. You do the census and some cleanup work from the ER; it's like being paid a day's salary for half the work.

At first, Lee would call in and say she was going to be late, but she'd show up not minutes late, but hours. The girls gossiped to me that when she got here she'd look like she'd just rolled out of bed. At first, I chalked it up to her waking up late and rushing. Now I'm not so sure."

"Why?" Tony asked.

"Her behavior was erratic—like she was on something—but there was never any alcohol or marijuana on her breath. Once, the girl I'd assigned to the first shift had a family picnic to go to, and after ten minutes of no Lee, she called me. I filled in, not imagining I'd end up working the whole shift. Lee waltzed in about an hour before the shift was over. I was so mad, I sent her straight home.

"A couple weekends, she'd call me at home, saying her car had broken down in some god forsaken place. I knew that those boys at her father's garage would go to hell and back to keep her car running, but she never bothered them. Other times, she'd wander in forty minutes late from lunch and leave early on others.

"Then one Sunday, when she came to relieve me, she brought a guy with her. You should've seen her. She was a mess. Makeup smudged, clothes wrinkled. She claimed he was going to keep her company while she worked. I told her that it was a breach of the patient's privacy. He got mouthy, so I called security, and they promptly escorted him out. I chewed her out real good."

"Did you know this guy she brought with her?"

"No, but he must have been one of the boys from the garage. He smelled like sweat and gasoline."

"Can you get me a list of the times that she didn't show up for work?"

"Sure," she said, moving to the filing cabinet on the wall opposite her desk. "It's unofficial, though. I keep it only for my reference, to complete my employee evaluations. Lee left me her badge with a note Friday night, saying that she quit."

From her top file drawer, she plucked a manila file folder with a red magic marker stripe running along the top of the front cover. It held several sheets of accounting paper filled with notations in red ink.

"She wasn't a bad girl," Dana said. "Foolish, yes. But she didn't deserve to die. She could be very sentimental—especially when something on the radio moved her. I remember her searching the dial, trying to find this one song. Originally, they played it so often you could set your watch by it. Then they phased it out, but every time she found it, she'd start crying her eyes out."

"What song was it?" Tony asked.

"I never caught the title. It was a 'lost-my-true-love song,' a twist on Pagliacci…."

Tony squinted at her. Was she dropping a clue in his lap? He waited to see what her interpretation was.

"Some guy singing about how he misses an old lover now that he's married. Lee would be blubbering by the end of it. There was a line about how he would see her face when making love to his wife. Lee would really lose it then."

Dana tapped the desktop with her finger, trying to mimic the rhythm. With a sigh, she gave up.

"I can't remember it for the life of me."

"I'm sure it'll come to you. I'll give you my card; when it does, call me."

"Breese… That is not how I imagined you'd spell it. Is it Irish?"

"No," he said. "Actually, it's Welsh, means agile and quick."

"Everyone around here is Irish. It's why Lee was so unusual—her Germanic name and looks, with that natural white blonde hair. I wish I knew more to tell you."

He rose from the chair. "Thanks, I'm sure this will help. I'll be in touch."

She rose and offered her hand to Tony to shake. When he clasped her right hand, she enveloped his with both of hers.

"Yes, please call me when you find out who did this. Lee didn't deserve to die."

"Thank you, Ms. Dawkins. I'll call as soon as we turn up anything important."

He started for the doorway, but something drew him back to her desk.

"Did she give a reason for quitting?" he asked.

"She mentioned something about a better job that involved

traveling, but that didn't ring true to me. With only her mother and her car, why would she take off and leave them behind?"

"Why indeed?" Tony intoned. "Thanks again."

October 1977

Love Unrequited

He leaned on the car horn blaring two long, then three short blasts announcing himself. She was looking hot in her chocolate suede boots and short stonewashed denim skirt. The black lace scarf tied around her waist accentuated the aqua sweater stretched tight across her breasts. She looked like Farrah Fawcett when she feathered her hair and bangs.

Lee knew the ride to the hospital would be all Mikey talking and her listening. Some of what he said made good sense, but most of it was over her head. She had a passion for things mechanical, but not like Mikey. He lived, ate, and breathed gears, servos, motors, and codes. He went from cars to computers to robots in a heartbeat. Slinging her fake black leather motorcycle jacket over one arm, and grabbing her purse off the kitchen table, she shouted goodbye to her mother.

"When you get off, Lee, take the car. I'll park in the usual spot. Don't forget to come back for me at 7:30. I'm too tired to do a double tonight," she responded.

"I won't need the car, Mom, I have a ride,"

"If you get stood up, we can eat at IHOP," Ann said. "I'll buy."

Corn pancakes with sausages sounded good, but Lee'd be sleeping off ribs from the Branding Iron. Dana was taking them there as a treat for achieving a month without absences.

"Bye Mom," Lee shouted before locking the front door.

"Hey, Mikey!" she yelled with a wave and a smile.

She seemed happy. Her freshly curled hair bounced as she walked, and her blue eyes sparkled. Mikey noticed something different about her; something he couldn't pin down. She seemed more voluptuous, more enticing to him than she ever had before. She had certainly matured from the dirty-faced kid fetching tools for her dad at the garage.

The customers at the garage didn't mind the mechanics taking their vehicles for test runs after they finished with them, as long as they didn't burn too much gas. The brown Plymouth Fury purred sweetly after its tune-up and muffler patch. Lee was glad the garage was still going strong.

Mikey knew what the others saw in this girl. Lee was different from all the good Irish Catholic "colleens" in so many ways. She was a playful, high-energy flirt. She made him feel good every time he saw her. She squeezed his arm.

"Whose car is this?" she asked." It looks familiar."

"Old Man Flannigan's. He calls her "Betty Grable;" says it was the name of his bomber from World War II. Everybody knows he flew in the war. Makes me want to charge him ten percent more for having to put up with listening to the same old stories."

"Yeah, you ought to charge him extra," she said, remembering how many times people called her Dad a Nazi right to his face when they didn't like the cost of the repairs. "Dad used to jack his price up at least fifteen percent so he could take it off and still break even after they haggled with him. Because he was born in Germany, they thought he was in the SS. But he was in Chicago long before the war. He served in the United States Army but was too proud of his roots to change his last name."

She changed the subject. "Mikey, you know I love the rides, but I need my wheels! When you gonna have my MG fixed?"

"You're the only one in the neighborhood with an English car. Your struggle buggy is a lot more trouble than you'd think."

"Don't call it a struggle buggy. You sound like my mother,"

Lee chided him petulantly.

Mikey eased into northbound lanes of Kedzie Avenue.

"We had to get a cover for your fuse box. It's why it wouldn't start on rainy days—the fuses were getting wet."

"Oh, you didn't like how I improvised with plastic wrap?" she asked.

He let out a low chuckle while turning west on 103rd Street.

"Jamie also found that the release bearing on your clutch was shot. He needed an alignment tool, so he called a guy from the MG Club to borrow one. When the guy brought out the tool, they saw another problem."

"I thought it was a leak in the master cylinder," said Lee thoughtfully.

"It was. They replaced that, too. Luckily, V&W's junkyard in Blue Island had a whole transmission cheaper instead of pieces. The good news is that the MG guy split the cost."

Mikey ran the yellow light to keep from having to look at Queen of Martyr's Catholic school sitting at the edge of a vast tract of land where he had spent most of his young life. He went from Martyr's grammar school with the nuns to high school with the Christian Brothers of Brother Rice. Those four years were torture because the girls at Mother McAuley High School were so close, yet so far away. When he enrolled in St. Xavier University, he thought he would get to know them, but the best and the brightest went to other schools and the rest wanted nothing to do with a boy like Mikey. Frustrated that his parents wouldn't finance a transfer to any institution of learning not connected to this one spot on earth, he dropped out of college after his first year. He wheedled the remainder of his tuition money from his grandfather to buy his share of the garage.

"Your dad was strictly business. He left a ton of records, but he didn't leave them in English. Why didn't he teach you German?"

"He didn't want people to discriminate against me," Lee sighed. She missed him badly. "He said it was bad enough to be blonde and blue eyed in a neighborhood of red-headed leprechauns; I didn't need to open my mouth and have sauerkraut fall out of it, too."

Mikey laughed. He ignored the twenty-mile-per-hour school speed zone. Nobody was in school on a Friday night. He made sure not to stop at the light on the north edge of the Brother Rice athletic field. He'd stood waiting for the bus on this corner too many cold days with an armload of books and a face full of pimples.

Lee was daydreaming, figuring how she could get to do the hospital census. It wouldn't be hard to ask Phyllis to give up the chore, but getting Dana to let her would be. As supervisor, Dana wanted to spread things around, make sure everyone had their share of work. But Lee needed to know where the vacancies were tonight. She had mischief on her mind.

"When was the last time you took a Friday night off?" Mikey asked.

"About two months ago," she said. "Spent it with Cara and the babies watching 'Wonder Woman' on TV."

"They're cute kids!" smiled Mikey. "I'm glad you give Cara a hand. She looks overwhelmed most of the time. I don't think she was ready for one kid, let alone two."

"Don't talk about her like that," Lee chided. "She loves those babies."

"I know she does," Mikey retorted. "But she is so… you know… on edge all the time."

"I know it looks like that, but she wasn't trained to be domestic."

"Dillon says if it wasn't for you, he'd never get a decent meal. Seems her cooking is as bad as her mood."

Lee smiled inwardly. Even the guys at the garage were finding out the good she was doing. Gazing out the window, she continued to defend her best friend.

"She was supposed to go to Vassar, you know, the exclusive college in upstate New York where all the blue bloods go? It fell through when the twins popped up. Her folks wouldn't pay for an off-campus apartment and babysitters. Besides, Dillon had registered and paid for his mechanics training at Coyne Technical Institute and couldn't get a refund."

Mikey chuckled as he made his turn onto Kostner, toward 95th Street. In a high, cracking falsetto, he imitated Cara's mother. "God's death, Cara! Look at ya! Ye've ruined yerself spreading your legs for a shanty Irish boy with no more future than a pissant!"

Lee laughed, but his mockery touched a festering wound inside her. It was the only thing she and Mrs. O'Toole agreed on. Cara *should* have kept her legs closed. She was supposed to go to the prom and take pictures with Dillon, not sneak off with him and get herself pregnant. Cara didn't even like him before Lee asked her to invite him to the dance. No, she should have left Beverly, gone to college, and married some rich boy from a big family of lace curtain, East Coast Irish. Someone related to the Kennedys or something. Someone Mrs. O'Toole would have approved of, maybe even liked. Sure, the twins were adorable, with their curly dark auburn hair, dimpled cheeks, and big sable eyes like their father. There was no denying that they were part of the Whelan family, not showing a trace of the bright-red haired, blazing green-eyed O'Tooles.

"Mrs. O'Toole is a piece of work. You sound just like her, with her high-handed manners. I can only imagine what she said to Cara in private."

Mikey drove to the back of the hospital lot, far away from the door before pulling into a spot.

"When are you going to start dating again?" he asked, a serious look on his face.

"Mikey, are you asking me out?" She smiled.

"Dillon's married now," he said, patting her hand gently.

"You need to find another guy. You need to get on with your life."

"I'm doing fine, Mikey, really I am," she said, quietly. "I got my job, I got Mama. What more do I need?"

"You need a boyfriend," he said, looking her in the eyes. "Listen, I got a friend who's a really good guy. You'd like him. He's an apprentice plumber, working big new construction jobs downtown. No filthy water or sewage—all new construction. He makes big money working all year long, no winters off drinking beer and pissing on the wall. You need to have some fun, go places, and do things."

Lee smiled at him. "Naw, I don't need to go anywhere right now, I'm in enough trouble with my boss," she replied. "I need to settle down and get back to being a good girl. But I do need my car back. I can't keep depending on you for rides to work."

"Sure you can, Lee."

Pulling even with the back entrance to the hospital, Mikey shot a glance at her with concerned eyes. "Me and the boys are always here for you. And your mom, too."

"I know, Mikey," she said patting his cheek softly before sliding out the car. "I know."

She shut the door gently and leaned into the half open window.

"Are you gonna go back to the garage tonight? Or, will I see you over at the Branding Iron later? Dana is buying tonight before she goes home. We'll be there early, around 6 o'clock."

He wanted to drive away, never to see her again, but he couldn't. His heart was beating hard in his chest from being so close to her. Her touch counteracted the "no" that should have come out of his mouth.

"I'll be at the Iron," he said, trying not to betray his disappointment.

"Oh goody." She kissed his ear.

Mikey wanted to confess his love to her, but he knew it wouldn't work. It wasn't the right time. She wasn't ready. She still had it bad, real bad for Dillon. There was nothing he could do. He was stuck.

"Thanks Mikey, I don't know what I'd do without you."

With the whirl of the revolving glass door, she quickly disappeared into the crowd of nurses, doctors, visitors, and patients who swirled about the lobby.

* * * *

In the dim rumbling roar of the bowling alley bar, when Mikey closed his eyes, he could feel the brush of her hand on his face. The aroma of her Navy cologne was fading from his memory as Albee and Jamie barged through the door, ready for beer and bullshit. They'd be good for passing the time until she came in for lunch. They might even bowl together to keep him busy until it was time to go back to the hospital to pick her up at eleven o'clock.

"Yo, Mikey," bellowed Albee, "what you doin' up here? I thought you were delivering old man Flannigan's car."

"He'll get it first thing in the morning," retorted Mikey. "I needed to take Lee to work since Jamie's still working on her clutch."

"Sure, sure," teased Jamie. "Blame me for taking Lee to work. I'll have you know the MG is now in tip-top shape. If you'd talked to me instead of running off half-cocked, she'd be driving it herself."

"I thought you had a couple more hours of work," Mikey replied. "Didn't the MG mechanic need to adjust something?"

"He finished fast," Jamie stated. "He's an expert."

"Yeah," chimed in Albee. "You, him, and everyone else who bought *Zen and the Art of Motorcycle Repair* are experts now."

"At least I know the difference between it and a *Haynes*

Manual," Jamie said as the bartender set a beer down on the dollar he'd slid across the bar.

Flummoxed, Albee waved a dollar in the air and barked at the bartender, "Hey, where's mine?"

"I wanted to be sure that's what you wanted," quipped the bartender as he reached for the flopping dollar.

"Mikey, you want to bowl a few lines tonight?" Jamie asked.

"Yeah, but I have to take a break around six. Lee and her co-workers are going to be here, and I want to join them."

"Listen man," said Albee. "You need to stay away from her. She's still not over Dillon."

"I hear you man," said Mikey, "but somebody has got to do something to wake her up. How long has it been now? Dillon doesn't have time to wipe his ass between working, two babies, and wife. Someone has got to make her see she needs to move on, start her life without him."

Jamie swallowed a mouthful of beer. "Mikey, man, you know how explosive Dillon is. Remember when he kicked a hole in the wall at the garage because he thought someone was making a joke about Lee? What do you think he'll do to you if he catches you sniffing around her?"

"For one thing, I'm not sniffing around her," Mikey said indignantly. "For another thing, I'm not scared of Dillon."

"Listen," Albee said. "You might know about a lot of things, but love ain't one of them. You need to keep away from Lee for a good while."

Before defending himself, Jamie stared him straight in the eyes, lowered his voice, and got serious.

"Mikey, you're like a little brother to me and Jamie. It's how Lee sees you—a little brother. You're not a man to her, I'm afraid. I don't think you'll ever be."

Mikey straightened up on the barstool and lit into Albee with a fury that startled him.

"You don't know shit. Lee loves me. She needs time is all.

She'll come around soon.You'll see."

Albee glanced at Jamie. Jamie raised his eyebrows and put his beer bottle to his lips. Albee followed suit. There was an awkward silence as they drank.

"You boys ready for another round?" the bartender asked, breaking the tension.

"Yeah," Albee barked. "And I'm paying this time. Send'em over to lane eight. Come on guys, let's get shoes and hit some pins."

* * * *

Lee scanned the lanes looking for Mikey. He was sitting while the other boys were rolling balls and laughing. She ambled over to their lane, grabbed an opened beer off the highboy and took a deep swig, nearly emptying it. In one bound, she was seated next to Mikey. She threw her arms around his neck, singing along with the song playing on the jukebox.

"I only have a few minutes," she cupped her hand to his ear and whispered. "I wanted to tell you I won't need a ride home tonight. You don't have to wait for me."

"Oh, okay," he said, shocked that she would have come all the way to the bowling alley to tell him he wasn't needed.

"I'm running back to the hospital. Hope you win!"

"So soon? What happened to your lunch? "

"Bette didn't come in, so we're going to wait for her. I'll be pulling a double because one of the night girls got sick."

Mikey didn't like the sound of it. He didn't know what to think about her landing nearly in his lap, petting him like a puppy in front of the guys. Her pupils were wider than he'd seen before. He wondered if she'd gotten something from the guy at the hospital's pharmacy—the one that gave leftover pills to his buddies.

"Did you take something to keep you awake?" asked Mikey, concerned.

"Yeah, I got some No-Doz from the gift shop. I'll be fine. Don't worry."

Lee was acting out of character, pawing at him, acting like she was high. He hoped it wasn't something that would hurt her. In her emotional state after her break-up with Dillon, she was vulnerable to bad choices.

"Do you want me to take you back to the office?" he asked.

"Pretty please. Then I can say that I was only on a break. If I wait for the shuttle, I might have to say I was using my lunch hour."

"Why don't you take Dana a barbecue sandwich?" Mikey asked. "I'll front you the cash if you don't have any today."

"Good idea. I need to keep her happy and quiet," Lee said.

She kissed him on the cheek, and scooping up a ball from the return, fired it down the lane toward a half empty pin deck.

"Finish my line," he said, "I don't know how long this is going to take."

She skipped to the door, waiting for Mikey to get the sandwich. Albee and Jamie looked at each other and shrugged.

Opening the car door for her, she slid across the bench seat toward the middle. As soon as Mikey twisted the key in the ignition, the radio came to life. Lee spun the dial, looking for a station that wasn't playing Lawrence Welk polkas. She hit a pop station, recognized the guitar lead, and began bouncing on the seat.

"I love this song," she squealed, turning the volume up.

Oh boy, Mikey thought. Five minutes of sheer hell. He suspected that Lee heard Dillon singing it instead of the lead singer. Why couldn't she see that Dillon didn't have it bad for her anymore and that he'd moved on with his life?

She sang loudly, holding her hands over her heart and tilting her face toward the roof of the car.

Mikey didn't know which rattled him more, her singing, or her grand delusion. The song summed up her hopes that Dillon would renege on his marriage to rescue Lee from her life of loneliness. Lee wanted Dillon to admit his mistake but Mikey knew Dillon was going to hurt Lee more as time went on.

She belted out the chorus, bouncing in time with the bass line of the song.

Mikey looked over at her, his jaw tightened in disgust. How the hell could she say she loved that song? It was her heartbreak song. He remembered the first time she'd heard it. She hadn't loved it then. It made her break down, silent tears first, then choked-back sobs that caused her to pound the dashboard as the reality of the words soaked in. She scared him. He'd pulled over to see if she was all right. She shook and sobbed in his arms. It was the only time she had ever let him hold her close.

Today, she sang with joy. Mikey's knuckles blanched white from clutching the steering wheel so tightly.

"Come on Mikey, sing it with me."

She punched his shoulder trying to get him to loosen up, to make him join in. He didn't look at her or take a hand off the wheel. He covered his anger by honking the horn at a guy and yelling "asshole" for an imaginary slight.

Mikey relented, managing to hum off key and out of time. As they pulled up to the main entrance of the hospital, the song ended. She hopped out the car and ran toward the door without even a glance over her shoulder.

Mikey sat thinking that one day he would be there to let her cry. He'd hand her tissues, sit patiently while she ranted, raved, and cried herself out. When she was done, he'd be there to tuck her under a blanket to sleep it off on his mom's couch. Yet she didn't even notice the look in his eyes. She didn't see that he was crazy in love with her, puppy dog faithful to the end. She never saw how he wanted to smash the radio every time the dumb song played. The lyrics said to him that the man was going to stay with his wife while dreaming about being with his former lover, not the other way round.

Wednesday, 18 Oct 1978, 15:10

Good Cop, Bad Cop

"I say we bring in this Whelan guy for questioning, and go at him hard. Everybody says that he and Lee were boyfriend and girlfriend before he got married, and—from what I heard from Murphy—afterwards, too. Sounds like the base angle of a love triangle if you ask me," Tony said as he sipped coffee from a white Styrofoam cup.

Rachael drove down 95th Street headed back to their Cottage Grove office. Tony might be right. All she got from Richard McDowell was a couple of girl's names whom she didn't think had enough moxie to commit a murder, much less a mutilation so vile. He added nothing new or compelling in the way of motive.

"What if this Whelan guy tells us to kiss his ass?" Rachael replied. "What then?"

"We play good cop, bad cop. I'll be the good cop because our Whelan won't succumb to your charms."

"Detective Breese, I'd appreciate it if you stopped referring to my 'charms.' Understood?"

"Don't be so touchy," he clucked. "All I meant was that he likes blondes or redheads, not brunettes."

"While we're on the subject, our last case wouldn't have been solved if I hadn't been the bad cop. Every one of those suspects expected the 'girl' cop to be the soft one. It totally rattled the asshole when I got in his face. He couldn't keep his lies straight."

She was proud the murderer had cracked for her. From the moment they'd seen the murder site she'd known who done it, and she'd been right. If only she and Tony had seen this case's actual murder scene, her gut would kick in, pointing them to the right suspect.

"Yeah," mused Tony. "It was gratifying watching the big son of a bitch shrink down to size when he realized he'd accidently confessed to you. He was trying so hard to be clever, but in the end, he didn't have a big enough brain."

"Yeah, it was. When they underestimate me, getting them dead to rights is sweet," she said.

"With this Dillon guy, let's keep it simple; bring him in, sweat him, close the case. Easy as pie."

Tony gulped the last of his coffee as they crossed one of the many railroad tracks bisecting 95th Street.

"I don't think so, Tony," replied Rachael flatly. "Stuffing her in a garbage can, slashing her up like that? No amount of bad Irish blood would make him do that. Not to her. They were sweethearts, lovers. You'd have to have deep-seated hatred to ruin someone's face like that."

"You're right but I still want to interrogate him. I want to see how he reacts under pressure. There's something about his involvement that I don't like. I can't put my finger on it, but the thought of him pisses me off."

In this partnership, Rachael often played the horrid cop, not the bad cop. The sergeant put them together because Tony was a ladies' man. It was a good call. She believed that Tony liked working with her better than he cared to admit.

"Rach, I keep telling you that this is an open-and-shut case of love and lust," Tony said. "Once you get on board with the lust part, you'll see it clear as day. Believe me."

At the street corner, a bunch of teenagers gathered heading for school. Maybe this was where it all began, inside school, Rachael thought.

"How 'bout we stop by Morgan Park High School instead. Have a chat with some of the teachers? Maybe something in Lee Nabb's background will shake loose."

"Good idea," Tony said.

Rachael turned south on Vincennes, toward the back door of the Beverly community.

Wednesday 18 Oct. 1978, 15:30

A Blind Alley

Rachael sat reading the transcript she and Tony obtained from Lee's high school. Leivald Nabb was an average student—getting mostly C's, a few B's, and a consistent A—in English. She got A's across the board, every semester. They even noted a few awards for poems and compositions. It meant she could express herself well. Rachael wondered why when they looked in her room, they hadn't seen any evidence of her writing. Not a poem, letter, diary entry, or anything. Ann Nabb hadn't time to throw away any incriminating evidence. The room hadn't been cleaned before they had arrived, so where were all of Lee's writings—her letters or cards?

"Tony, what would make you throw away all your love letters from a girlfriend?"

"Breakup," he answered without skipping a beat.

"Yeah, gotcha. But if you were in love again, crazy in love, wouldn't you be keeping anything that revealed it?

"There are always a lot of trinkets in the courtship stage of a new relationship. Cards, letters, hearts, and pressed flowers—girly kind of stuff. But you know that, Rach."

She picked up the yearbook that the school librarian lent them and leafed through the pages.

"This girl was a writer. Take a look at the transcript. This yearbook shows awards for poetry, she's in advance placement English classes, and a writer for the school newspaper. There should be piles of clippings, copies of her work, all in her bedroom. Even the most private person has something lying around. Where's her stuff, where's her writing?"

It was a rhetorical question that Rachael needed to voice.

"We find the purse, we find the notebooks. Deep inside one of them, there's a construction paper heart with a knife through it with the name of the one who done her wrong. Case closed. If you think about it, wouldn't she have given all the poems and letters to the object of her affections? Why would there be anything in her room to point us in the right direction? Everything should be in the hand of her beloved, not under her dirty clothes, right?"

"I'm thinking, if she were a writer, she'd be mulling over something all the time. Snippets, notes, entries. But somewhere there's an entry, a name, half a poem, something that would narrow down the cast of characters down to a manageable few," Rachael said.

She had written down names of all the boys on the school paper or involved in any activity that Lee participated in.

Tony had his head in a different book, the yearbook that chronicled the year Cara started at Morgan Park High. He was amazed that her folks hadn't transferred her to Morgan Park Academy, the private school on the top of Longwood Hill, where the doctors, lawyers, and judges sent their kids. He wrote down names of girls he thought they should talk to for background. Interviewing teachers would be okay, but they wouldn't know her internal life, her deep secrets, unless there had been a very close connection. Perhaps one of them might have been a confidante. Since Rachael mentioned the writing connection, he took down all the names in the English department—including the drama club teacher.

"I don't see Cara involved in any of the things Lee was in. Wonder how they ended up being friends?"

"Who knows?" replied Rachael. "Girls make friends in the bathrooms over hairdos or lipsticks, in the cafeteria griping about the food, or over a broken-down car. Maybe Lee rescued her from a dead battery or something?"

"You don't think this thing has a lesbian leaning, do you?" Tony asked.

Rachael tilted her head and looked at Tony. With all the damage done to her face, jealousy was definitely part of the motive. Among high school girls an unrequited love was rarely admitted to a family member, but a third party might have known about it.

"This means a whole other set of girls to interview, in addition to the candy stripers and the hospital crew. You can have this book when I'm done. You do the females, I'll do the males," she sighed as she put aside her hope that this case was going to be solved relatively quickly. School, hospital, garage, carnival. Where else did this alleged 'homebody' hang out?

Tony picked up the desk phone on the second ring. It was the boss of the carnival Rachael had called earlier. Tony handed the phone to her and took a walk down the hall. When he returned, the call was almost over.

"Yes, thank you," Rachael said cradling the receiver on her shoulder as she jotted down numbers of an address and phone number. You've been very helpful."

Ending the call, she dialed a number and waited for the connection.

"Hello, is this Darlene?" she asked.

"My name is Detective Culpepper. I got your number from Mr. Washbrand. He said you might be able to talk to me about a girl named Lee Nabb. Could me and my partner come by and pick you up? It would be easier to talk in our office."

Rachael verified the address in her book and slid it across the desk to Tony. They didn't have far to go to get her. She lived in an apartment building on Cottage Grove Avenue north of the Pullman neighborhood. Tony pulled the squad car keys out of the desk drawer, stood, and stretched.

"This might be interesting," he said to Rachael, ignoring the last of his cold coffee.

"Or it'll be a walk down a blind alley," sighed Rachael. "From what I could tell, this one is a chatter box. I hope she can listen long enough to answer us."

November 1977

Bed Rest for Cara

“Hello,” said the nurse into the white phone hanging from the wall of the exam room, “May I please speak to Mrs. Teagan O’Toole?”

As the nurse waited, tears streamed down Cara’s face. She hadn’t done anything wrong. She took her vitamins, ate moderately, and made sure she drank twice the amount of water she normally did. But look where it had gotten her. The doctor was putting her on bed rest because her ankles were swelling. The books on pregnancy she’d read said that swollen ankles sometimes happened, but they didn’t say that bed rest was the cure. She wished she’d lied about how long they’d been swollen. Now she was on her way to the hospital for observation. If everything was okay, then home to bed rest. But there was no one at home to take care of her. She’d have to go to her mother and Mrs. O’Flynn for help.

“Hello Mrs. O’Toole, I’m Doris, Doctor Riley’s nurse. I’m calling to tell you we’re admitting Cara for observation.”

The pause was longer than it should have been for a simple “yes, thank you.” And the nurse’s tone changed drastically when she was allowed to speak again.

“Yes ma’am, I am aware she is married and no longer on your insurance….”

Another uncomfortable pause.

“Yes ma’am, I am aware I need to notify her husband…” countered the nurse, but she was cut off again. Cara overheard her mother’s strong angry voice leaking into the silent exam room.

"... Because ma'am," said the nurse slowly, "We can't get through to Mr. Whelan at this time, and you're the secondary contact listed on your daughter's file."

The pain shifted from Cara's navel to a point outside her huge belly. She looked like a woman who was ready to deliver instead of being six months along. The twins were growing fast. Doctor Riley said something about her cervix—whatever that was—thinning from the weight, and that if she continued to remain upright, she would go into labor and the babies would be born premature. He was sending her for a battery of tests, keeping her in the hospital for a few days to check everything out. If there were no more complications, he would send her home to lie down until February.

The nurse said that from here on, Cara would need help doing everything. Bathing, going to the toilet, eating, and sleeping. Cara had to admit that sometimes the pain was so bad that she barely could stand up long enough to make a cup of soup.

She regretted that she'd prayed for a miscarriage when one seemed imminent. It hadn't come soon enough for her to escape to Vassar, so what was the use now? It would only make Dillon and his family mad at her for having spent money for an apartment and second-hand furniture. It certainly wouldn't do anything to repair the damage done between her and her mother. If it happened today, she wouldn't be able to get into junior college until January.

"Thank you, ma'am," said the nurse flatly. "She'll be in a room on the South Wing in about 45 minutes. Yes, ma'am, I'm absolutely going to keep trying to contact Mr. Whelan. Goodbye, ma'am."

Hanging up the phone, the nurse leaned over to pat Cara's arm as she lay on the exam table. If she'd had lollipops in her pocket like when she'd worked Peds, she'd have given Cara two. The grandmother-to-be was as cold as a night on the Mount Everest without a tent.

"I'm sorry, but I had to notify your next of kin, even if she isn't happy about the news. I'll keep trying to get in touch with your husband to let him know where you are, okay?"

"Okay," sniffed Cara, putting on as brave a face as possible while lumbering to the wheelchair the nurse had pushed over next to the exam table.

"They'll keep you for observation, but after a few days, we have to let you go home for bed rest until the twins decide to make their entrance," the nurse said, smiling, trying to cushion the blow.

All Cara was able to think about was how to get out of being at her mother's for three whole months. Dillon's mother worked every day in the beauty shop, so she'd be of no help. All of her girlfriends were off at college, and even if they hadn't been, their mothers wouldn't let them come around her for fear that her wantonness might rub off on them. Even Lee, who couldn't afford college, worked. So there was no one to help her. If she had any money of her own, she'd give it all to Mrs. O'Flynn, her mother's housekeeper, to have her find someone for her. But she'd spent every dime Daddy had given her on baby clothes when she moved out because there would be no baby shower, just as there had been no wedding shower or reception. As she was rolled down the hallway toward the elevators, all she could think was, thank goodness that the tissues the nurse had given her were free.

Wednesday, 18 Oct 1978, 15:35

Dillon's Grief

"Why is it that every place this guy is supposed to be working is either shut down, closed for the day, or they haven't heard of him?"

Tony grumbled as he wheeled the car out of the parking lot of the motorcycle dealership, bound for another place on their list of where to contact Mr. Whelan. "Who in the hell runs a shop only open on the weekend?"

"Guess they figure Saturday and Sunday is when the bikers need 'em, so they shifted their weekend to the middle of the week," Rachael answered with a yawn. "Kinda like what we're supposed to do with our lives—adjust them to fit the needs of the public."

"Oh, shit," he exclaimed. "Now you're sounding like one of those old-ass sergeants I had when I was working the streets."

She had no comeback. It was a hundred percent true. She was raised on the company line; she'd heard it around the family dinner table often enough from her father, his friends, her uncles, and even her mother. Everyone in her family worked for institutions that ran twenty-four-hour days, seven days a week. It could've been their official family motto.

"And another thing," Tony said as he sped along at fifty miles per hour to keep up with street traffic, "These people out here drive way too fast. They think every street wider than two lanes is an expressway."

Rachael didn't mention the posted limit was forty-five. Tony's eyes darted from mirror to mirror. He was definitely going to be the bad cop in the interrogation today, if they found their intended subject.

The old guy who identified himself as “interim manager” of the McDonald’s had set the tone for the day. Because they were across the border of Chicago in the suburb of Blue Island, the manager said that he didn’t have to talk to them without a warrant. Tony quietly informed him that no matter where they stood, failure to reply to his questions was obstruction of justice, which carried a minimum of six months in the Cook County Jail. It was then that manager told them that Whelan no longer worked there. Asking when he had left, the man gave Tony an exact date, without even looking at a calendar.

Riding past apartments sandwiched between factories comprising the closest south suburbs, Tony vented his anger at the insult.

“I bet if I’d gone to any other Mickey Dee’s in the area, we’d find that he’s worked at every one of them in the past.”

“Either his friends are ignorant, or they think they’re doing him a favor by leading us on a wild goose chase. Don’t they know that makes him look guilty?” Rachael mused, watching the traffic around them.

Midlothian wasn’t known as a high-crime area, but there were dope dealers living everywhere. To the dealer, any unmarked car posed a threat. When they saw a plain wrapper, they automatically hit the gas and sped off because they assumed that the police were after them. Rachael ignored the temptation to chase them.

“I wonder how many of those so-called friends of Whelan’s were screwed over by him,” Tony asked.

They drove on, quietly, looking for the sign to the entrance of the railroad freight yard. Rachael had a feeling of déjà vu as they drove down a dusty road into a place people seldom noticed even though it was vital to their lives.

The urban sprawl spread right up to the edge of the

embankment that separated commuter train tracks from the vast web of steel arteries in the train yard. A tall gray concrete control tower was where the detectives headed. Threading their way through parked semis, giant forklifts, and a maze of containers, they found the workers' parking lot. Rachael took down all the license plate numbers, makes, and models.

"Looks like he's here," she said. "See the little red Chevy Luv pickup over there? That's what he's supposed to be driving."

"Yeah, somewhere here," sighed Tony. "Look at the size of this place—not to mention all these train cars, heavy equipment, containers, and tracks. Shit, you could hide a couple of marching bands in here and we'd have a hard time finding them. I sure hope none of his smart-ass friends work here. One wrong word, and he'll flee."

"I don't think he's up to running on foot. I'm willing to sit on the bed of his truck and wait for him."

Smiling at Rachael, Tony decided to up the ante. Turning the engine over, he inched the car's bumper against the back bumper of the truck. The wall of the maintenance shed helped to block his escape route.

Stepping out of the car, Rachael adjusted her gun, and Tony stretched his arms. "Nice idea, partner. I wouldn't want to have to run down the tower steps, trying to prevent Mr. Whelan from avoiding questioning," Rachael said before walking over to the base of the control tower.Climbing the steep metal staircase snaking around the outside of the tower gave them a good view of the surrounding tracks. The effort of the climb made Tony crankier. Rachael didn't say anything, as another flash of déjà vu had swept over her. Like the original Mount Trashmore crime scene, Tony didn't like anything that reminded him of a ladder. He muttered about his safety all the way up. She had to admit that whoever designed the structure didn't consider its being located in a region where cold wind and rain could turn exposed wrought iron stair treads and handrails into an ice coated death climb.

The door to the control room was unlocked. Tony shrugged at this breach of security. He had seen too many World War II movies, but trains here were too slow and unimportant to be hijacked. Besides, you'd only end up in Canada or Mexico. Hijackers targeted airplanes these days because they wanted to go to Cuba.

With badge case in hand, he showed the occupants that he had a good reason for making the steep climb. Rachael stood behind him in a defensive position.

"Good morning, gentlemen," he said. "Could you tell me where I might find Dillon Whelan?"

The four men stared past Tony toward Rachael. They were not accustomed to having female company. Tony cleared his throat. A man wearing a telephone operator's headset, punched a button on his console to call Whelan to the tower.

Rachael quickly moved over to him, bending slightly to place her hand over the mouthpiece.

"Don't tell him who we are, okay?"

The guy nodded, wide-eyed, without taking his eyes off Rachael's face, as he replied to Dillon's supervisor.

"We need him to move his truck."

Rachael smiled. Although he had come up with the wrong excuse, one that might make Dillon run when he recognized their plain wrapper blocking him in, it was an acceptable ruse.

The other men went back to their jobs, glancing occasionally at Rachael.

"Can I ask what this is all about?" inquired the guy with rolled up sleeves and a thick grease pencil behind his ear.

"We need to ask him some questions in reference to a homicide investigation we're conducting. Sorry, but it's all I can say at this time," replied Tony.

"Oh, yeah" he said wide-eyed. "Gotcha—an investigation."

He went back to his chart table of codes and numbers. The other guys stared out of the window and talked into their radios, flipping switches. Rachael took up a position behind the door. Tony stood waiting for it to open. Their patience was rewarded when an annoyed man burst through the door, his dark eyes flashing anger as he yelled across the room.

"I don't get you guys. You call me up here about *my* truck, but there's a cop car blocking *me* in!"

The yellow hard hat he was wearing was tipped back as far as it could go, showing his thick auburn curls. He wore a safety vest, black turtleneck, navy sweatshirt, and dark blue overalls. A heavy chrome chain looped from his back pocket to the belt loop near his side pocket. His black work boots could double as dance wear in any of the leather bars on the North Side.

Crossing his arms over his chest, he stopped in the middle of the room. Tony stepped toward him, extending his shiny badge at eye level. The dimples in his cheeks showed as he smiled at Tony.

"So the cop car is for me," he said.

"Mr. Whelan, we would like you to come in for questioning," Tony said in an official tone.

"About what?"

Rachael walked up behind him.

"We want to talk to you about the murder of Leivald Nabb," she said.

He stared at Rachael in amused disbelief.

"What did you say?" he asked.

"Come with us to our office. We want you to help us with the murder of Lee Nabb," she repeated.

"Get the fuck out of here, lady," he guffawed. "Which one of these sick bastards put you up to this lousy joke?"

Before she could answer, Dillon spun around to look at his co-workers, searching each face for the glimmer of a smile that would tell Dillon the joke was on him. But nobody made a move or looked away.

"Come on you ass wipes," he hissed. "Fess the fuck up!"

He focused squarely on each face. "Answer my fucking question!" he demanded. "Which one of you?"

Tony watched him clinch his fists into a ball as if preparing to pummel the answer out of the men.

Rachael reached into her jacket pocket for the Polaroid photo of Lee on the morgue gurney showing her birth-marked leg and long blonde hair. Moving toward Dillon, she extended the photo to him.

"It's not a joke, Dillon," she said solemnly. "Look at this picture."

He took the photo from her, looked at it briefly, and lowered his head reverently. Lifting the picture to his eyes again, he studied it for an exceedingly long time as large tears began to well in them and spill down his face. "It's her," he said. It's Lee," he sobbed. "Oh my God. Lee, what did they *do* to you?"

"You'll need to go with us to our office for routine questioning," Rachael said.

"Take the rest of the day off, Whelan," the yard boss said.

Dillon shook his head as though in disbelief, still clutching the Polaroid photo in his hand.

As the reality that Lee was dead settled into his consciousness, the bravado that had been on display moments earlier, before the news had been broken, was displaced by a spasm of mournful sobbing that overtook him. During a brief break in his outpouring of grief, in a manly gesture that Tony read as Dillon's attempt to suppress a show of weakness, he pushed his hard hat firmly down on his head. Looking Tony straight in the eye, he finally spoke in a resolute voice.

"I'll do anything I can to help," he said, wiping a tear on the cuff of his sleeve. Summoning control of his emotions, he quietly followed the two detectives out the door and down the metal staircase.

Wednesday, 18 Oct 1978, 16:41

Dillon's Interrogation

The room was small, plain, with nothing to aid escape. A thick cast iron ring sprouted out of the wall, scarred from years of rage and handcuffs. The table was bolted to the floor but not the chairs. It was one of the nicer rooms, with a window facing Cottage Grove Avenue, covered by City of Chicago circle 'Y" logos made into a green iron screening big enough to let sparrows in but not let humans out.

Dillon walked in calmly, and flopped into the chair closest to the window. He wasn't at all freaked out about the station or the ride over. Tony and Rachael stood near the door. As he wasn't under arrest, they couldn't restrain him in any way. They had to make excuses for leaving him there to stew. Being the "girl" cop, Rachael extended the hospitality of the station to him.

"Mr. Whelan, would you like something to drink? Coffee, or water, or perhaps a Coke?"

"Naw, I'm good," he replied flatly, stretching his legs out, scooting his butt to the edge of the chair and resting the back of his head against the top of the straight wooden back, looking at the ceiling.

Rachael looked away from his bored schoolboy act to Tony.

"Coffee, black, thanks," said Tony.

Watching Dillon ogle Rachael's rear end as she left, Tony saw a faint lecherous smile play for a few seconds at the edges of his mouth. It faded fast. This boy liked women, no doubt. Tony knew it would be an advantage, but Rachael would have to play more than the "good" cop. She would do best to play the "interested" cop. Dillon would either lie to impress her and trip himself up, or tell her more than he intended in trying to be friendly. Either way, it could close the case. Tony believed that Dillon was the cause of all the trouble.

Tony stood by the door, watching. He knew Rachael would be at the end of the hallway soon, pad under her arm, coffee in hand. He was waiting for the right moment to excuse himself. He would say he had to go to the can, walking down the hallway to join her. They would sip coffee in silence, letting Dillon cool his heels even more. But before he did, Tony would get some work done.

"How did you know Leivald Nabb?" Tony asked.

"We used to be boyfriend and girlfriend. But that was a few years ago. We're only friends now. I'm married, with kids. Twin baby girls. Wanna see their picture?"

He grabbed the chrome chain of his trucker's wallet to haul it out of his pocket without changing his position in the chair. Tony was impressed that he had pictures. He pulled out a fuzzy dog-eared Polaroid of two swaddled babies sleeping on a bed. Their faces filled the shot, telling nothing about them. They could've been rubber dolls on a toy store shelf. Dillon handed the photo to Tony. He made no effort to add any information.

"Cute," said Tony as he handed the photo back.

"I hope you get whoever did this to Lee," Dillon said softly, replacing the photo in the well-worn wallet. "She didn't deserve to die."

Tony thought he heard a suppressed sniffle. Dillon's eyes looked watery, as if one more detail would make tears flow.

"Why do you think someone did that to Lee?" Tony asked.

"I think someone was trying to take some from her," Dillon said as he leaned over the desk to whisper to Tony looking him straight in the eyes. "If you know what I mean. She liked to do it, no doubt, but she was selective. She didn't go for every hairy Tom's fat dick."

Tony hadn't expected the interview to get off to a quick start. He hadn't expected Dillon to step into Lee's sex life without prodding. After all, Dillon and Lee had been an "item."

"Lee was a scrapper. She fought like a dude. With no brothers to defend her, she had to be rough. Back at Morgan Park, she beat the piss out of some ugly ass freshman who had the nerve to say he'd fucked her. You need to look for someone with a lot of damage done to him. She wouldn't have let 'em get away clean."

"Thanks for the advice," said Tony, "Would you mind if I made a note in my case file?"

"No, I don't mind. Write down whatever you want," he said, sliding back into his original position in the chair, but with his hands laced together behind his head. His body language said he was open, cooperative. He didn't break eye contact with Tony. His facial expression went from placid to evil. "I hope you find the motherfucker and quick. Be sure to take down my number."

Tony wrote it down. Looking up, Dillon continued defiantly. "You call me when you do; let me have a couple of minutes with him. I can do things to him you can't do."

Dillon patted his front jean pocket, winking at Tony. Tony was glad they'd patted him down. Guys like him were mercurial, dangerous when cornered, like alley rats.

"I keep bail money in my pocket. Cara bitches at me about holding out, but you know how it is. Beer makes guys brave, knuckles make 'em quiet. She'd bitch even more if I'd spend days in jail."

"Yeah, I know what you mean."

Tony knew whatever he had in his pocket wouldn't cover the crime he was discussing. Aggravated battery gets a hefty bail—in the thousands—even at ten percent. He figured it might be a card for a bail bondsman in his wallet. With Dillon feeling comfortable, rocking on the back legs of the chair, it was a good place to make a break in the proceedings.

"Listen, I'll be right back. Gotta tap a kidney."

"You must be my uncle's age; he can't hold his pee either."

Tony left the room. He wanted to hear a case-breaking answer to put "closed" on the file box to make the arrest, and hand everything over to the state's attorney with a smile. Disappointed that it hadn't happened by now, he headed down the hall where Rachael was. She handed him his mug of coffee, while he sipped without a word.

"No confession yet?"

Rachael knew Tony's mood. Not that he was an open book, but in the time they'd been together, she'd learned to read him. And right now, he wasn't happy.

"The son of a bitch is probably innocent. He admits to being her lover in the past, but not now. He admits to being a brawler but nothing else."

"Well, let me have a crack at him and see what shakes out," Rachael said.

"Don't try too hard to crack him. He was watching you when you left. He is more interested in your ass than your fists. He thinks he's a lady's man. Think you can use it against him?"

"His interest in my ass might get his thrown in jail," Rachael said. "Find out anything else?"

"That he's gonna ride the "wife and kids" alibi to death. He showed me a picture of the twins. Bet he ain't going to show it to you. The young dad thing has no sex appeal to you. Five bucks says you'll have to ask to see it."

Rachael held out a pinky for Tony to hook.

"Better than five bucks; the winner has to do all the reports for the next week."

They sealed the bet, touching their thumbs together.

She handed her book and pen to Tony, popped open the third button down on her shirt then pulled her shirttail out of her pants. Reaching behind, she twisted it into a tight knot before tucking it back into her waistband. The Quiana fabric stretched across her torso, hugging her breasts as tight as a Playboy Bunny costume. Tony was impressed enough to want to call foul, but was intrigued enough to let her play it out.

She got no reaction from Dillon. Moving her chair to the side of the table close to him and crossing her legs, she started the interrogation. With her murder book in hand, she asked about the guys she'd found in the yearbooks, hoping if she poked hard enough, something useful would come out.

"Did Lee know Billy Ryan?"

"Yeah, we all knew Billy Ryan. Went to grammar school with him."

"Would you consider him one of her boyfriends?"

"Billy Ryan? A boyfriend? Naw."

"What about Mikey Shaw?"

"Nope, not Mikey. He's like a little brother. He hung out at the garage helping her dad. Him and my cousins bought the place when her dad died. And no, she didn't date them either."

"Thank you. I'll make a note of that." She smiled at him and he loosened up a bit, sliding back into his chair. Rachael assumed it was to get a better look at her.

"What about Declan McGuire? Did she go out with him?"

"You kidding? He's not even hand job material," he blurted out, "Excuse the phrase."

"Not a problem," she smiled coyly. "Would it be the same with Dirk Foley?"

"Definitely. Carnival gypsies wouldn't get to first base. Work the summer, blow through their cash by Thanksgiving. Sponge off some lonely bitch for the rest of the winter. Lee don't take in strays."

Rachael took a couple of notes, not about his answers, but about Dillon's demeanor. He was showing a twinge of jealousy underneath his show of calm. His eyes were focused on Rachael's face. She flipped a few pages, searching for more names she'd taken from the yearbook.

"Didn't Kyle Allred go to school with Lee?"

"Yeah, that egghead went to school with us, but he didn't pay her any attention. He was in the library all the time."

"Damien Burke?"

"He wasn't hitting for our team, if ya get what I mean."

"No, I don't know what you mean. Help me out."

He straightened up in the chair. His lips curled into a wicked smile.

"He's a goddamn fag."

"Oh, okay. But you're sure he wasn't one of Lee's friends? Don't they hang with girls because they aren't 'on your team'?"

"He didn't hang with Lee. She didn't like them as much as I don't like them. Look, I know you pulled my juvie record. There's a lot of fights on there, especially up in the 18th District. Most of those fights weren't really fights. They're me having fun kicking some fairy's ass."

"I see."

She'd seen a number of arrests on his rap sheet, but because of his age, she thought it might have been some sort of rivalry between him and kids from Holy Name Cathedral School or Loyola. Now she knew he was a fag basher and proud of it.

"Juan Contras, maybe"

"She didn't do Mexicans. He 'no habla de englase.' She 'no habla' assholes who rode up here on a lettuce truck, okay?"

"Ryan Fleming."

"He didn't stand a ghost of a chance with her. We called him Flem 'cause every time you saw him he'd be wiping his snotty nose with a big ass bandana he bunched in his pocket."

Rachael wrote under Dillon: "bully, taunts others," but she also wrote "bandana" under Ryan Fleming, wondering if he had a handkerchief like the one found in Lee's clenched fist.

"Douglas Smith"

"Naw."

"Billy Huff?"

"Billy the Stuff was a senior when we started there."

"William Daniels?"

"I told you, she didn't do ethnics. Not Mexicans, not blacks, not even Polacks. Lee wasn't a liberal kind of girl. She wasn't one of those Beverly brats, singing cum-by-yaw, let's visit the ghetto. She was a Mount Greenwood girl, through and through. She stayed on her side of the tracks. Got it?"

"Got it."

Rachael made another quick note. She was pushing, but she didn't want him to flash hot in case he wasn't the killer. If he hadn't done it, she needed the information he had so she could continue without backtracking.

"Did Lee keep a diary? Would you know where she might have hidden it?"

"I don't ever remember seeing her write anything beyond a grocery list. Lee typed fast, but a diary, nope. She didn't have one."

He was so emphatic that Rachael wanted to ask more, but she knew that Tony had a thing about the purse and he was going to follow up on it. She went back to the list of possible lovers.

"Any of the McMahon boys?"

"Look, lady," he said with a suck of his teeth, "the last boyfriend she had was me. And we haven't been together that way for a long time. Me being married kinda puts a kink in the romance, if you get what I mean. She and Cara are close friends. She loves my kids, spends as much time with them as she can. I know she hasn't hooked up with anyone that way since we broke up. She dated a couple of guys from the hospital, but it didn't go anywhere."

"I see."

Rachael scribbled, letting him seethe a bit.

"Tell me Dillon, what happened between you two?"

"Nothing."

"Why did you break up?"

"Because of a dance."

He didn't want to tell the story. He didn't want to have it out on the desk in the detective woman's papers, in her files. He'd tamped it down into his gut every minute since they told him she was found dead. He'd squeezed it tight, not letting it loose. If he'd been faithful, if he'd been sweeter, if he'd kept his dick in his pants, none of this would have happened.

He didn't want to realize she was never going to come back. Not ever. He hadn't had that moment, and he sure as hell didn't want it here in front of the lady cop. His lips tightened into a circle, nostrils flaring. His dark brown curls wiggled as his head wagged in an unspoken no. He looked up into Rachael's eyes. She didn't break the spell.

"Lady, we were dating; she got mad at me. I took Cara to the prom instead. She was a good little catholic girl. What kind of trouble could I get in with her, right?"

He sniffed hard once.

"I had to get greedy. It didn't mean anything. Me and Lee were going to get married. We couldn't see Cara had plans. I didn't know she had the hots for me. I thought Cara would be a straight arrow for one night."

He sat back in the chair, scratching his nose to cover wiping away a tear.

"Cara was on me like a blanket. She started buying me stuff. Records, ID bracelet, wrenches. She got me a whole ninety-nine-piece Craftsman tool special from Sears, because I worked on cars. It was like Christmas. The more I said no, take it back, the more she'd get the next time. I gave up. Her dad's a fire captain, her mom some kind of Irish princess; she had cash to burn."

She hoped Tony was still listening outside the door.

"Cara bought me some fancy dress shoes so I wouldn't have to wear rented ones. Got me a set of heart cufflinks and studs to make me different from the other guys renting from Gingiss."

"We were going to the Branding Iron, hanging out at Palermo's because she was paying for everything. Lee got pissy about it. We had a fight, and I told Lee to fuck off. It was her fault. She said I didn't have to knock Cara up at prom. Everyone knows virgins don't get knocked up because of all the blood from popping their cherry, so Lee said I'd been screwing Cara regular, so she was finished with me. That's how we left it. Broken."

He was sitting there, lips tight against snot and tears. He went back to fixing an imaginary spot on the floor with his foot. Tony decided to make a reappearance, to break the mood.

"Sorry about taking so long, got caught by the sergeant down the hall," Tony chirped as if he hadn't heard a word. Rachael noticed Dillon hadn't raised his head. Even the scrape of Tony's chair across the floor didn't divert has gaze.

"Mr. Whelan," Tony asked, "where were you on Saturday night? 'Round about three A.M."

"Is that when it happened, three A.M.?" Dillon asked.

Tony waited for the answer.

"I was home, sleeping."

Tony glanced at Rachael. She shrugged but didn't say a word.

"And do you know of anyone who would want Leivald dead? Anyone who was mad at her?"

"Like I was telling the lady, Lee kept to herself. All those people she was asking me about, Lee knew 'em but didn't hang with them. She went to work, hung out at the garage, and went home. She'd come by to help Cara with the twins early in the morning, but by the time I got home, she was gone. I didn't make it home until way past five. Seven, if I stopped by the garage to catch up with the guys."

He locked his gaze on Tony. Dillon stretched across the table to get closer to Tony.

"If I knew who," he said through his teeth, "I'd bring the fucker in myself. And he'd be happy to come, believe me."

They stared at each other for a few seconds. Dillon's voice broke the peace.

"You check out those hospital folks. There's a guy in the pharmacy watching her, waiting for an opening. A manager for housekeeping was sniffing 'round her, too."

"You sure none of the guys from high school were hanging out with her?" asked Rachael.

"I'm sure," he replied. "Cara would've told me if they were."

Dillon continued to answer the mundane questions, but all the fire had left him. Shoulders hunched, eyes squinted, he looked like he'd lost his whole world. Without a word, Rachael wrote "still lovers," then closed her notepad so Dillon wouldn't see them. When Tony finished, no one seated at the table was satisfied.

Wednesday, 18 Oct 1978, 18:45

Darlene, the Carnival Worker

Darlene stood three feet, ten inches tall. She wore sheer pink lip-gloss, not lipstick in a color that would make her face look more like an adult's. Her small head gave her eyes a puppy-like appearance. Her Cupid's bow lips and heavy mascara enhanced the kewpie doll look. As she drove, Rachael glanced at her in the rear-view mirror, trying to figure out if Darlene had painted herself that way because she wanted to be treated like a juvenile, or if it was a ploy to manipulate people.

Sitting in the interview room chair, her feet swung half way between the floor and the seat. Her legs, covered in hot pink tights, were as well-proportioned and shapely as any other woman's. Rachael wondered if Darlene had gotten the tights in the children's department. It disturbed Rachael to see such tiny feet in spike heel shoes, because the added height didn't help much. Darlene was a walking dichotomy of innocence and sensuality, child and adult.

"I hope I can help y'all," she said as she shifted from one butt cheek to the other to get her little skirt underneath her.

Because Darlene wasn't a suspect, Rachael and Tony interviewed her in one of the better rooms in the station. It had a big window in the door opposite a large unbarred window that faced the street.

"I was with the carnival all summer this year. Last year, I went to the hospital half way through the darn season. A drunk fell on me at the hot dog booth, and broke a couple of my ribs. That sent me home before we finished the churches on the West Side. We go there first, before the weather gets real hot. Those folks are too rowdy in the heat, if you know what I mean." She gazed at Tony, and then smiled at Rachael.

"I missed out on a lot of money, staying home alone waiting for bones to knit together. I couldn't even sit on a stool to be cashier because it hurt too much. If I took my pain pills, I'd miscount the money or fall asleep as soon as the sun went down."

Darlene shifted her gaze from Rachael to Tony and then lowered her chin to look at him through her thick eyelashes.

Rachael slid a yearbook picture of Lee across the table towards her.

"What can you tell us about this girl?" she asked.

Darlene looked at the photo, then back at Tony. When she sat back in the office chair, she was swallowed up, like a child in her Grandpa's recliner.

"I worked the cotton candy booth this year. They made a wide wooden ledge for me to walk on between the machine and the counter. I loved it. When I was up there, my head was on the same level as the six-foot-tall men. I had a great view of the aisle, plus the backs of the Fun House and the Ski Jump."

The detectives nodded as Darlene sighed. Before Rachael asked what it all had to do with Lee, Darlene started up again.

"When we set up, they always make a triangle of the food booths, with the Fun House on one side and the Ski Jump on the other. That way, we get the folks before they get all shook up on the Jump or have the crap scared out of them by the freaks in the Fun House. The Jump is lit from the front and it's real tall; the Fun House is a big solid tent lit up with black lights; the back side of them makes a nice shield from the Midway. They put us nice and tidy, at the end of two walkways. We put our supplies back there, easy to use and keep an eye on. It also makes it a great lover's lane, but only if you know about it. Occasionally, some of the kids figure it for a make-out spot. We shag them outta there, 'cause we don't want any trouble with the bosses, but we don't say anything to the ride operators who take their lunch back there or do some horse trading, if you know what I mean. We watch out for husbands or boyfriends, or sneak a peek at the action." Darlene scrunched her nose and pulled in her lips like a naughty little kid.

"Because my ledge goes all the way around to my machine, I have a great view. I can make a whole board of cotton candy and fifteen cones while someone's back there busy makin' bacon."

She demurely put her tiny hand over her mouth before locking eyes on Tony. Her soft apologetic giggle showed Rachael that she parlayed her small stature in getting what she wanted. As Rachael wondered if it would work with Tony, Darlene repeatedly poked the nose of the girl in the picture with her forefinger.

"Now I recognize her. Oh yeah, she's the one back there first with Tiny McGuire, then Dirk Foley, and then a lot of times with some local boy. We never knew his name because he didn't work for us, but he sure knew Dirk and Tiny. We girls called him Romeo. Hell, I didn't even know her name, come to think of it. We called her Juliette once she swore off our crew. Once Tiny showed her how to get in, it became their home away from home. They followed us from Holy Redeemer on 95th Street to the Greek Orthodox Church on 103rd in Oak Lawn, all around Alsip for a month, then over to the Scottsdale Shopping Plaza for our two-week run in August, and finally to the Alderman's Fair on 115th down by I-57. They were so regular, we should've charged them rent."

Darlene hid a smile behind her hands. Then she took a big swig of the diet Coke, nearly finishing it in one gulp. When she set it back on the table, she squared her shoulders and began talking without prompting.

"See, the carnival doesn't charge admission, but we do funnel you through a gate and keep a count for safety. That makes my stack of sugar bags the cheapest honey hole in town. When those two would hit the gate, it was the only time any of the guys ever volunteered to relieve me to sell candy. Those fools nearly gave the candy away they were so busy trying to look over their shoulders to watch 'em. And let me tell you, she didn't mind one bit. Neither did her boyfriend. She was always strutting around, looking hot in her sundresses. Juliette never wore shorts or pants. She never wore panties under them, either. Too limiting I guess."

"Are you sure this is the girl?" Tony asked.

"Oh yeah. Definitely her. Another reason I remember is most girls who play with Tiny only give him a hand job, but not this one. When he brought her behind the Jump, he sat her on top of a stack of sugar bags. At first, all I saw was the back of her. She leaned back, way back and halfway through she had her hands stretched over her head, touching the ground. Near the end, she was almost upside down. I got a good look at her face because it wasn't quite dark. That hair of hers glistens green in the neon lights. That's her, no doubt. She came back several times. Tiny was much easier to work with when she was around. See, we don't call him Tiny 'cause of his shoe size, if you know what I mean. He usually gets a girl once, and then she runs away, so he didn't think twice when she left him alone.

"I won a C-note after Alsip, betting she'd show up at the next site. I could've lost because by then, cause she'd sworn off both Tiny and Dirk, but the bet was only that she'd show up. She was exclusive with that local boy. They were real cute together. So much in love."

Tony took note on his pad. Darlene had given them a few more people to question.

"Darlene," asked Rachael, "how much do you know about what goes on in the front office?"

Darlene smiled broadly. "Like they say on TV, I have my sources. What you wanna know?"

"Did that girl come to work for the carnival?"

"Nope," said Darlene with a shake of her head. "By the time she applied, it was too late. Ya see, the office staff drops down to two—one lady answering the phone from her house during the offseason and the boss. They send the guys with the equipment to Florida, a one-week deal. The guys get non-refundable one-way airplane tickets to come home. The return trip to do the pickup is in April. If you don't know how to drive an eighteen-wheeler, the boss doesn't need ya. The rest of us go on unemployment for the winter."

"Did her boyfriend know how to drive an eighteen-wheeler?" asked Tony.

"Not that I heard," said Darlene licking her lips as she leaned on the table, her chin resting on her elbows. "I only heard him moaning and groaning. He was kinda loud, if you know what I mean.… "

Her eyes fastened on Tony.

"Darlene, are any of the guys you mentioned still in the area?" asked Rachael, trying to break the connection. Darlene shifted her entire body toward Rachael.

"Sure, Tiny and his mom live in a trailer park in Worth. Dirk has an apartment on 127th Street in Blue Island."

Rachael flipped her notepad to a blank page, laid her pen across it, and slipped it across the table to Darlene.

"Give us the addresses, please?"

"Sure, I'll give you Chuck, Peter, and Bill too, but they wouldn't know anything about her. They were too old for her. Myself, I like older guys. They're more mature, make better lovers."

She glanced at Tony with a smile before she started writing down phone numbers and addresses. When she finished, she slid the paper slowly across the table.

"Is there any way I could get a ride back home?" she asked as she pushed the pad towards Tony. "I don't like taking the bus. People pick on me 'cause I'm little."

"Oh, of course we'll take you," replied Tony. "It's the least we can do for your help."

Darlene smiled wide, crossing her tiny legs.

December 1977

Lee's Moment of Truth

Sizzler Steakhouse down on Southwest Highway always had a long line on Friday nights. Why the girls thought it was a good place to have lunch for second shift was beyond Lee, but to keep in good graces with her co-workers, she piled into Bette's car and went along.

"Cut?" asked Pete McEvoy, the lanky kid working the grill. He called out as politely as possible to get over the hubbub of the patrons in line. Holding up a steak pulled from the iced pan, he would bark, "How do you want it?"

Moving the meat on the grill from one side to the other, Pete pointed his tongs at each person in the glut of patrons ahead of Bette, Phyllis, and Lee, getting their orders and moving them through as efficiently as the sizzling steaks would allow.

Finally, after several verbal exchanges, the girls were directly in front of him. His serious look turned to a big toothy grin when he saw Phyllis, but Bette in her usual abruptness spoke up.

"New York Strip," she snapped, "medium rare, onions, and mushrooms."

"Medium red Strip, mush and o's," he repeated, slinging a steak on the hot grill without showing it to her. Pointing his tongs at Phyllis, he asked with a big smile and a wink, "Your cut, miss?"

"T-Bone, please," demurred Phyllis, batting her freshly mascara laden lashes at him then tucking her chin into her collarbone. She always liked Pete, thought he looked handsome, pimples and all, but even back in high school, she never had the nerve to tell him.

"How would you like yours cooked?" he asked, watching her face color.

"Medium well, thank you."

"Can I interest you in sautéed mushrooms or smothered onions?" he asked slowly, grinning at her.

"Mushrooms only," she said wrinkling her nose at him, "if you please. Onions are good for the digestion, but bad for the breath."

"Sure thing, Phyllis," he smiled broadly. He didn't even look away to flip Bette's steak before he grabbed a T-Bone from the iced pans resting at the lip of the grill. "You can have it any way you want," he sighed, "any way at all."

Before Phyllis could luxuriate in his attention, a voice from ahead of them in the line bellowed a protest at him holding up the line to be nice to her.

"Hey, asshole, you're burning my steak!"

Lee glanced to see Dillon taking all the romance out of Phyllis's moment in the buffet line. She turned her back to him, ducking behind Bette, as Pete flipped the steak one last time on the grill and grabbed a platter. With a deft flop, the meat landed in the center of the china. A snap of tongs topped it with onions, and, with a remorseful look, Pete reached over the counter and said he was sorry.

In his anger, Dillon didn't see Lee standing there. With so many things on his mind, all he managed was taking his plate down the line, picking up a baked potato, an ear of corn, and a dinner roll. Screw the salad. Cara fed him enough cut-up lettuce to last a lifetime. Now that she was back with her mother, he wasn't going to eat any more California yard clippings. He stomped to the cashier at the end, threw his money at her, and strode into the dining room without waiting for the change.

Lee stood frozen in place. She didn't know if she should walk past him and the very pregnant Cara, or if she should turn and make her exit. The guy behind her decided it for her.

"Hey, Lady," he barked, "ya want to move down? My kids are hungry."

Seeing she couldn't push between four big high-school-aged boys, their linebacker of a father, and the rest of the line, she turned. Moving toward Pete, she ordered quickly before he could ask.

"New York Strip, well done, mushrooms and onions."

He flipped her steak onto the grill as he put Phyllis's on a clean platter and garnished it with a spoonful of mushrooms before handing it to her politely. "Here you are Miss, medium rare."

Several people moved around Lee, getting their steaks rare as hers cooked. With the line moving, Lee was perilously close to her moment of truth. She hadn't turned to look in Dillon's direction all the time that she had waited. When she handed the cashier her money would be soon enough.

Picking out her corn, deciding on salad fixings, and choosing a dessert, bought her more time to avoid seeing Cara in her "condition." At the cash register, Lee fished in her purse like an old lady, looking for her wallet, counting and recounting singles. When she couldn't stall any more, she turned and scanned the room, bracing herself for her moment of shame. She hadn't seen Cara since the Fourth of July blow up, when the twins made themselves known. She'd dreaded seeing her all round and rosy, carrying Dillon's children.

To Lee's surprise, there would be no shame tonight. Dillon was sitting alone, with Cara nowhere in sight. Lee reasoned that the twins were now big enough to be dancing on her bladder, so she was probably in the ladies room.

Moving quickly, she sat at the table Bette chose, a good vantage point somewhat hidden behind a short divider wall. She wondered if Bette had sat there on purpose, but it didn't matter. Now she would be able to see Cara waddle between the rows of tables on what was probably their six-month wedding anniversary. For an intelligent girl, Cara was silly like that. Lee stabbed her steak with a fork, tearing it angrily with the steak knife.

"Isn't he cute?" Phyllis asked, striking up a conversation to divert Bette and Lee.

"Who?" asked Bette, scanning the room.

"Peter," replied Phyllis, smiling in his direction, hoping the line thinned enough for him to see her and smile back.

"Really Phyllis," huffed Bette, "It's only a step up from flipping burgers because the meat here isn't ground into patties. You're an absolute goose."

"Bette you are so-o-o negative," pouted Phyllis. "Don't you ever give a guy a break?"

"No, I don't. And no, I don't think he is cute. I'm mad at him. Talking to you, he burned my steak."

Phyllis put a piece of meat in her mouth, eyeing her plate. Lee chewed in silence, switching her attention from the door to the ladies room watching for Cara and then Dillon, who was gulping down his food. Halfway through the meal, Lee realized that there was no place setting opposite him, so there wouldn't be Cara emerging from the bathroom or anywhere else. She hopped up, grabbed her purse, and went into the bathroom to be sure.

"Well, that was nice," quipped Bette. "She doesn't say one word this whole time, then bolts for the bathroom. We should leave her, make her walk back to the hospital. It would serve her right."

"That would be mean," replied Phyllis, "and not practical. We wouldn't get everything done tonight without her. I don't want to stay late, not tonight. I have Christmas shopping to do in the morning."

Inside the washroom, the FM station piped in was loud to rise above the clatter of silverware against dishes. Lee checked the stalls. Each one was empty. As she passed the mirror, a lyric struck her ears in the empty room and stopped her in her tracks.

She'd been listening to the song for months. Now, she took it as an omen. If Cara wasn't here with him on a Friday night, something had gone wrong. This was her moment. The song was telling her what to do, and she wasn't going to ignore its advice. She marched through the door, straight down the aisle, to Dillon's table.

When Phyllis saw where Lee was heading and who was sitting there, she hissed, "Oh-ma-ha, Nebraska."

"What the hell are you talking about?" Bette asked.

"Look over by the windows," she whispered. "You won't believe it."

Phyllis was right. Bette didn't believe what she was seeing: Lee standing beside Dillon with her hand stretched out as if for a handshake. Phyllis grabbed Bette's forearm as they watched him take Lee's hand, draw it to his lips and kiss it gently. When Dillon rose from his chair, Phyllis was squeezing Bette's wrist. Over the din of the dining room, the song played inside Lee's head.

He took Lee in his arms for a hug, slipping his hands under Lee's soft blond hair to cup her head. He pulled her close and kissed her.

As the kiss ended, the last lyrics of the song floated down to Lee's ears. Dillon's hands slipped down to settle around her waist.

No one in the dining room, except Bette and Phyllis, were paying any attention when they left the restaurant. Stunned, the girls watched the couple climb into his red pickup truck and drive out of the parking lot headed down Cicero Avenue.

"Bette, wasn't that…"

"Dillon Whelan, ah ha, it was," said Bette, chewing the last bit of her steak.

"But isn't he… married to Cara O'Toole?"

"Yup, before God and witnesses since July and two babies."

"Bette, tell me I did not see Lee kiss her best friend's husband, then walk out of here with him?"

"No Phyllis," said Bette, putting her knife down on her plate. "What you saw was your Christmas shopping trip evaporate before your eyes."

"But when they're finished talking, he'll drive her back to the hospital, won't he? He knows where to drop her off so the guards can't rat her out to Dana."

Bette tilted her head and stared at Phyllis before blowing out a breath of exasperation.

"You *were* hatched from an egg, weren't you?" Bette moaned, "How did you manage to sleep through all the sex education classes? Those two are headed down motel row, to the first vacancy sign they see. They won't be coming up for air until check out time, which is eleven A.M. tomorrow morning. Way too late to help us finish the stack of work we have."

"But, but," stuttered Phyllis, dropping her fork. It clattered onto the plate. "You mean we have to finish without her?"

"Yup," Bette stated flatly. "And when I get back to the hospital I'm going to the time clock, punch her card, and put it on Dana's desk with a note. Unless you have a reason for me not to. As you'll be going straight to Ford City to shop, I suggest we hightail it back to the office and key as fast as our little fingers will go. Otherwise, we'll both be leaving tomorrow around noon."

"She'll come back to help us," quavered Phyllis's voice in an attempt to reassure herself and defend her friend. "Won't she?"

Bette shook her head no.

"Bette, she knows how big a pile of stuff we have back there. I'd come back as soon as I finished talking to him. Honest I would."

"And if he *were* Pete, I wouldn't expect to see you for week. That's how long it would take for the two of you to figure out what *they're* going to do in the next few hours."

Phyllis looked out the window, hoping for a glimpse of the little red truck heading in the direction of the hospital. Every vehicle she saw seemed to have turned dirty white or salt-speckled gray. The last words Bette said sank in and confused her. She couldn't stop herself from asking.

"They'll be done in a little while right," asked Phyllis hopefully. "Then she'll be coming back?"

Bette sighed, "P-L-E-A-S-E Phyllis, shut up."

Thursday 19 Oct. 1978, 04:57

Night Musing

Rachael awoke with a start, the case twisting her stomach into knots. The burning sensation gnawed her awake. Her cat Napoleon flicked his tail agitatedly at her for disturbing his rest. Blinking his green eyes as Rachel slipped off the bed, he lazily licked his paw as she walked down the hallway to the bathroom.

Tony said repeatedly that this was a simple love triangle, but Rachael had maintained that it was more like a polygon. How did one young woman generate such bad feelings to precipitate her murder?

If you followed the trail of lust, it led to five males; if you followed the jealousy route, three or four females. If you followed the money, the path was much shorter. Neither the mother nor Lee were rich enough for it to have been the motive.

It was startling that Lee hadn't done the wild child things that Rachael had expected. She didn't offer sex for money or for clothes. She didn't deal dope—even within the crowd she ran with—which Tony thought odd. The opportunity was certainly there, but there was not a shred of evidence. It just didn't add up. With both mother and daughter struggling to live off their meager salaries, it was only logical for them to try to supplement their income.

Rachael stood barefooted, shaking Tums out the bottle. The clock glowed orange. It was four fifty-seven A.M. She wondered where Tony had spent his night off. She wanted to talk things out, but she knew if he were home alone, it wasn't fair to call him at four in the morning to discuss a case.

She sat back on the edge of her bed. Her mind wandered back to the current cause of her stomach problems—the unsolved murder. Tony still suspected Dillon of the murder because of his juvie record, his quick temper, and the history of his rocky relationship with Lee. But that didn't add up. It was clear that Lee was his safety valve, his means of escaping the confines of his marriage to Cara. A married man, he had to be responsible for a family, but with way too little income. Lee provided a glimpse of how his life might have been, so why would he kill her? From all accounts, she didn't appear to be demanding. She lured him away from home when she could. The fights he picked were his way to get out of the house. It all seemed typical of an extramarital affair. The only thing that was out of the ordinary was their ages. Dillon and Cara still should have been trying to figure out who they were, not trapped in a marriage with the responsibility of raising two children.

The arguments between Dillon and Cara more than likely had taken their toll. Perhaps he transferred this anger to Lee, which, according to the therapists, people did all the time. Rachael knew from working the streets, the "fight tonight, make love tomorrow" syndrome—the pattern for many of the domestic calls a cop goes on.

Dillon had been seen fighting with Lee in public several times and was known to fight Cara behind closed doors and in front of neighbors. That he had an explosive temper was obvious.

But why didn't it feel to Rachael like Dillon was the one? Why didn't it ring true?

Rachael grabbed her robe and pushed her feet into her slippers. Wide awake and unable to go back to sleep, she put on a pot of coffee.

While the pot brewed, she took out a giant newsprint pad that she often used to outline the facts that emerged in solving a case. She looked in the junk drawer for a box of multicolored markers. Flipping to a blank page of the pad, the strategy helped clear her mind.

Sipping coffee, she wrote a thumbnail biography of each of the principals in the case. The sun had broken through the kitchen window when the phone rang. It was seven A.M.

"Morning, Rachael. Sorry to call so early. I hope I didn't wake you up." It was Tony on the other line.

"I was just having a cup of coffee. What's up?" she asked. He wasn't one to call her so early, unless it was something important.

"I'm in the neighborhood. At the Fifth Wheel. Do you know the place?"

"The restaurant at 116th and Western? What about it?"

"The Leivald Nabb case has been running around in my head all night. I woke up at about five and couldn't get back to sleep. I've got a theory I want to run by you before we get to the office. How about meeting me here for breakfast? I'm buying."

"Give me ten minutes."

"Bring a steno pad if you got one."

She and Tony were on the same wavelength, which had been happening more and more, the longer they worked together as a team.

January 1978

An Evening Rendezvous

Dillon leaned over the fender of his black '58 Rambler, his dark hair covered by a blue bandana. He was replacing the spark plug wires one by one, just like the old man Nabb had taught him. Starting at the cylinder and moving back to the distributor cap, he snapped one end off and then one end on before moving to the next one. A logical way to do it, but many guys run to the *Chilton's Manual* because they would get the firing order messed up by pulling things apart and not paying attention when it came time to reconnect them. The old man was methodical, precise, and he instilled those traits in his young apprentices. He would never have left a car misfiring or running ragged.

At the garage, Dillon, and the rest of the boys had shadowed the hulking blonde guy with the foreign accent since the time they were big enough to ride their bikes to the corner. Once they'd overcome their fear of him, they started helping by carrying tools, washing cars, and absorbing his deep knowledge about engines. In turn, they became the sons he never had.

Dillon's tee shirt clung to his sweaty torso, revealing a package of well-developed muscles. He didn't have time to go to the gym because he had too many irons in the fire, what with a family and all.

Busy with apprentice school, working at the railyard, and delivering pizza on the side, his hot rod had sat in the corner of the garage lot for over month. The guys had been nice enough to cover it with a tarp to protect it from the elements, looking out for the custom flake paint job Dillon had paid for before his finances had evaporated. Nobody had told him that babies were expensive. It was a good thing the hot rod was nearly finished when his family obligations began to suck his pockets dry. Now all he could afford was competition grade wires and plugs. He couldn't even manage the price of a couple of trips down the lane at the U.S. 30 drag strip on "Run-What-Ya-Brung-Night" to blow the car out on the track.

Disposable diapers, baby formula, and clothes ate away every paycheck, not to mention keeping up on the rent, phone, electric, and gas. With groceries, he was left with barely enough to buy a pack of ciggies, beer, and chips. He didn't know what he would do if he hadn't gotten help from his friends. The garage crew were his saviors. One day, he was going to win the Irish Sweepstakes and pay back each and every one of them.

Most of the time it wasn't money; it was a hamburger here, a beer there, a quart of oil or trans fluid, and maybe a new tool thrown into his toolbox that no one would claim responsibility for. Sometimes it was a detail job they made a customer wait for him to do so he could earn some pocket change. They even went so far as to hide a five or a ten under the back seat for him to find. This generosity wasn't lost on him. He noticed everything. When he broached the subject to Mikey, Jamie, and Albee, they played it off, pretending they didn't know anything. How many times could Wonder Burger make the same mistake of adding an extra burger to the bag? He'd make it all up to them, one day, in spades. Albee disturbed his musing, calling him from the office door.

"Hey Dillon," he cried out over the hiss of the compressor and the radio. "I got a call for you."

"Is it one of those damn bill collectors, Albee? I can't answer the phone at home without 'em," he said.

"Naw, it's some girl from the hospital. Says she got test results for you."

Albee returned to finish the oil change he was doing.

Dillon closed the door to the office as he picked up the phone from the outdated calendar blotter lying atop the desk. He reared back in the wooden chair. If the call was from the hospital, he knew who was on the other end.

"Hello, this is Dillon Whelan, what can I do for you?"

"Mr. Whelan, this is hospital census calling. We have several vacancies in the private rooms on the 7th floor this evening."

Dillon smiled. Lee liked to play games. She was always saying something to bring a smile to his face.

"And what would I do with a private room on the 7th floor?" he asked. "I don't feel sick."

"Really, Mr. Whelan?" I have test results right here saying that you need to be admitted for some medicine the doctor has prescribed."

When Lee wanted something, she'd purr like a kitten. Over the phone, he imagined the look on her face. She'd be smiling enough to show the jagged edge of her left front tooth. The tooth she chipped on the steering wheel of her MG when she ran it up over a curb in Dan Ryan Woods one summer night.

"How do you know I'm sick?" he countered, spurring her on.

"Because I'm in charge of special treatments and I can hear your need over the phone. Your breathing is beginning to quicken, and in a few moments, you'll begin to feel pressure in your groin."

"Really?" he said.

"Yes. You're thinking about the last time I gave you one of my special treatments, and your body is reacting to the prospect of getting another one."

"As a matter of fact, when I look down at my jeans, I can see you're right. The mention of your 'special' treatment has me tingling all over. Why, I think I see some swelling."

"Yes, Mr. Whelan. Swelling is a symptom that shouldn't be ignored. You better come in tonight to see about it. Looking at my schedule, either at nine or eleven o'clock for a half-hour session. Which would be more convenient for you?"

Dillon pressed his hand on the bulge. He hadn't planned on seeing her, but since he was already away from the apartment, he didn't see any harm in a quick run up to the hospital. Looking at his watch, he decided spark plug wires weren't so important.

"Is there any way you could move the appointment back to 7 P.M.? I'm finishing up a car here and can make it there by seven. Is that okay?"

There was a slight hesitation before Lee answered. She should've explained it to him straight instead of being cute and playing this game. She wanted him there right now, but she needed him to wait until her workmates were on their lunch breaks, the visiting hours over, the housekeeping staff had moved past the room she had picked out, security had done their patrol, and the moon had risen high enough so they wouldn't need to use the room lights. All these conditions had to be met to make the tryst work.

Dillon had never tried to negotiate their time together before, so why now? she wondered. Stifling her annoyance, Lee explained things to him as briefly as possible. She didn't want to ruin the fantasy.

"I'm sorry Mr. Whelan, if you can't come at either 9 P.M. or 11 P.M., we'll have to reschedule for another day."

To him, her voice sounded coldly professional, with all of the fun drained away. He remembered that they couldn't risk being early. Later yes, but early was always bad. They needed the hospital to quiet down, to become a slumbering place where they could go undetected. Dillon was smart about cars but not so smart about other things.

"I can make 11 P.M.," he conceded,

Her voice softened, but she kept up the charade to the

very end.

“Wonderful. At the North elevators, get a visitor’s pass to see Mr. Abbott, proceed to the basement level. You’ll be met there by the technician and taken to your room.”

Dillon loved it when Lee played games. Everything she asked him to do heightened the excitement.

“Eleven P.M., North Elevator, visitor’s pass for Mr. Abbott. Then basement level to wait for my escort.”

“Very good Mr. Whelan. Very good. Bye for now,”she said.

Lee giggled at how calm and professional she had sounded. Her body began to react at the prospect of the rendezvous. She returned to work with renewed vigor. It all had to be done before her lunch break at eleven. Humming along with the radio, she plowed into the ER reports on her desk.

Dillon hung up the phone, suppressing the urge to smile. Albee didn’t need to know. Moving toward his car, he heard Albee’s voice from under the Dart.

“Not bad news was it?”

“Naw, a blood test the doc ordered for the apprenticeship program I’m enrolling in.

“Whew, I was worried. I need you to go with me to drop off Old Lady Garvey’s Dart.”

The two wiped the Garvey car off, making sure everything was in place. Dillon moved toward his car, lowering the hood and re-covering it with the tarp. The car symbolized everything he had to do without in his life now. It wasn’t Cara’s or even Lee’s fault. It was the way things had worked out. Sadness welled up in him, causing his eyes to burn. Clearing his throat, he gathered his resolve, heading toward the car across the garage.

“Ready whenever you are, Albee,” he said.

Albee threw an old bedsheet over the front seat to keep dirt and oil off the tan vinyl upholstery.Newspaper on the floor mats was a bit much, but it was one of those special touches that made the folks from the neighborhood come back to the garage instead of the dealerships along Western Avenue. Albee eased it out through the big overhead door, stopping next to Dillon in his red mini-pickup.

"Did Mrs. Garvey say what kind of cookies she was making us this time?"

"I'm sure she did," said Albee, "but I tuned her out somewhere after the Hello. She's nice, but she sounds like my mother."

Dillon followed Albee down 107th Street driving west towards Avers and Mrs. Garvey's house.

Thursday, 19 Oct. 1978, 13:25

At the Home of the Lady O'Toole

Bordering the bottom of the only hill in all of Chicago, Longwood Drive is the spine of the Beverly Hills neighborhood, providing the only geologic justification for its name. Starting at 95th Street and meandering south, the east side of Longwood slopes quickly into a depression that could swallow a three-story building. Unlike most of the city's arrow straight streets, it wiggles to compensate for Mother Nature's caprice. Its topography exemplifies the hierarchy of the city. The rich and powerful live at the apex, the middle class on the lower east side, and the working class lives across the tracks extending into the neighboring community of Morgan Park.

The address marker at the foot of the driveway hung on a wrought iron lamppost made to look like a tree trunk. From the address, Rachael should have known that the house was situated atop the hill, but she had assumed that because of Mr. O'Toole's profession as a city firefighter, the home she was seeking was either a coach house located behind a mansion or one of the more modest homes on the low side. She glanced at Tony as they turned up the long driveway stopping at the stately brick home that might have been transplanted from Chicago's Gold Coast.

"Not too shabby," intoned Tony with a low whistle, "Guess what they say about the fire department is true."

"What do they say?" Rachael inquired. "That they all have second full-time jobs, or they get paid more than we do?"

"Yeah, that, and a few other things...."

Tony got out of the car, stretching his legs and twisting his body. A burgundy Mercedes convertible, white Mustang II, and a black Buick Estate station wagon were parked in front of the brick garage. Tony wondered if the home was furnished with mismatched furniture from Goodwill to justify these outward trappings of wealth. Even with the prices of Beverly Hills homes dropping because of the white flight to the suburbs, this beauty wouldn't be on the bargain list.

Rachael noted on her pad each vehicle, make, model, and license plate. She grabbed her case and joined Tony at the edge of the cobblestone walkway.

"This is really nice," she said in a whisper.

"Yeah, really, really nice." Tony replied with a wink. "You sure we got the right address?"

"Double checked it," she said.

The large wooden door was stained a rich oak with a sparkling cut-glass inset oval sunburst. The doorbell was surrounded by a highly polished brass frame that burnished like gold. The two detectives stood on a front step finished with terrazzo tile, in the center of which was a thick welcome mat with the name "O'Tooles" etched in the center. Even a deputy veteran fire chief didn't make the kind of money to afford such a home, not even with two jobs and a shrewd investment broker. It screamed old money, in sums large enough to endow museums and hospital wings.

A woman answered the door wearing a long black skirt, black cardigan, gleaming white shirt, and sensible shoes. Her ruddy hair was swept into a long thick braid. She wore only a utilitarian Timex watch on her left wrist. She could have been a nun without the veil.

"How might I help you?" she asked with a voice tinged with the lilt of Ireland, despite having lived in Chicago for decades.

"Mrs. O'Toole is expecting us. I'm Detective Culpepper, and this is my partner Detective Breese."

"Ah yes. She said ye'd be popping by. Please come in,"

the housekeeper said.

After they entered the marble-tiled foyer, she carefully closed the door and locked it before motioning for them to follow her.

"Right this way. She'll be coming down—momentarily."

Standing in a parlor larger than some Northside studio apartments, its tall windows catching the afternoon sun, the woman introduced herself.

"I'm Mrs. O'Flynn, housekeeper for the O'Tooles," she said proudly, "Please make yourselves at home." She motioned toward a grouping of two white and pale yellow flowered silk couches, two winged chairs, and a dark mahogany coffee table.

"Might ye take refreshment while ye wait?" she asked as they seated themselves. She motioned toward a large enameled tray on the elegantly carved coffee table. It held an ornate silver service and three of everything, bottles of Perrier sweating condensation into collars of folded linen napkins, sparkling cut crystal tumblers, and daintily flowered porcelain cups on saucers, accompanied by a purple blown glass plate of Danish cookies.

She hovered, smiling sweetly, pointing to each item on the tray.

"Tea, please," said Rachael.

"Just water," replied Tony to her gestures.

Wordlessly, she poured a glassful of Perrier for Tony and then prepared hot tea for Rachael. Holding the sugar bowl, she offered the tongs to Rachael. Tony smiled. It reminded him of his childhood days at Morse Manor, before he went to St. John's Military Academy in Wisconsin.

Just as the housekeeper poured another cup of tea, Mrs. O'Toole floated into the room, as if on cue. With a straight back and practiced tone, Mrs. O'Flynn announced the arrival of the mistress of the house.

"Detectives Culpepper and Breese, this is Mrs. Teagan

Fitzwalter O'Toole."

Tony stood, and Rachael followed suit. Mrs. O'Toole extended her manicured hand, allowing them both to shake it in a gesture of well-practiced politeness. She stood ramrod straight. She'd swept her dark auburn hair into a loose, low pony tail. Deep green eyes sparkled like emeralds beneath thick dark eyebrows in a smooth heart-shaped face. She was impressive, down to the tiny cleft in her chin, Rachael thought.

"Please, take a seat, Detectives," she said in a sweetly lilting brogue much like Mrs. O'Flynn's. "How might I help ye?"

She pinched a cheesecloth swaddled lemon into her cup as Tony spoke about the on-going investigation. Without taking her eyes off his face, she picked up her saucer delicately, and stirred precisely four times. She placed the spoon on a painted china rest and sipped as Tony finished up his "If you would be so kind" speech.

"I don't know what I'd add to the inquiry, Detective."

Rachael let Tony take the lead, as Mrs. O'Toole was ignoring her entirely. She guessed that the woman didn't approve of women detectives.

"We're hoping that, as the mother of Lee's best friend, you might be able to provide us with some background information."

Mrs. O'Toole sipped calmly before answering.

"Well, sorry to say, ye've come on a fool's errand. I've only seen the lass a few times."

"Really?" Tony said in an off handed amused tone. "I thought she would have visited here often."

"No. She didn't like grown up eyes on her. She weren't Cara's *best* friend, simply an acquaintance."

"Did she and Cara have a place where they liked to hang out?"

"None that I knew of," she said between sips, "but me

Cara became secretive after she friended those blaggards. Left to me, she'd ne'er met them."

"Why's that?" queried Tony.

"'Twas Cara's father's idea for her to attend a public school instead of finishing at Francis Parker. He reckoned for her to be a lawyer, she needed to rub elbows with the hoi polloi. Buying this house, moving out of Edison Park when Mr. O'Toole became a lieutenant was his excuse. I wanted her to go to Morgan Park Academy, not Morgan Park High School."

"I see. When did she transfer?" Tony asked, jotting a note on his pad.

"At the beginning of her junior year, but that's not when I first met Miss Lee Nabb. 'Twas after Christmas. They had a class together, but don't go asking me which one."

"Tell me what you know about Lee Nabb," Tony asked quietly. He poised his pen, waiting for her answer.

"Practically nothin', other than she's got no fither. He died a bit ago, left 'em poor as church mice."

Rachael sipped tea as she observed Mrs. O'Toole's every move. This woman genuinely disliked Lee Nabb. At any mention of her, she would cringe slightly, almost imperceptibly. When she spoke Lee's name, the corner of her lips would curl as if she wanted to spit. If she hadn't been so prim and proper, she would have risen to the top of Rachael's list of suspects, but women like her didn't do their own dirty work. They hired hit men to keep from breaking their nails.

"And what can you tell us about her relationship to Dillon Whelan, your son-in-law?"

"Not much actually. Pure piss and vinegar, that one. He's empty pockets and honeyed words. His life's dream is owning a grease monkey place where he can work on cars, dying of starvation and deep in debt. He never would have bothered with my daughter if the Nabb girl's father had lived. Dillon would've charmed the old Nazi, married Lee, whelped her fast, and everything would have been right as rain. But the old man's dying changed everything. Dillon couldn't afford to buy that hole in the wall, so he turned his eyes to my Cara."

Rachael noted Mrs. O'Toole had a lot of information that she claimed not to have.

"Did he ask her for a loan?" Tony asked.

"No, they weren't that daft. Insidiously clever, those two. First, Leivald began to come around, all friendly like. She tried to charm me, but I was having none of it. She was sniffing out how much money we had. I can smell a fortune hunter a mile away. My money's been both a blessing and a curse. I learned long ago that smiles are not always given from the heart; they can be arrows aimed at your wallet."

She'd said it so proudly that Rachael knew there was something at work here, something under the surface of her dislike for Lee and Dillon. She'd certainly interchanged the last name of Nabb with Nazi easily enough. Perhaps she'd lived her early life in England despite her Irish brogue, surviving the privation and pain after World War II, blaming all Germans for her suffering.

"Ya see, Dillon seduced my innocent. He taught her how to lie, filled her head with pretty words and her belly with his foul seedlings. A true man doesn't do that; a rake does. Cruelest of all, he did it when she was standing at the door to her shining future. He not only stole her innocence, he killed her dreams. Now, she's a shanty mum with babies hanging off her like possum kits."

She hadn't raised her voice or changed her expression as she delivered the pronouncement. Now, the interview was over. She sipped her tea with all the grace of a woman enjoying lunch at the Art Institute or a matinee at the Civic Opera House. Tony, knowing her type, knew better than to press her further. It was time to finish their drinks politely and go.

Closing his notepad, he thanked her for her hospitality, not the information she provided. Rachael nodded politely, but didn't speak, not wanting to break the mood. She was hoping perhaps, that Mrs. O'Toole would release something stuck in her craw before they left. And she was right. The woman accompanied Tony from the sofa to the door, engaging in harmless chit chat. But when they entered the foyer, she circled back to the case.

"From what I do know about that unfortunate girl, there's a boy at the garage who was moon-eyed over her. Michael or Mickey or something. Violent temper on that one. He came here before the prom to talk to Cara, and before you knew it, he was screaming like a banshee and running for his car. N'er did figure what 'twas about."

"Thank you again Mrs. O'Toole," Tony said, standing with Rachael at the door.

"Good Day, Mrs. O'Toole," Rachael said. "Thank you for your time."

"County Cork or Kildare?" asked Mrs. O'Toole, speaking directly to Rachael.

"Kildare," answered Rachael with a small smile.

"I've spent time there. Lovely county," she replied with a sigh. Then she turned back into the house and disappeared behind the staircase. Like a well-rehearsed magic trick, a smiling Mrs. Flynn appeared out of nowhere to close and secure the door.

Mrs. O'Toole's acknowledgment of Rachael's Irish heritage was a subtle move not lost on either of the detectives. Once the car turned out of the long driveway onto Longwood Drive, Tony brought it up.

"What do you think she was trying to pull with her question about Ireland?" he asked.

"She spent so much time making friends with you, that she must have felt the need to make me one of her distant relatives," Rachael laughed.

"Well, you didn't ask her one question throughout the interrogation," Tony said.

"Wouldn't have done any good; she was busy pointing the finger at Dillon and Mikey."

"Yeah, she was devoid of any grandmotherly instinct, too. Calling her granddaughters 'possum kits.'"

"A lot of mothers live vicariously through their daughters. She's bitter and disappointed at Cara for getting pregnant and dashing her dreams," Rachael said as she looked from the mansions on the hill to the bungalows on the east side of Longwood. "Cara's fallen from the hill to the valley in her eyes. Against all her work and her wishes."

January 1978

Caught Trespassing

Illuminated by a glimmer from a nightlight, he drew his hands over the curve of her hips. In the glow, she hooked her feet together at the small of his back. With the twinkle of the streetlights far below them playing on the ceiling, she braced herself against the mattress, arching her back, letting her breasts brush his lips. He ignored the fleshy offerings of her nipples to concentrate on thrusting into her, deeper, harder, faster. She groaned as he sank in deeper.

She squeezed him with her thighs, enjoying the feel of him. He responded by gathering her ass in his hands, pulling her hard against his pelvis, burying himself all the way in. She gulped at the force, purring deep in her throat. Sweat was beginning to rise on them. She was riding a wave of small orgasms that were building in response to his increased tempo.

He broke her thigh's hold on his waist by pushing them down to the mattress on both sides of her body. By standing at the side of the bed, he applied more leverage as he pumped in and out. She jammed the back of her hand in her mouth to keep from letting a loud noise escape.

He was the best lover she'd ever had, strong and voracious as she was. If she had her way, she'd be in bed with him every day. They were a well-matched pair.

With three hard grunting jerks, it was over for them both. She was panting, floating on the needles and pins of a huge climax. He leaned over, the upper half of his body on hers, letting her legs stretch out. She wrapped her arms around his neck, kissing the side of his face.

"Damn, baby, that was good. I'm glad you thought of this," he whispered.

"Yeah, I needed that more than I imagined. You were extra special tonight."

He laughed as he kissed her quickly on the lips and began to pull away from her embrace. She pouted but released him. He reached down to pull up his jeans. She pulled down the two tabs of her body suit, snapping them together between her legs. Smoothing down her stone-washed denim skirt, she ran her hands through her hair.

Grabbing his black leather jacket off a nearby chair, he spun around to watch her slip into blue canvas shoes. Now, they looked ready to return to reality, but he wasn't—at least not yet.

He pulled her into his arms, crushed her against his chest and the buckles of his jacket. She hoped the buckles would leave a bruise, so she could have a visual token of this episode.

She hugged him tight, savoring the kiss tangling their tongues together. In these sweet moments, she couldn't imagine anyone ever replacing him. And as she was relaxing into the glorious feeling, he pulled away again.

She knew he was right, that it was time to leave.

Peeking out into the hallway, he waved for her to follow him. As they made their way toward the back staircase, a security guard on his rounds hit the top stair as they opened the door.

"Excuse me," he said standing between the couple and their escape route, "What're you doing here?"

"We work here," she said with a big smile.

"Then I need to see your ID cards," demanded Officer Murphy.

Lee dug into her purse, but Dillon made no move. Officer Murphy was nobody's fool. He'd done 37 years on the Chicago PD before retiring to this job. He knew the guy didn't belong. Watching him closely, he waited until she'd retrieved a handmade plastic lanyard with her photo ID attached. Handing it to him with a smile, she thought they were out of danger. Old coots like him were easy to charm. Besides, he didn't have any way to know what they had been doing. She thought that he had no reason to detain them.

Murphy checked it out, but kept it in his hand, "Can I see your ID, sir?"

"I don't have one." Dillon replied, "I'm with her."

"Do you have any form of ID?"

Murphy might have left the streets, but the streets had not left him. Shifting his stance, he readied himself for Dillon's resistance or flight.

"I have a driver's license," Dillon said.

Murphy didn't answer. He watched as Dillon reached for his wallet in the back pocket of his jeans. After looking at the license, Murphy stared at the girl, with her tousled hair, flushed face, and damp temples.

"Step over here please, Miss Nabb," he said, pointing at a spot out of earshot, away from Dillon.

As she moved, Murphy watched for any tell-tale shifts in Dillon's body language.

"I'll be with you in a moment, sir," he said.

Even though it was after midnight and suspicious, Murphy didn't like sending people to jail on things that were more discretionary than criminal. If they weren't hiding stolen goods, he would make up a case file of his own, forgoing the official channels. However, if it happened again, he would follow protocol and go through the official channels without a moment's hesitation.

Watching every move Dillon made, Murphy began his interrogation.

"I'm really sorry to trouble you," Lee said. "We met for my lunch hour. We had some things we needed to discuss, so we came up here to have some privacy."

Murphy knew why they needed privacy, and it wasn't called "discussion" where he came from.

"Is he your boyfriend?"

Sheepishly, she whispered "yes," looking down at the floor. Murphy had a hunch she lying.

"Did you know he's trespassing on hospital property?"

"I didn't realize it was trespassing," she responded.

She was looking directly into Murphy's eyes, putting her best little girl pout on, ratcheting up her innocent act into high gear.

"That sounds awful. It's not his fault. I didn't think it would matter. He was with me all the time, and we were talking. Honest." Tears welled up in her eyes. "I promise it won't happen again."

"How long have you been up here?"

"About half an hour," she said softly. "We were in the cafeteria, but my girlfriend works for food service. She's nosey, so we couldn't talk with her around."

"Don't you have to get back to work?"

"No, my shift is done. I saved my lunch for the last half hour," she said blinking repentant blue eyes, "and that's how I lost track of the time. We really didn't intend to be here so long."

"All right then, Miss Nabb, but if I see Mr. Dillon Whelan on the premises after visiting hours again, he'll be arrested for trespassing."

"Oh, thank you, thank you," she exclaimed. Straining to see the name tag on the officer's shirt, she addressed him by name. "Thank you, Officer Murphy."

"Now, I'm going to go over there and explain to him that I'm giving him back his ID," he said. "That is, after he turns his pockets inside out for me. If I don't find anything wrong, then you both are going to walk out of here with me and go about your business. Is that clear?"

"Yes, sir. Thank you, sir," Lee said.

Thursday, 19 Oct. 1978, 18:24

Lee's Visitation

Rachael hadn't been in McGann's Funeral Home in a very long time. Amid the candles and flowers, nervous young people filed in for the visitation.

Some were coming face-to-face with the reality of their own mortality for the first time, and it made them uncomfortable. Lee had been with them only a few days before, vibrant and happy. Now she was lying still, never to stir again. She was a warning beacon, but for what type of bad behavior wasn't exactly clear to them. In order not to jeopardize the investigation into her death, the full extent of what happened to her couldn't be revealed, and because of the condition of the body, there was only a picture of her on an easel next to the casket to remind them of her pert face, sunny blonde hair, and bright blue eyes.

Rachael listened to the organist as she watched the mourners gather. The hymns were calm and traditional, sprinkled in with some of the Lee's favorite songs. It was strange to hear "How Deep Is Your Love" and "You Don't Bring Me Flowers" played on the mini pipe organ, but it did speak to the state of mind of Leivald Nabb. Her mother had taken the songs off of a home-recorded cassette left in Lee's Walkman. Mrs. Nabb asked the young organist to incorporate them into the music for the wake. Tony made note of each selection as it was played.

Mrs. Nabb tried not to cry, but she couldn't contain her sorrow. Even sadder was the fact she had no family to comfort her. She sat alone on the front pew sobbing until one of the girls from Lee's graduating class, in a burst of compassion, went to hug her.

Halfway through the visitation, Tony moved close to Rachael as she occupied a back pew. The room was surprisingly full, with many people from the neighborhood. Rachael thought Lee was a bit of a loner, but it seems she was very well liked by both young and old.

"I want a copy of that guest book," Tony whispered. "There could be some good leads in there."

"Yeah, I'll bet our murderer was one of the first ones to sign," Rachael said in a hushed tone.

"Probably. The deed is done, it's time to observe the reactions of the people around the victim," whispered Tony.

"A thrill kill for one of these boys?" Rachael wondered aloud, squinting to see if the word "maniac" was stamped on someone's forehead that only a detective could see.

"If it had been a thrill kill, she'd have been a lot more beaten up than she was. This murder seems more like it was inspired by passionate rage. Look at all these different people here to pay their respects. We got a wide range of ages, and from the dress of them, an equally wide range of economic strata, too. Check out the lady in the black mink coat. That cost a pretty penny."

Rachael saw what Tony was saying. From cheap gym shoes on geek boys to a North Michigan Avenue maven; there were a lot of people to sift through.

"I'm going to see if I can find a guide," Rachael whispered. "Perhaps one of those guys from the old man's garage can help me narrow the field."

"With your luck, you'll be talking to the murderer himself," Tony whispered.

"Remember it's all those slashes to her face that made this a closed coffin affair. Jealously could be a motive, too."

Tony watched Rachael slip out of the pew. She had a knack for knowing how to blend into a crowd. Dressed for undercover work in a shoulder-padded midnight blue suit, fluffy hair, and navy faux snakeskin pumps, she looked like an older sister of one of the former teen queens who arrived in tandem. Tony marveled at his partner's chameleon-like ability to change her appearance and demeanor to suit the occasion. He had seen her switch from playing helpless victim decoy to ferocious martial artist taking down a formidable scumbag. He hoped it wouldn't happen tonight. It wasn't a pretty sight.

This time, Rachael wore a vulnerable, confused mien, which meant that the men would respond to her in a protective way. She approached one young man leaning against the railing of the staircase leading from the street to the door.

"Nice turnout isn't it?" she remarked.

"Yes, fine bunch of phonies," he said, a twinge of anger in his voice. "Most of them haven't seen Lee in months."

"Really?" Rachael noticed his moist eyes. This one had a story to tell.

"They either worked with her and her mom, or they graduated high school with her. Some of them were last seen at her father's funeral. They have a good case of the guilt is all."

"Guilt is a big emotion," said Rachael. "It can have many causes."

"Well, most of these folks are guilty of abandoning Mrs. Nabb. They didn't like Mr. Nabb because he was German. He moved here long before World War II and was American through and through even though he spoke with an accent."

Rachael made a mental note of this assessment before attempting to go to the well again. The young man knew things. Before saying anything more, he piped up. "I'm glad you're on the case. I hope you'll be able to see through some of these innocent faces spewing pretty lies."

"How'd you know I'm on the case?" she asked.

"Simple," he smiled looking her straight in her eyes. "I know everyone in the neighborhood. I know most of the folks from the hospital. And you're too pretty to be working for the funeral home."

"Thank you," she replied, acknowledging the compliment. She extended her hand for him to shake. "Rachael Culpepper. I'm from the Chicago Police Department. I'm one of the detectives assigned to the case."

"I'm Albee Meegan," he answered as he took her hand. "Pleased to meet you. If I can help you in any way, just ask."

"Thanks, Albee. I appreciate it. You weren't at the garage when we talked to the others. While we're standing here perhaps you can tell me about the folks we haven't met yet?"

"Sure thing."

Rachael looked for someone in the crowd. Sighting a tall man lighting a candle, she decided to see how much Albee Meegan was willing to share.

"Who's the man lighting a candle?" she asked.

"Peter Finch, Lee's next-door neighbor. He's a bit cracked. He became a Jesus freak after he got home from 'Nam. I think he has a bullet or some shrapnel in his head."

"Is there more to him than that?" Rachael asked, noticing that none of the others went near the rack of votives.

"Naw, Peter's a straight arrow. He was a few years too old for Lee."

"It must be really tough on Mrs. Nabb, to be all alone now."

"She ain't exactly all alone," said Albee quietly. "She's got us down at the garage. Jamie, Mikey, and me will do anything for her. Mr. Nabb was too good to us. We'd never leave her in the lurch."

"Which one is Jamie?" Rachael asked.

"The one over there, across the aisle from Mrs. Nabb. He's wearing a navy-blue shirt. Jamie don't own a suit jacket. He's taking this hard, too. At one time, Lee was going to be his sister-in-law. That was a couple of years back, when Lee was engaged to his baby brother, Dillon."

"Really?" said Rachael, realizing that she'd cozied up to the right guy. She glanced about to see what Tony was up to.

He was chatting intensely with a girl half his age, but from the look on his face Rachael couldn't tell if it was for business or pleasure. She turned her attention back to Albee.

"What happened to the engagement?"

"There was a bad breakup. Lee and Dillon had been together since the seventh grade. They fought because neither of them knew how to say, 'Hey, how about we go to a dance with someone else and see what it's like?' They had a big blowout, said horrible things to each other in the middle of the school parking lot. Wouldn't have been so bad, but Dillon always goes overboard in everything he does. He went around telling everyone that Lee had an abortion, killed his baby without telling him. It wasn't true, but it ruined Lee's chances with anyone else. These good Irish boys can't be with a woman like that. It ain't Catholic. And her being Lutheran didn't help, either."

"I see," Rachael said, filing this nugget away for later analysis. "Interesting. After that, she wouldn't take him back."

"She would have, but he couldn't go back. By the time it was all over, Dillon had to get married."

"Why?" Rachael asked.

"While Dillon was being a son of a bitch, Cara was his rebound chick. She had listened to his ranting and raving about Lee and let him cry on her shoulder about the dead baby, giving him what she thought he wanted. And she got pregnant. Wouldn't have been so bad, but Cara and Lee were best friends. They stayed friends even beyond all of that. When the twins arrived, Lee was always there to help. Now, they won't know their 'Auntie Lee.'"

He stopped talking as his voice began to crack. He turned away from her, his shoulders heaving. Taking a couple of deep breaths, he walked away, into the main parlor. She watched him go to the front row and sit next to Ann Nabb.

Tony walked up beside Rachael and whispered, "Good job. You put him in tears."

"He's torn up about this. He did help me fit together a couple of puzzle pieces. I'm going to the restroom and make some notes. I'll be right back."

Tony stood looking at people signing the guest book, watching for someone who wanted to talk. He didn't have long to wait before a dark-haired beauty walked up next to him. She was older than most of the crowd, elegantly dressed in a black wool suit and black patent leather pumps.

"Terrible, isn't it?" he said quietly.

"Yes, we're going to miss Lee at the hospital."

"You worked with her there?" Tony asked, hoping that she was one of the people he had scheduled to talk to in the next few days.

"Yes, I work in Personnel," the woman said sadly. "Lee came to me when she had decided to quit about a month ago. I couldn't talk her out of it. Unfortunate, really. Now there won't be any insurance money to help her mother. We saw something coming. Her attendance was very erratic. We didn't know what she was doing, but we knew it wasn't normal. We weren't as shocked to hear about her death as some of her friends were."

"I'm one of the detectives working the case," Tony said.

The woman looked him up and down, slowly, taking note of his tanned skin, well-trimmed hair, wool sports jacket, and wing tip shoes. She should've known he was a cop because everyone else was wearing Quiana shirts, polyester pants, mullet haircuts, beards, and platform shoes. She reached into her purse, fishing out a small wallet of business cards and offered one to Tony.

"Nice to meet you, officer," she said. "I'm Tabitha Harris. I hope you'll come and talk to me about Lee. I want to help you find who did this to her. I liked Lee, and I didn't want to fire her, but she was forcing my hand. She had only one warning left. I had no idea her leaving would lead to this."

Tony pulled a card from his jacket pocket and offered it to her.

"Thank you, Ms. Harris. I will. I hope the day after the funeral won't be too soon."

"I can talk to you tonight if you have the time. I'll put my address and phone number on the back of my card. I'm an insomniac, so don't worry about the hour."

He returned her card. She wrote quickly. With a nod and a smile, she gave it back to him.

"Bring your notepad. I have lots to tell you," she whispered. She left him to pay her respects to Mrs. Nabb, and then placed a single peach-colored rose wrapped in a lace handkerchief atop the casket.

Tony watched Ms. Harris and Ann Nabb embrace each other. Whatever words of comfort she offered the grieving mother only seemed to make matters worse. Sobbing loudly now, Mrs. Nabb clung to Tabitha, verging on hysterics. The priest and funeral director came to rescue both women from the eyes of the crowd, escorting them into a small alcove opposite the main parlor.

Rachael moved next to Tony as the mourners in their cliques went back to their quiet conversations.

Friday, 20 Oct. 1978, 09:17

Lee's MG Is Found

"Saddle up!" Rachael yelled to Tony, who was standing by the coffee pot about to pour his second cup of the day. "They found her car."

"Yeah? We gotta make a trip to the pound?" he asked as he walked back to the desk.

"You're gonna love this. It's still at the scene and has been since she went missing, apparently."

"Shit, that means there'll be dozens of sets of prints from the neighborhood kids…."

"Oh no," Rachael said, wagging a finger. "This car is special. It's has been hidden far from the public's eye."

Tony gathered up his files, and as he slipped his arms into his sports jacket, Rachael crossed hers.

"Don't you have another jacket? Something less dressy?" she asked. "You're not going to meet another girl to add to your harem," she teased.

"Ha! Ha!" he said in a deadpan. "Don't tell me the car was found in a southern Illinois coal pit and we have to drive down there to get it," he said.

"Almost, but not quite." Rachael pulled a sweater and a pair of gym shoes out of her bottom drawer and slipped off her pumps with a giggle.

"You're enjoying this, aren't you? Keeping me in suspense…. "

Rachael glanced up from tying her shoe. She *was* enjoying it.

"I've never complained about you warning me. Now,

I'm returning the favor. I know how much you love that blue jacket." She decided that she'd held back long enough.

"The forest preserve police were alerted by hikers that a car was on a path where it didn't belong. When they ran the plates, they called us. Hopefully, the hikers didn't contaminate the evidence."

"Great," Tony said, fishing in his desk for his keys. "I hate the woods. Bugs, and birds, and animal scat. Saddle up, indeed."

"Officer Miller will be waiting for us. He'll lead us to the car's location. When we're done they're gonna hook it up and tow it over to the 103rd Street pound for the lab boys to go over it."

"What do you think we'll find in the car?" Tony asked as they drove across 95th Street heading west.

"I'm hoping we find a diary or a journal or an address book. I assume there might be some clues in it still."

"Do you think Lee was dating anyone from the hospital?"

"It's possible," Tony answered. "And maybe someone was pitching in some cash to cover for the overtime she said she was doing."

"Could be. Or, maybe Mama knew it in her heart, but didn't really want to accept it. Lee was all she had left in the world. Why make yourself crazy? Fix it in your heart that she is a good girl, and leave it that way."

"Makes sense." Rachael breezed past the White Castle and the IHOP standing sentry on opposite sides of the road. "Hang on, there's the last set of tracks."

Tony grabbed the dashboard. The small lump in the pavement didn't even make an impression.

"I'm wondering what we'll find in the car. If I were the suspect, I'd have left it open on the street or parked in a nice dark corner on the lower level of the parking lot back at Evergreen Plaza. This looks more suspicious to me, but then again, we see it every day."

"What I don't get is how the car got here, but the body ended up back in the 19th Ward's garbage," Rachael replied.

"That's why they pay us the big bucks. This is quite a gap in time and space. It's looking more and more like it might be a two-suspect job. It's not like you can walk away from the scene, unless you're a competitive hiker. I guess if the killers really needed to, they could have hitched a ride."

They passed the Sabre Room with the oversized genie leaning on his scimitar. The white and gold Forest Preserves Police squad car soon came into view. Rachael made a left turn off 95th Street to pull in behind the occupied car.

Officer Miller was tall and stood erect in his beige shirt and dark green uniform pants. He shook Tony's hand first and then reached out to shake Rachael's. His shirt cuffs were tucked under, exposing well-tanned wrists.

"Good to meet you Officer Miller," Rachael said. "How far do we have to go to see the car?"

"It's down by Morrell Meadow, on 107th off La Grange Road. Most folks aren't familiar with the preserves, so my sergeant decided I should take you there. Is there a tow truck on its way?"

"Dispatch said they're sending one. Let me go and check on it," Tony volunteered.

Not long afterward, the tow truck pulled up. Rachael tossed the keys to Tony and walked around to the passenger side.

"With all these trees and bushes, I'd have pulled over to the side and rolled her out of the car. There's a hell of a drop off over there. No jogger would even look down there. It would have taken us longer to find her if they had dumped her body down there, and there wouldn't have been much left to identify once the animals got a hold of her," remarked Tony.

"Someone hated her for sure; that's why they killed her," Rachael said. "Yet, looking at it from a twisted point of view, she was protected, not dumped. She was put in a relatively clean garbage can and covered with newsprint, not garbage, not placed out here, left to the elements. If they'd left her out here, the case wouldn't have been assigned to us."

The car was located off the road quite a ways. Someone had driven it to the end of the gravel turnaround that served as the parking lot and bypassed the big horizontal log that was the trail head marker. It was an amazing feat to clear the log because MGs don't have much ground clearance. It would have been difficult enough for a Jeep or a Land Rover to get around it, let alone a small sports car.

The car was left down the trail, near where part of the lake formed a pond on the other side of the road. The bushes and trees thickened as the land sloped. The hard-packed dirt gave way to loose, shifting gravel.

"You and Miller go ahead," Tony directed Rachael. "Me and the tow truck drivers will be there in a minute. They'll have to run some cable, and I want to take some notes about this location."

"Okay,"she said.

Following Miller into the turning leaves, Rachael hurried to catch up. When she did, Tony was standing at the rear bumper of the car. The hunter green MG blended in with the foliage perfectly. It was only a few yards off the path, the front end pushed up and caught on the ragged stump of a fallen tree. It was hard to tell if this had been done accidentally or on purpose.

"Officer Miller, what do you make of it being here?" Rachael asked.

"Detective Culpepper, call me Dan," he smiled. "This ain't the kind of car you take for a trail ride. Someone was trying to hide it."

"That's what I was thinking too, Dan," she said. She walked around Miller gingerly, expecting the earth to be soft underfoot, but it felt as hard as concrete.

"You don't have to worry about your footing here because it isn't wet," Miller said. "This is a kettle moraine sloping into a spring-fed lake, so no marshland leads up to it. It's probably why they didn't leave the body out here. The ground is too hard to try to dig even a shallow grave without a backhoe. You'll hit solid rock a couple of feet down."

"Tony and I were wondering why the victim and car were separated."

Pulling a pair of exam gloves out of her pocket, Rachael saw Tony and two big guys wearing dark blue coveralls with city flag patches on the sleeves approach. One counted his footsteps aloud. With his notebook open, he calculated the distance, converting footsteps into yards. She opened the passenger side door to the car. There were no bloodstains on either seat. The floor mats were clean too. She searched for the lever to flip the seat back forward, and finding it, she got a good look at the space between the seats and the back wall. It was a litter of rumpled clothes, crumpled computer reports, discarded magazines, cassettes, and empty paper bags. Poking the pile, her flashlight picked up a couple of glints from the odd earring or broken bracelet, but no weapon. Rachael stopped, looking up when she heard the tow truck guy.

"Shit Hank, we're gonna have to put the extender on the cable. This thing's way past the 50-yard line."

Turning to Tony, Steve, whose name was stitched in red above his left shirt pocket in a white circle, explained the plan. "I'm going to help him feed out the cable as we move the truck a little closer. Good thing we came out in Big Bertha; she's got a heavy-duty winch. We're going to need every ounce of torque to get that baby off that stump. That's one hell of a bad spot. What'cha bet we'll have to jack it up? And after all that, the steering's probably busted from going over those logs, rocks, and bumps back there."

"No rush," Tony said, looking up the trail at them. "We want to look it over before you hook it up anyways."

"You know, if it wasn't for that chunk of deadwood, this car would have been submerged in the water, and we wouldn't have found it," Officer Dan Miller said.

"Did you boys bring gloves?" Tony inquired.

Steve patted his deep pocket. "Me and Hank always keep some rubbers in our wallets for occasions like these. We don't want to be on the suspect list—if you know what I mean."

Tony knew, indeed. He nodded to Steve, looked back up the trail, and then turned to look toward the finger of the lake in the distance. All of them stood there, looking through the trees to the sun glinting off the distant calm water. Dan was right. Whoever dumped the car was aiming for the lake.

Friday, 20 Oct. 1978, 11:47

A Talk with Timothy O'Toole

Rachael wished Tony had ridden with her instead of the tow truck drivers, but they had to maintain the chain of evidence. They both had had cases blown by the technicality of the car being ferried all over Chicago before being taken to the crime lab impound lot. They needed a break in the case, and this car might be it.

On the way back down 111th Street, the tow truck driver cleverly jetted across the entrance to Holy Sepulchre Cemetery before a hearse turned in, sticking Rachael to wait for nearly 80 cars to clear the left turn. Once the procession entered, the truck was out of sight. Rachael smiled, thinking Tony was in a worse position than she was.

Past Central Avenue, a freight train stopped her progress for another five or six minutes. She figured that by now, Tony was at the pound. At the first gas station beyond the train tracks, she stopped. Rummaging in the glove compartment, she found a tattered FOP guidebook. Thumbing through to find the telephone number to the impound lot, she moved to the pay phone.

"Hello, this is Detective Culpepper. Do you have a Detective Breese checking in a green MG by any chance?"

"Yeah, hold on."

She heard the phone drop on the desk with a thump as the male voice yelled for Tony. After a long pause and a rustle of papers, he picked up.

"Detective Breese, how can I help you?"

"Tony, it's me Rachael. I managed to get caught behind

two funerals and a train."

"I wondered what happened. My guys drove like their asses were on fire. Told 'em I wanted to take a girl to lunch and they hauled it."

"Is she there?" Rachael asked.

"Oh yeah, Debbie's here, and she's hungry. You can take your time. I'm going to let her drive me over to the Sauer's on 23rd Street. Do you think there's something you could do for about an hour, hour and a half?"

"I'll get a bite to eat at the Paragon, and then try to find one of those candy stripers for a few questions. How about we rendezvous at 3 o'clock?"

"Sounds like a plan. I'll have her drop me at the office when we're done."

Rachael got back into the car. At the next light, she heard a horn. In the driver's seat of the black pick up next to her was Cara's father. He rolled down the window. She followed suit.

"Arrested that asshole son-in-law of mine yet?" he shouted.

Rachael was a bit stunned by the bluntness of the accusation. Dillon wasn't a suspect in her mind, but she answered in an official way.

"We're still gathering evidence, Mr. O'Toole."

The light changed to green. She had expected him to speed away in a huff, but he fooled her.

"Come on, follow me. We need to talk. Things I can't say in front of the wife or the guys at the firehouse."

He jetted across the intersection, forcing Rachael to floor it to catch up. At Cicero, he made a left and headed north. After they crossed 107th Street, he got in the right-hand lane and put on his turn signal. Two blocks later, he pulled into the parking lot of Huck Finn's Restaurant and parked at the edge of the lot. Rachael followed and met him at the door.

"Don't look surprised." He smiled as he opened the doors for her. "Firemen like coffee and donuts, too. I didn't think you wanted to talk in a bar, being on duty and all."

"Very considerate of you, Mr. O'Toole," she said.

The perky hostess took them to a semi-secluded booth near a window.

Before they sat, Mr. O'Toole asked the hostess, "Is this one of Betty's tables?"

"She's not working today. Would you like to sit somewhere else?"

"No, no," he clucked, "this'll be fine."

The girl put the menus on the table with a huge smile and bounced back to her podium. "Thank goodness that old gossipmonger isn't here today; otherwise, half our conversation would have to be in code. She knows my wife."

Before he got started, another young redhead stood at the table, poised to take their order.

"Hello Mr. O'Toole. How's Cara?" she asked.

"She's doing fine, Lauren," he smiled. "How are you?"

"I'm doing great. I'll be leaving for France next month; I'm going to study literature there for a whole year and then I'll be back to finish up at Loyola. Tell Cara we miss her. She never comes in with the twins."

"I'll tell her," he said with the trace of a wince. "Will you bring us a pot of coffee and six glazed donuts?"

"Sure, Mr. O'Toole. Be right back."

He didn't watch her leave, but he leaned over the table to whisper to Rachael. His face had a tight, pained expression.

"See what that bastard Dillon took from her? My Cara's a smart girl, except when it comes to the world. She was supposed to be going to college, studying abroad, living the life her mother and I worked hard to give her. But this asshole comes along and ruins everything. He was doing fine with Lee. She's his type. They had nothing and they wanted nothing, being together with nothing would have suited them fine...."

Lauren returned with the plate of donuts and a Thermos of

coffee. Mr. O'Toole sat back in the booth, faking a smile for her. She poured the coffee skillfully.

"Anything else," she smiled brightly, "you wave. I'll be around."

Rachael had her notepad and pen lying on the table, in case something he had to say was important enough to note. So far, she felt that she was being a sounding board for the price of a cup of coffee and donuts.

"I make no bones about not liking my son-in-law. He wasn't my choice. He wasn't really Cara's choice, either. She was a spite date for him. I know it sounds bad, but Dillon and Lee were nice enough, but they didn't have any ambition, no drive to improve themselves. Lee was going to go to a trade school and learn mechanics, of all things. She was going to spend her life in that damn garage under her father's wings, never going past 79th Street unless it was to see the Sox play the Crosstown at Wrigley or a Bears game on the Lakefront. And Dillon was going to be right along with her, greasy from head to foot."

Rachael sipped coffee, waiting for him to tell her more. If nothing came of this, at least she'd have a story to tell Tony.

"Cara's mother nearly died when she found out our daughter was pregnant. She had no idea anything had happened on prom night. Dillon got her home at the curfew we set. Come to find out, they went, danced once, got in line for the picture, and then he ruined my baby in a cheap hotel room…."

His voice trailed off, and he hid himself in the upturned coffee cup. Rachael sipped too, letting him recover.

"I wanted to have her take care of it differently, to send her to a boarding school in Michigan specializing in that kind of thing. She would have been there over the summer and through her first year of college. When the baby came in February, it would have been put up for adoption. She would have been home in the spring and on with her life."

He took another sip of coffee and a bite of donut. Rachael

waited. She wanted him to get it all off his chest.

"I don't want you to think my wife is vindictive. She's from the old country. She has a different idea where morals are concerned. When the pregnancy was discovered, she wasn't keen on my solution. Don't ask me why, but she took over, and you can see where it got Cara. Married, stuck on a dead-end street, across from the cemetery, wallowing in depression."

Rachael was disappointed. So far, he was offering nothing important. From his fervor, she'd thought he had a lot more to give.

"I love my little girl. I want her to have a good life. I want her to get over this marriage. He isn't right for her. He doesn't really love her. Lee was his true love and perhaps now he'll divorce my Cara, out of grief, of course, and we can all get on with our lives."

He poured another cup of steaming hot coffee. There was a brief silence between them. Rachael decided to break it as gently as she could.

"Mr. O'Toole, do you think Dillon might have done this to Lee?"

Timothy O'Toole glared at her with a set jaw. He wanted to tell her yes, but his conscience wouldn't let him.

"Dillon's a devil for sure, but even with all his anger, he wouldn't kill Lee. He's trapped, like my Cara, but there's no reason for him to go after Lee."

"Not even if she were seeing someone else? Someone say, from the other side of the expressway?"

O'Toole sipped the cooling coffee, thinking for a moment before answering.

"I don't think Dillon cares about black folks. He's been known to do some fag bashing over on the north side or in East Chicago, but for all his faults, he's not a racist. And for some strange reason, he doesn't seem to have a jealous bone in his body, either. I can't figure it out. I guess it's because Lee isn't… I mean wasn't dating anyone. She's been as chaste as a nun since summer, according to the neighborhood scuttlebutt."

Rachael scribbled down the phrases "not dating" and "not a racist" with the initials next to the notes. Not big revelations, but they might help.

"Where do you think I should be looking, Mr. O'Toole?" she asked, biting into a glazed donut.

"I think it was someone weird, someone outside of the neighborhood. Someone who came in to find a nice young girl. A Richard Speck, or like that Laskey guy over in Cincinnati, or that Manson dude. Someone like that got to her."

It was an interesting theory, one that reminded Rachael why she was the police and he was a firefighter. People like that didn't kill one person and then stop.

"We'll definitely explore those angles, Mr. O'Toole."

"Can I ask you a question, Detective Culpepper?"

Rachael nodded, putting her cup back on the table.

"You got any kids?"

"No, I don't. I have nieces whom I love dearly, but no kids of my own."

"Well, let me tell you," he said in a serious tone. "When you have some of your own, all you'll want for them is the best. The absolute best. You'll move heaven and earth to give it to them. I work two jobs. I have a few investments. I spend as much time as I can at home. My wife keeps a beautiful house. She had two miscarriages before Cara. That was hard on her. The last one nearly unhinged her. She was six months along when she woke up bleeding. Screamed like a banshee all the way to the hospital. They had to sedate her. When she awoke, they told her she'd had a D&C to get out all of the placenta. She was frantic; she said they'd made her sin against God. She believed they'd performed an unnecessary abortion on her. We had to take her to the morgue to show her the baby. It was too deformed to survive. She was devastated. The doctors told her she wouldn't get pregnant again. We weren't going to have the big Irish family she wanted. I was okay with it because I had Teagan, but she wanted to have a house of full of children, like in the old country."

He sipped again, holding the cup in both his hands like a chalice. Peering into the cup, he continued.

"After about four or five months, Teagan found she was pregnant with Cara. She was thrilled. She went to Mass every morning and prayed a rosary to St. Mary and St. Brenna every other day. She stayed in bed for seven months because Cara was our miracle. She was Teagan's redemption, her gift from God. She still believes Cara is a miracle. It's why she was so disappointed, so hurt when Cara made her mistake."

"Thank you Mr. O'Toole. You didn't have to tell me all of this, you know."

"Yeah, but I want you to understand why Teagan and I are the way we are. I apologize for wasting your time, but I thought it was important. After I said what I did about Dillon, I felt bad. I wanted you to understand where I was coming from. He ruined my baby, and I can't erase that fact. But there is nothing I would actually *do* to him. Know what I mean?"

"I do, Mr. O'Toole."

"As a matter of fact, I invested in the old garage where he works. I put up some money so the boys wouldn't lose it. When the babies were first born, it was the only place Dillon was working. It was in my best interest to keep it going. I'm a silent partner, only Mikey Shaw knows I have a piece of the place. I'd like it to stay that way, if you can manage it."

Rachael recorded it on her notepad. This was an important fact. She put an asterisk behind it and the words "silent and secret partner" in parentheses.

"I hope I haven't ruined your morning." He smiled weakly as he rose from the booth, reaching in his back pocket for his wallet. "I should've let you go on your way, but I've never seen you without your partner."

He ended the meeting and fingered his open wallet for a

tip. Rachael didn't know whether to be insulted or flattered by the comment, whether it was intended as a flirtation or whether it was an admission that Tony made him uncomfortable. He dropped a couple of dollars on the table as Rachael slid across the vinyl seat.

"Catch the murderer for me, Detective," he said narrowing his gray eyes, "I didn't care for Lee, but she didn't deserve to be killed. Whoever he is, he needs to be put behind bars."

Rachael put out her hand for him to shake. He took it in his strong grip, pumping it gently. He strode through the tables showing more raw physicality than she had noticed earlier. She would note that on her pad when she got back to the car.

March 1978

Cara Feels Abandoned

"Lee, I have a bad feeling," Cara sighed. "A very bad feeling."

"Cara, you're paranoid. You've got everything you could possible wish for: two beautiful baby girls, your own apartment, a car, and a good husband."

"I wasn't supposed to be here, Lee. I was supposed to be in upstate New York, getting an education. I was supposed to be studying, not changing diapers. My mother hasn't even spoken to me since the twins were baptized."

"She'll come around," Lee said, tenderly rocking one of the twins in her arms. "How could she resist such a precious little one like this?"

"Don't act like you don't know my mother. You know she was mortified by my pregnancy."

"She's just an old fuddy-duddy, not ready to be a grandmother. But if you keep taking these precious angels over there, she'll eventually melt. Wait until they start to crawl. They'll have her down on the floor crawling with them!"

"Now I know you're dreaming," Cara sighed.

She gently placed the sleeping twin in a bassinet with the name "Hanna" written in pink magic marker on a piece of masking tape. The baby wiggled slightly, trying to put a cloth-covered fist in its tiny mouth. Lee continued to cuddle the other twin in her arms. Cara paced the open floor nervously.

"You don't understand, Lee," she said, her hands pushed into her jeans pockets. "I'm all alone. No one comes to see me, except you. All of my other friends have abandoned me.

Dillon is off working. My mother doesn't help, and she won't let any of her friends help, either."

Tears rolled down Cara's face, and settled on her baby-food-spotted blouse. The jeans she wore were several sizes too big, reminders of her pregnancy. She hated wearing them, but on Dillon's meager salary, it was the best she could do. They were good for housework and baby drool, but not as good as the ones her dad used to let her put on his Field's charge account.

"Cara, your friends will come around," said Lee, rocking slowly as if she were listening to a folk tune inside her head. "Half of them are still away at school. Vacation doesn't start at the same time everywhere."

"No, it doesn't, Lee," Cara replied sharply. "Champaign-Urbana lets out next week, along with Northern in DeKalb, and Southern. Northwestern's term ends closer to the holiday, and the University of Chicago and Yale are already out. Lindsey and Marge should be home by now, and I haven't had a phone call from either one of them."

Cara sat dejectedly in the small brown glider rocker near the window overlooking the train tracks. It was supposed to be where she would breastfeed the babies, but she used it as her personal refuge instead. When she couldn't produce enough milk to feed them both, she happily followed doctor's orders and put them on Similac. Inwardly, Cara was glad that her body wouldn't provide it. Wasn't it enough to carry them all the way to term without having them attached to her like leeches?

She couldn't have had an abortion; she was a good Catholic girl. Her timing couldn't have been worse. She wanted to conceal her condition until after graduation, spend the summer in hiding, and then have the baby—at the time she thought it was only one—and go to college, but she'd exploded like the Goodyear Blimp in month four, ruining all her plans. Twins indeed. She couldn't have one tiny baby like other girls.

"They'll come over as soon as they can get out of their families' clutches, Cara. Most of them have never been away from home before, you know."

Cara watched Lee, content to be holding little Lorna, as though the baby belonged to her. It grated softly on Cara's nerves, seeing her sitting on the cast-off couch where Dillon should be. She should have been grateful that Lee was spending time helping her instead of hanging out with the boys from her father's old garage, but tonight something felt different to her. There was something smug about Lee, but Cara couldn't put her finger on it. She shook her head slightly as if to clear the thought from her head. The one that replaced it was equally troublesome. It nearly made her cry.

Cara's other so-called friends were down at Eric the Red's, listening to music, drinking dollar beers and flirting. That's where she should be, not stuck in this one-bedroom kitchenette prison with two tiny wardens demanding her constant attention.

"Lee, they're not coming up here to listen to the train whistles and watch me change diapers."

"Well, when you put it that way, Cara, no. But they've got to want to see these little cuties. Everyone loves babies. I know they'll want to hold them and play with them."

"The problem is none of them like Dillon," said Cara flatly. "They all think he is a bum. They won't come around. They don't want to run into him. They don't think I should have married him."

"They, they, they….Don't pay those snooty bitches any attention. They don't know a good man when they see one," huffed Lee. "Dillon is working his ass off for you and the babies. Isn't he doing overtime right now?"

Cara looked past the tracks into the western edge of Mount Greenwood Cemetery, counting tombstones to calm her anger. Mentally, she would wish every person who had irritated her into one of those graves, dead and quiet, far away from her.

"Yes, Lee, he does work hard, but the paychecks are always the same. Somehow, the more time he spends at work, the less money he brings home. Between the taxes and the currency exchange fees, it almost doesn't make sense for him to work overtime."

"Yeah, that happens to me, too. If I do a lot of OT, it feels like I get shafted, but with it being Mom and me, I take all the OT I can get," Lee returned.

"It's not *that*, Lee," she sighed. "I miss him. I've got nobody to talk to but you and him, and you can't be here all the time. He needs to be here, helping me with these babies. But when he is, all he wants to do is sleep."

"Cara, he's doing the best he can. It's hard work unloading those trucks at the railroad yard. I'm sure he's really, really tired when he comes home. You've got to give him a break. He was lucky his friend Jake knew the foreman, or he'd be at Burger King, flipping burgers. You know that wasn't enough money to support all of you."

Lee seemed so quick to defend Dillon that Cara felt a pang of jealousy. He must have been talking to Lee about his feelings instead of her.

"I know, Lee," she said, resignation in her voice. "I know."

As Lee played with the babies, Cara didn't think Lee knew how precious her freedom was. She had no idea how horridly loud it was in this tiny apartment. Lee was used to listening to freight trains blow their horns day and night, but her bedroom was in the back of the house, not so close that the engineers could wink and wave as they passed. Lee had no clue how loud the fire trucks were when they pulled out from the station down the block, scaring babies into howling fits after they'd finally fallen asleep. She didn't hear the ugly, embarrassing noises of the drunken neighbors penetrating the thin walls. She didn't know how much Cara wanted to be back home in her beautiful aqua bedroom—her oasis of comfort and peace, her safe haven closed with an actual hasp and padlock bolted into the good woodwork the day her mother found out that she was pregnant. Mother hadn't allowed Cara to remove any of her personal items. She wondered if she ever even opened the locked door and gone into her room.

She had been exiled to sleeping on the couch in the rec room while the two families negotiated her fate. Her punishment was no abortion, no home for wayward girls, no going to college with her friends because the twins had stretched her belly to nine-month dimensions by the end of the fourth month. She had to go to city hall to marry Dillon before a judge. Their honeymoon was in a bedroom off the kitchen in Dillon's mother's house. When the doctor ordered bed rest, her mother took her back in—temporarily—but put her in the guest room that she had outfitted like a hospital room.

Right before the babies came, Dillon rented this beige hellhole of an apartment. Seventeen steps up from the narrow, rutted gravel street that abutted the train embankment. Lee had no idea how precious quiet really was.

Lee moved gently, slowly rising from the couch. Baby Lorna was sleeping soundly in her arms. Lee deposited her into her labeled bassinette, covered her with a thin cotton blanket, carefully tucking in the sides. She saw Hanna was lying uncovered, reached in, and tucked her in too. She wouldn't mention that babies slept longer if they were warm. Cara would learn these things eventually.

"I'm gonna go, Cara," she said. "Mom and I are going to the Pancake House when she gets off tonight. I'll see you day after tomorrow. I won't forget your doctor's appointment."

Cara barely looked away from the window; she had sunk deep into the maw of her nightly depression.

"Yeah, okay," she mumbled. "The doctor's office."

Stopping at the door, Lee bent over to pick up her purse. Most of the time, Lee went to work looking unkempt according to Cara's standards, but tonight, she looked as if she were going to walk the half-mile down 111th Street to Eric the

Red's. She had on her shiny black cowgirl boots, nice jeans, and a big yellow sweater. Even her hair was combed. She wasn't that dressed up to eat pancakes with her mother. She was out on the prowl. Cara would bet money on it.

"See you later. Don't forget to lock the door."

Cara nodded. Her anger bubbled up in her throat, preventing her from speaking. She tasted bile, felt the heat of tears at the back of her eyes. She stared at the tombstones, biting her tongue, feeling totally lost.

When Lee let herself out, she ran down the wrought iron steps. Throwing the bag behind the passenger seat of her MG, she slid behind the wheel with a big smile. It was a visceral pleasure for her to turn the key and hear the engine roar to life. Heading in the direction of the hospital, the radio blared under the canvas top. Passing the hospital, she headed for the corner of 95th and Cicero. Instead of pulling into the lot of the blue A-frame International House of Pancakes, she continued over the railroad tracks, to the driveway of the Miami Motel. Going past the office without a glance, she parked next to a red Chevy pickup. Grabbing her purse, she knocked on the door of a room where she was greeted by strong, bare outstretched arms that pulled her into the room and kissed her passionately.

Friday, 20 Oct. 1978, 19:13

A Love Song Leaves a Clue

Rachael stretched. It had been an incredibly long time since she'd been so tightly wound. She'd seen brutal murders before—many times. She'd witnessed the aftermath of countless vicious attacks, domestic disturbances, and mayhem, but this case was different. She couldn't reconcile the act of violence perpetrated on Lee Nabb's face without any signs of struggle or reaction. There was no fighting back, no skin underneath the nails, no hair or fibers stuck to her palms, nothing to indicate a struggle of any kind. Surely, Lee had gone somewhere secretly to meet someone she knew. She'd trusted the person. Didn't fear them. That fact was clear.

Perhaps she'd been lured by the promise of sex, or she'd gone to help someone out, or maybe had been going about her business when she was blindsided. Whatever had happened, the killer had made their hatred known. Rachael wondered if they had made their feelings known to Lee before they killed her. And why did they kill her? From the photos of Lee that she'd gotten from her mother, she was a vivacious girl. Who'd she have pissed off so much that it led to her murder and mutilation?

The brutality of her disfigurement was even more disturbing. It wasn't the cause of her death but it was part and parcel of the murder. When someone slashes your face once and you don't put up your hands to defend yourself, either you're unconscious or restrained. Yet Lee's arms weren't bruised or red to indicate any kind of mechanical restraint, ropes, or cuffs. There were no finger marks left on her wrists; no bruises shaped from handprints. Not a drop of glue or adhesive of any kind. Strange. Very strange.

Even stranger was the fact there was so much blood and so many cuts. It seemed odd to inflict so many slashes on such a small surface of her body. Rachael had surmised that the slashing started at the hairline because of the propensity for foreheads to bleed. Blood running down the face thick and red might obstruct vision, but it didn't justify the lack of defense. There were no slashes on the outside of her wrists, where they should be if a fight had ensued.

Rachael's cat, Napoleon, stretched out his front legs, flexing his paws, in a show of comfort and ease. He reinforced what she knew to be true; if you didn't trust those around you, you couldn't relax. Lee had been caught off guard and hadn't expected the murderer to attack her so viciously.

It could have been one of her boyfriends from the carnival. Perhaps they went out to the woods, headed off the road. There might have been a car waiting nearby. After having committed the act, she got pushed into the back seat of the waiting car. If the murderer drove fast enough, rigor mortis wouldn't have set in before he got back to the neighborhood. And then, in the middle of the night, when traffic was at its lightest, it would've been probably fifteen or twenty minutes—tops. But if they got stopped on the wrong side of a freight train, then it could take half an hour or more, as there were four active tracks between the McMahon Woods and the garbage can in the 19th Ward.

Or even simpler, Lee had gone to the woods to meet her lover, gotten in the back seat of his car, ready for some action, and got killed instead. Then the lover had to make her car disappear by pushing it back into the deep brush.

Rachael still couldn't fathom what Lee might have done to make the murderer mutilate her. Pure anger and hatred were all that came to mind. She didn't have enough money for it to have been a motive. She was pretty enough to have a herd of suitors, though. And while there were a lot of boys in her life, they seemed to be kept at the fringes. Of the girls who'd come forward, none appeared to be the violent kind. At most, they might douse a rival's clothes with a drink, pull out a fistful of hair, land a few open hand slaps, or throw a shoe, but these were girls from "good" families from upscale neighborhoods. Of all of them, Lee was the bad ass, the tough girl, and the one with an axe to grind.

Yet, the one thing that kept coming up was that damn song. Tony had heard about it from Dana, her supervisor. Lee must have sung it over and over again for them to remember it so vividly. What was she trying to tell them?

It was the only time Rachael wished she'd spent more time listening to the pop stations on the way to and from work. The city didn't put FM radios in unmarked cars—only police band Motorolas. All they heard were the radio calls on Citywide because they needed to know what was going on around them. No one wanted to get caught in the crossfire from a gun battle, drive into the midst of a riot unprepared, or miss an "officer needs help" call.

She went to the stereo, and tuning the dial, hunted for an FM pop station. Her tastes tended toward classical and jazz, so she'd have to search for one. She wondered how many love songs she'd have to suffer through before the song she wanted to hear came up in the play list. One song in particular reminded her why she had crossed over to jazz.

She poured herself a glass of wine from the fridge to the strains of another song about a couple drifting apart. As she listened, she thought the words fit Lee's predicament. It was a song about lost love and reconciliation, but the chorus was too hopeful to make a girl cry every time she heard it, no matter how sensitive a soul she might have been.

Unsettled, Rachael re-read her notes from the interview with Mikey. They were a scattered collection of scribbled disconnected ideas covering the gamut of emotion. He had rambled over the place: Ideas about why Lee had been killed and how it happened; yet he didn't mention her being pregnant. He was heartsick about her death, but didn't know why the coffin was closed. He would go over to Mrs. Nabb's house, but half the time he would sit in his car and not go in. He did a lot of talking. It revealed that he was infatuated with Lee. Yet of all the people she and Tony talked to, he gave the best insight into her character. Both he and Dana mentioned the song she sang and cried to. What ruled him out as a suspect in Rachael's mind was his sweet nature. There were no signs of hidden psychopathic tendencies in him, no gut feeling that he was hiding anything.

After suffering through a few one-hit wonders and a disco number or two, the strains of a ballad floated across the room. One long song, like Mikey said. The lyrics unfolded telling the lifecycle of loss, remorse and remembrance, which could be reconciliation if you were in the right frame of mind. Rachael jotted the lyrics down, hoping it was the song that Lee was reputed to have sung and cried over, so much so that her friends and co-workers sat up and took notice.

Pushing into her shoes before the last stanza finished, she was determined to get a copy of the song to play for Tony. Glancing at the clock, she saw that she could easily make it to Evergreen Plaza before they closed. She was confident that the kids in the record store would know who the recording artist was from her notes.

Friday, 20 Oct. 1978, 20:15

Mikey's Grief

Some people wear beer goggles; the more they drink the better things look. Mikey was different. The more he drank, the better he thought his memory served him. Lee's murder had obsessed him from the moment he had heard about it, but tonight he was determined to solve it for himself. He ordered another tall Jim Beam and ginger ale.

The lady detective was nice, and seemed really concerned, but she didn't know Lee like he did. The guy detective was okay, but he didn't seem to care as much, so it was up to Mikey to try his hand at cracking the case. Hell, his mother watched every detective show on television. He'd sat through hours of "Columbo," "Kojak," and "Barnaby Jones." He'd picked up a few tricks of interrogation. He'd use what he'd learned on the O'Casey Triplets as soon as they came into the bar. Somebody in the neighborhood was responsible, and he was going to get to the bottom of this tonight, one way or another. All the guys had the hots for Lee. He would get information they had, and then he would call the cop lady and have her lock the killer up, like the guys on TV.

Mikey formulated his questions, such as "when was the last time you saw Lee Nabb?" That was always the best way to start. And he'd have to be sure to watch the guy squirm because you're pinpointing his whereabouts on the night in question. The more he protested and squirmed, the guiltier he was. If he has an alibi, who or what was it? That question always makes the killer nervous. Remember to watch his eyes. Look for a twitch or a tick. The guilty have twitchy faces.

As he was formulating more questions to ask, the first of the O'Casey Brothers, Rory, walked through the door, heading for his usual stool near the end of the bar. Grabbing his drink, Mikey headed toward him. The bartender placed a Guinness Stout down, and Mikey jumped onto the stool next to Rory.

"Hallo there!"

"Hi Mikey," Rory answered. He was annoyed that Mikey was drunker than he wanted to be bothered with. "Been here for a while I see," he said sarcastically.

"I have. And it's a fine thing for a Friday night, too." He patted Rory on the upper arm. "I have something on my mind that you might be able to help me with."

"And what might that be?" Rory asked.

Mikey hadn't noticed that Rory's two brothers had arrived. They came to stand behind him. Seamus was known for his unruly hair and his propensity for fighting. He was twice Mikey's size—all muscle from working the lumberyard delivery truck. Quinn was an inch shorter, but solid as both his brothers. He slung packages for UPS, while he studied business at Saint Xavier's University. The three brothers glanced at each other as the bartender pulled one Bud and one Harp.

"Where were you Thursday, three weeks ago?" Mikey asked. While Rory answered, his brothers chugged down half their glasses in the first swallow.

"I was where I always am on a Thursday night—sitting here with my brothers having a beer."

It wasn't going to be as easy as it looked, Mikey thought. He wondered what to ask next, but before the thought came to him, Rory went on the defensive.

"What the hell you asking me for?"

Rory peered at him over the rim of the glass. The brothers standing behind Mikey bit their lips to keep from laughing out loud. Undeterred, Mikey fired off another question.

"Can someone other than your brothers corroborate or vouch for your whereabouts?"

Rory slowly sipped his beer before he answered, obviously annoyed.

"Why do I need someone to corroborate my whereabouts?" he seethed.

Mikey stared at Rory's impassive face. Mikey was the only one who had cared about Lee, the only one who wanted to get to the bottom of who had murdered her. He wanted to go to Mrs. Nabb, reassure her that justice would be done, and confess that he should have been there to protect her. Without knowing who had done it, none of that was possible. Overcome with a sense of futility, tears started rolling down his cheeks. His body began to shake, and he broke down, sobbing uncontrollably.

"Look at what ya done," Quinn bellowed, moving around to hit his brother Seamus in the chest.

"I've done nothing," he pushed him back. "You were the one doin' all the talking."

"Insulted him, ya' have," Rory chimed in, as he wrapped his arms around the sobbing Mikey.

"I did not!" Seamus said. "He started it all by asking me where the hell I was, like it were any business of his."

The bartender and the other regulars moved to the back of the bar to see what the commotion was all about. The triplets could be a handful, and a good fight could be entertaining. But tonight wasn't the night for it. Mikey tried to collect himself, but when he saw the faces surrounding him, he broke down again.

"What the hell did you do to him?" the bartender asked.

"Not one bloody thing," said Seamus. "He was asking me some stupid questions, and when I answered him, he broke down. I don't know what's wrong with him."

"Get him a beer," one of the patrons in the crowd said. "Whatever he was drinking needs to be flushed from his system."

"Here," said Quinn, pulling the unfolded cocktail napkin

from under Mikey's drink and pushing it into his hand, "your damn nose is running."

Mikey wiped his face and uttered a thank-you in the general direction of the crowd.

"I want to know…" he sniffed, "… who could do such a thing…."

They waited for him pull himself together. They knew better than to speak. They'd seen many a man reconcile his pain on a barstool.

"She was so beautiful," he sighed. They waited.

"She would have married me, if I'd asked her. I was going to ask her—I was, this week. But I didn't want to do it around Halloween. I didn't want her to think it was a joke."

He took a slug of the beer the bartender had put in front of him.

"She should've been over him by now, you know. I knew I had to wait. Ya can't walk up to a woman and say 'He dumped you, marry me' … it doesn't work. I wouldn't have minded being Mr. Rebound Man. I loved her. But ya know, ya have to time it right."

He looked around at the sympathetic faces. They nodded in agreement, listening to him pour out his sorrow. Some of them knew who the "she" was, but those who didn't understood what he was going through.

"I did everything. I took her to work; I let her cry on my shoulder. I didn't push. I waited… and waited… too damn l-l-long"

He started bawling again, putting his head on the bar. From the crowd came an old man's brogue. "Steady on lad, we've all been there once and again. Women are the most unknowable things in all of God's universe. Ye can't be blaming yerself."

Mikey raised his head from the bar and glared at the old man. "But I can blame the son of a bitch that killed her!"

As Mikey leaned forward at the bar, the crowd began to

disperse. The triplets stood around him, drinking silently, nearing the bottom of their mugs. Suddenly, Mikey jumped to his feet.

"Some son-of-a-bitch killed her. I want to know who. I wanna beat his ass good. I want his blood on me. I wanna put my hands 'round the bastard's neck, drag him to the station, and throw him in a cell myself."

"I hope you find him, Mikey," Seamus said with a consoling pat on the back, "I really do."

Signaling to the bartender for refills, the Triplets left Mikey to recover himself.

"He's got it bad," Rory said to Seamus, "but then again, he always did have the hot's for Lee. Wonder if he's gonna take the test and get on the department now."

"Yeah, he could hunt down her killer, like on TV," quipped Quinn. "He was acting like a cop when I first got here. Somebody needs to pay him for it if that's what he's gonna do."

"Yeah, he'd need the weight of a badge on his chest to get answers, but he can't fight his way out of a paper bag on his best day," Quinn put in. "But he does have a good head when he keeps his heart out of it."

June 1978

Carnival Ride

Holy Redeemer's carnival was in full swing. Rides ringed the fences of the parking lot bordering 95th Street. The sounds of controlled fear mixed with laughter echoed everywhere.

Jimmy Conklin was running the Tilt-A-Whirl, which meant that Dillon Whelan didn't need any tickets. Jimmy knew that even in a crowd this large, there were always times when the ride would have empty seats.

The girl had her hood pulled up and tied tight around her face even though it was a summer night. Only the old and the dead were cold on a night like this, but she needed to keep her locks hidden.

Dillon hugged her close as they ran toward the open Tilt-A-Whirl. Jimmy pretended to take a ticket from them, winking as he lowered the bar across their laps. She giggled as Dillon's hand slipped around her ribs to cup her breast. They were tingling like when she had hit puberty. She moaned loud enough for him to hear her. He smiled and squeezed harder. She reached up and kissed his neck. As the ride started spinning, they stroked and groped one another, kissing deeply. She didn't know if she was dizzy from the excitement of his touch or the motion of the ride.

When the car came to a stop, Dillon didn't. Parents hurried their kids along, diverting their attention from the bad example of teenage necking. Jimmy ran over to break up the party.

"Hey, Dillon, wanna get a room so I can keep my job?"

Dillon pulled away from the girl's mouth, looking up at Jimmy with a smirk.

"Give me a break, Jimmy. This is some sweet stuff. Let us ride one more time and we'll be out of your life for the night."

"All right, but wait until the ride starts before you shoot your load on the seat, will ya?"

Dillon laughed as he squeezed her breast, making the noise of a honking clown's horn. Jimmy spun the car around so that they were facing the hedge-covered fence. Seeing that they had a modicum of privacy, Dillon stepped up his fondling by sliding his hand underneath her tunic. He was happy to find that she had worn a pair of pants with a convenient split in the crotch. As the other riders loaded into their cars, he snaked his fingers into her and felt her shiver in his arms.

"My little girl scout. Always prepared," he told her through hungry kisses.

"My boy scout, always ready," she whispered as the ride began to build momentum.

The shrieks of the other riders covered her squeals. When the ride stopped, she pulled quickly away from Dillon. She didn't want to get Jimmy in trouble. She pushed up the lap bar, jumped out of the car, and pranced to the exit. Stopping short, she turned to see if he was chasing her. He yelled after her, pushing at his tumescent crotch with one hand and pointing to it with the other.

The girl strutted away with a seductive sway to her hips. Several people exiting the ride gave him dirty looks, which made him feel even more excited. Dillon stepped off the ride, laughing as he adjusted himself in his tight black jeans. As she passed Jimmy, the hood fell off, revealing her identity. Smiling, she blew him a mischievous kiss before continuing down the path.

As Dillon passed through the gate to follow her, Jimmy grabbed him by the bicep and stopped him. With eyebrows knitted and nostrils flaring above his tight lips, he hissed, "I thought it was your wife with you, Dude."

"Naw, I wanted to have some fun."

"Dillon, you need to leave that girl alone. You have a steady piece now; one you can get every night of the week and twice on Sunday. Why don't you give the rest of us guys a chance?"

Dillon wanted to respond to Jimmy, but he didn't. He knew Jimmy's chances with his girl were the same as a snowball's chance in hell, but he wasn't going to be the one to say it. Their eyes locked in contempt, but Jimmy released Dillon's arm with a shove.

Dillon shrugged and followed Lee to the parking lot.

Friday, 20 Oct. 1978, 15:51

The McAuley Girls Get Questioned

Bette Wilson was pensive, and Phyllis White panicky as Tony drove them from the hospital to the office on Cottage Grove. Once they crossed the Rock Island commuter train tracks, they were in foreign territory for Phyllis.

Now, as they walked through the halls with Rachael in the lead, Phyllis was on the verge of hysteria. She'd never been in a police station before. Although the old building where the detectives worked was no longer used as a district, the ambience of jail was still there. The woodwork was darkened by age and gouged by use. The walls were painted the same green as the public schools built in the early 1900s, a telltale sign that it had been built with the city's money. The dark brown linoleum floor was polished to a reflective shine. The furniture, thick and heavy, had been made for long, hard use. Once you passed through the thick wooden doors, the place smelled of coffee, cigarettes, after shave, and fear.

Everywhere you looked were men in states of anger, seriousness, or dread. Not a happy face in the crowd. Through the open doors, men handcuffed to big iron rings in the wall, waiting to be questioned or taken to jail were visible.

The detectives walked like gunslingers from an old Western, their guns riding tight against their bodies in dark leather laced through their belts or in shoulder holsters with straps that crisscrossed the backs of their shirts. An occasional female office worker broke up the select fraternity, along with a few uniformed cops.

Everything about the place made Phyllis nervous. She

reached out and grabbed Bette's strong hand as Tony led them up the stairs, looking for an open interrogation room on the second floor.

When she was finally ushered into a room, the frightened girl retreated to the chair farthest from the door. Bette followed her, dragging a loose chair behind her. Once the door was closed, Rachael began the questioning.

"Thank you both for coming to help us. We need information about Lee Nabb to solve her murder and find her killer. You want that too, right?" she asked in as solicitous tone she could muster.

Both girls nodded, but neither spoke. Tony gave them Styrofoam cups of water to drink while Rachael opened her notepad.

Addressing Bette, Rachael cut to the chase.

"So tell me, Betty, when was the last time you saw Lee Nabb?"

"It's pronounced 'Bette,' like the singer, 'Bette Midler,' not 'Betty,'" she corrected her. "And I haven't seen Lee to actually talk to her since the hospital gave the candy stripers a bowling party at Bleeker's a few weeks ago."

"Exactly how long ago was that?" Rachael returned.

"About a month ago now. It was the first Sunday, wasn't it Phyllis?"

Phyllis nodded in agreement.

"I've seen her car around, but it doesn't really matter," Bette volunteered. "But it wasn't always her driving the little green thing. The boys from her father's garage drove it too."

Again, Phyllis's head bobbed in agreement as she appeared to take her cue from Bette. Rachael made a note of it.

"Did either of you socialize with her?"

Bette chimed in quickly. "Not really, ma'am. She hung around with the crowd from Morgan Park High School mostly. We're both Mother McAuley girls."

Still, not a word came out of Phyllis's mouth, but she

seemed to want to say something. Rachael continued the line of general questioning, hoping to draw Phyllis out of her shell with the innocuous queries.

"Are both of you girls still in school?"

"We certainly are," Bette spoke up proudly. "Phyllis goes to Moraine Valley, and I'm at Saint Xavier."

"What about Lee? Was she taking classes anywhere to your knowledge?" asked Rachael, hoping that the answer would come out of Phyllis's mouth.

"No," Bette said flatly, teetering between boredom and annoyance. "She didn't have the money to go anywhere. She had to help her mother. They were deep in debt."

Tony was watching them. Phyllis was holding onto Bette's hand for dear life. It made him wonder if it was for more than just security. As Rachael asked more questions, Phyllis appeared to calm down, but she didn't let go of Bette's hand.

"Did you know any of her boyfriends?" Rachael asked.

"Most of the boys we know are from Brother Rice or Marist High School," Bette answered.

"I take that to mean no," Rachael said with an emphatic nod of her head. "She didn't talk about any guys with you?"

"She didn't talk much," Bette said. "But from the phone calls she got, what I *do* know is, that Mikey was her puppy dog. He was so in love with her that it was sickening. He lives somewhere around the garage down on Kedzie, but it's Dillon who she's in love with. They broke up early in their senior year. She never said why, but I know she's still after him. I'm sorry but I don't know his last name or where he lives."

"That's okay," Rachael said. "Did she have a particular place where she liked to hang out?"

"With the Morgan Parkers probably, but where, I'm not sure."

"Did you know any of her other friends? Other girls she talked to?" Rachael inquired.

Again, it was Bette who answered. "The only one we

know is Cara O'Toole. She used to be in Irish dance with us but, we lost track of her when she transferred to Morgan Park in her junior year."

"Does Cara work at the hospital?" Rachael asked, hoping the line of questioning would draw Phyllis into the conversation.

"Oh no. She's married now, with babies to raise already. Got pregnant the first time she had sex, too, or so I heard. My mother always said public school boys were full of germs," Bette giggled. "Guess she was right."

Rachael wrote the word "foe" next to Bette's name. So far, these girls weren't adding much to the case.

"Okay. Let's go back to Lee. Do you know whether she was stealing from the hospital, or dealing drugs?" Rachael asked point blank.

"If she was, she was a terrible at it. She barely kept that hunk of junk of hers going. Dope dealers drive new sports cars, not ones pieced together from the scrap yard."

"Do you think she might've been hiding something?"

"No," Bette snapped. "She was an open book. Everything she felt showed on her face. She couldn't lie for squat. Her baby blue eyes would give her away."

"Nothing to hide in her life that you know of? No one she owed money to?" Rachael asked, trying to shake loose some little known fact.

"Lee may have had a few problems, but I wasn't her confessor," Bette said.

Tony had had enough of Bette's attitude and flip answers. He moved to sit on the side of the desk closest to Phyllis, who cowered under his glance. She peeked at him and then cast her eyes at her feet. Bette narrowed her eyes at him. He gave Bette a quick reassuring wink before he started in on Phyllis.

"Phyllis, it's okay," he said in a soothing voice. "We understand that none of this is your fault. But we really need your help, even though you had absolutely nothing to do with

Lee's death."

She nodded in agreement, biting her bottom lip.

He touched her forearm lightly.

Seeking an answer in Rachael's expression, she detected a slight smile. Though Rachael had no idea what Tony was up to, she wouldn't negate his actions in any way.

Phyllis turned towards Tony.

"Now, close your eyes," he told her. She gave Bette a quick glance as if seeking her approval, as Tony clarified his intentions. "It'll be okay. We're all friends here. And Detective Culpepper and Bette won't leave the room. Okay?"

"Okay," she whispered weakly.

"See, it's not so hard," Tony purred, "give yourself a moment to relax. Take a nice breath. It'll clear the clouds from your memory. There. Keep your eyes closed until I tell you to open them."

Bette and Rachael watched, fascinated. Tony commanded the entire room, talking slowly, calmly. He covered Phyllis's wrist with his palm, curling his fingers around her arm, pressing ever so slightly.

"Very good, Phyllis. Now, all the clouds are gone. You'll be able to answer questions easily. When I remove my hand, you'll open your eyes. Even with your eyes open, you'll be able to see the answers to the questions in your mind's eye. Understood?"

"Yes, Detective Breese," she answered in a strong voice that amazed Rachael and Bette. "I understand completely."

"Now Phyllis, please open your eyes."

As she opened them, he pulled his hand away and asked Phyllis to tell him about the last time she saw Lee.

"It was the day of the candy striper's Annual Luncheon. It was Sunday, October 1st. I was very excited because Hospital Administration asked our department to set up the tables and handle the gifts, so it would be a surprise for the little 'candies.' We were being paid four hours of double time, no matter what. Lee was there. She arrived only a few minutes late and she stayed for about an hour and forty-five minutes. She pushed hard and worked super-fast. By the time the decorations were done and the gift table was set up, she'd disappeared. I'm sure she was using us for an alibi. I haven't seen her since."

Tony not only had gotten her to talk, he got her to deliver a speech. Then the "trick" seemed to be working on Bette, too. She started talking without being asked. Rachael was impressed.

"We were all happy to go and help with the party, except for Lee. We only had to blow up some balloons, and string up some crepe paper. Then we got to bowl a line or two, have free beer, eat, and have fun. Lee seemed pissed that we were cutting in on her off time…."

"Bette, you shouldn't be mad at Lee. She was sick that day. I heard her in the ladies room. She was upchucking a lot," Phyllis admonished her.

"Why should I be nice about her having a hangover? She jammed me up plenty of times. Do you know how many weekends I've had to work for her?"

While the girls bickered, ignoring the detectives, Tony listened and watched, pencil poised, waiting for something significant to drop.

"You shouldn't speak ill of the dead, Bette. It isn't nice," Phyllis said.

She shut down when Bette shot her a withering glance. At that point, Rachael decided to insinuate herself into the interrogation to keep the flood gates open.

"Phyllis, what do you think made her throw up?" she asked.

"I'm not entirely sure. She hadn't eaten anything, so I don't think it was a hangover…"

"She was either hung over or out screwing around. Wasn't that always the way, with girls like her?" Bette said.

Tony and Rachael inferred that Bette was a party girl too, but she was proud that she managed her drinking and carousing well, so it didn't interfere with her working. Rachael continued to focus her attention on Phyllis.

"Do you know who any of her boyfriends were?"

The two girls stared at each other; then Phyllis answered.

"Nope, she was pretty quiet about her lovers," Bette said highhandedly. "But there was talk about an intern and a pharmacy guy buzzing around her."

"Bette! You don't know that to be true!" Phyllis blurted out.

Bette shot her a dirty look.

"Okay, Bette, so what do you think made Lee late so often?" Rachael asked.

"Like I said, she was out with a guy."

"Did you ever see anybody drop her off or pick her up after work?"

"There's always a car waiting at the main door, no matter how late it is. But when I'm going in, she would still be in the office. Some of the men were waiting for nurses, too. Lots of the women get picked up. Being alone at night scares them."

Rachael glanced at Bette; she wasn't one who shied away from the dark of night. She was sizing up Tony, eyeing his hair, and checking out his muscles through the fabric of his shirt when she thought no one was looking.

"And you didn't recognize any of them as her friends?"

"Sorry ma'am. Most of the time I was busy trying to beat the time clock. I really didn't notice."

"Did Lee ever ask you to work in her place, Phyllis?" Rachael asked.

"No ma'am. I mostly work third shift. When I'd come in to relieve Lee, lots of times she'd already left. She was supposed to stay to give me turnover notes, but she would leave me a bin full of reports to be keyed in or a messed-up census that had to be fixed."

"Messed-up censuses?" Rachael asked.

"The hospital censuses. We control what rooms the patients are assigned. If you have two male patients in the ER needing beds and two females alone in different rooms, you need to move them together, so the males can be housed in one of the vacated rooms. Sometimes she would put the patients in the wrong places, mix the genders, overcrowd a ward room, or shift all the male beds to one floor."

"Why would she do that?" Rachael inquired.

"I don't know," Phyllis said, looking down at her shoes. She knew, but she wasn't going to tell, Rachael thought.

Bette chimed in. "Because she didn't have time to do it right or wanted to vacate the upper floor. Oldest trick in the book, really. Dana teaches us to clear the upper floors as much as possible because that's where the private rooms are. Insurance companies don't like to pay for private rooms, so we keep try to keep them empty. They're for overflow, special cases, or isolation. Some nights, doctors will come to you and pay to have the penthouse cleared. That's what they call it. They like to sneak up there to sleep, with or without company. Lee would too. She'd have boys sneak in."

"Do you know this for a fact?" Rachael asked, looking at Phyllis for her reaction.

The shy girl bowed her head. She knew it too, but she apparently was trying to salvage Lee's reputation.

"Yes," Bette answered. "The guards caught her a couple of times. They were nice to her because of her mom. They like her mom. She's very sweet. But, they told Dana."

Rachael squinted at Tony. She had given up on getting anything useful out of these two.

"Ladies, you've been very helpful. Give us a few moments to check with our boss, and we'll take you back to the hospital," Tony said.

The girls sipped their water, warm by now, and waited. Tony and Rachael left the room, shut the door behind them and walked a few doors down the hallway to confer.

"Where the hell did the 'laying on of the hands' trick come from, Tony?"

"It's not a 'trick,' it's a certified psychological technique."

"Seriously?" Rachael asked.

"It's straight from Sigmund Freud's 'Selected Papers on Hysteria.' I read 'The Case History of Miss Lucie R' last night. Freud used it on patients who were resistant to hypnotism, so I decided to try it. I think it works as well today as it did back in 1892...."

"You were up reading last night?" Rachael quipped. "The women of Tony's world must be on strike."

"I don't go out every night. I have to have time to maintain myself," he huffed.

With a shake of her head and a roll of her eyes, Rachael sighed.

"Let's get these poor girls out of here. They didn't add a thing of value to the case. I think it would be better for their psyches to take them down the back stairs to the parking lot, don't you?"

"Ah, you never know," Tony grinned. "This little trip to the other side of the world might keep them out of trouble for a long time. Did you see the size of Phyllis's eyes when we walked her past the old lockup? I don't think she'll throw a gum wrapper on the sidewalk from now on."

October 1978

A Domestic Disturbance

Trains thundering by the tiny apartment seldom awakened them anymore. The babies became immune to the engines' roar and the clacks of the rails so close to their bassinettes. Cara was too tired after a day tending them, and Dillon was simply exhausted from working two jobs. They slept back to back, like strangers, on the hand-me-down bed they got from his Aunt Megan.

In the apartment buildings next to the cemetery, people made noises all times of the day and night. Each apartment was so close to its neighbor that you felt the noises before you heard them. If it wasn't the people, it was the trains. If it wasn't the train, it was the traffic on 111th Street, the fire trucks, the ambulance or the police. Car tires screeched on the rails. When pickup trucks crossed the tracks, their contents clunked, rumbled, or banged.

Once a week, when the night finally quieted down, the garbage trucks would rumble in, disturbing sleep with the men clanging cans and whistling to the driver to stop. Cara wasn't used to this. It wasn't at all like where she'd grown up: in tame, tidy Beverly, where the only train intersecting the neighborhood was the regularly scheduled Rock Island commuter line. It was loud, but it genteelly shut down operations after midnight. Anyone who was anyone, was home by then. If not, they'd stay in a hotel room in the Loop or spring for a cab ride. The good citizens of the neighborhood expected to sleep through the night without interruption. Doctors, lawyers, businessmen, and judges had to be bright-eyed and bushy-tailed to keep the city running smoothly.

Where Cara lived now wasn't even a good part of Mount Greenwood. It was scarcely twenty feet beyond the tracks, where the rent was dirt cheap because the grass of the graves was the front yard. The two yellow brick apartment buildings looked like undersized no-tell motels, where rooms rented by the hour, complete with the smell of sex and alcohol. This wasn't the kind of place Cara's mother had expected her daughter to end up living. Not that she would set her foot on the few feet of gravel that served as a sidewalk, parking space, and playground.

Several trains passed every night; most blowing their horns for the 111th street crossing while they passed through the golf course before reaching the cemetery. This deep into the night, some would forego the warning blasts, regardless of the regulations. Tonight, was different, though. The engineer lay hard on the horn, frantic blasts, long and loud, starting several blocks before the crossing. From the cab of the locomotive, he could see something on the tracks, an object that he knew he couldn't stop the heavy load from hitting unless it got out of the way fast. He prayed that the horn would awaken whoever was in the stalled vehicle.

The long howling blasts, the rumbling breaks, and the shifting load so close to their tiny apartment, nearly dumped Cara and Dillon out of their bed. The apartment's windows rattled and the doors shook. The screeching of the steel wheels with air brakes hissing and bells clanging were loud enough to rouse the dead in the cemetery across the right of way. The final howling blast sounded as the engine pulled even with their window.

Seconds later, colliding with a sickening crunch of metal on metal, the train crashed into an old rusty pickup, shoving it far down the rails. When it finally came to a stop, the badly mangled truck tumbled down the slight slope of the tracks, to rest on the chain link fence of Mount Olivet Cemetery.

"You hit my truck, you stupid son of a bitch!" hollered the driver from the pavement of the intersection, "You hit my fucking truck!"

The drunken driver jumped up and down near the crossing, screaming. Further down the tracks, a head popped out of the train's high window as air breaks hissed and couplings groaned.

"Your truck?" shouted the exasperated engineer "Anybody in it?"

"No asshole. Nobody's in the truck! But look at what you did to it!"

The train was blocking 111th Street with gondola cars piled high with coal. They were nearly done for the night—almost in their bunks in the caboose. A few more miles and it would have been over. Now, the engineer and the crew would be up for hours writing reports, answering stupid questions, and pissing in cups.

"I didn't park on working railroad tracks, moron. And don't call me an asshole again."

The engineer pulled his head back in, snatching the radio's mike off its hook. Barking into it, he alerted the control tower at the Harvey Yard, letting them know what had happened. Flopping levers and punching buttons, he put the trio of SD45 engines into a low idle. Even though the yard was close, it would be quite a while before a supervisor got to the accident site to inspect the damage.

"I'll call you asshole if I want to, you blind sack of shit!" hollered the drunk. His whiskey-stoked courage began to wane as he looked down the tracks. A single light could be seen swinging slightly as the switchman made the long walk from caboose towards the engine.

The drunk ran frantically to the two apartment buildings nestled along the tracks. He was angry. He needed help. He started knocking on the doors of the first-floor apartments yelling like a fiend.

“Help me, help me! The train hit my truck! Let me in. Call the police!!”

Each door he banged on stayed firmly shut, but curtains moved enough for the residents to see that it wasn’t someone they knew. While the drunk banged on the last door, above him hovered Dillon, pissed off and clad only in his boxer shorts. Dark curls piled atop his head, stubble shadowing his face, with his furry chest and legs exposed, he looked like a small bear. Grabbing the railing of the balcony, he leaned over to reason with the drunk.

“Pipe down,” he hissed. “We called the cops already. They’re on the way. I got two babies up here sleeping, so calm down before you wake them up.”

“Pipe down, my ass! Did you see what that asshole did to my truck? He killed it! He hit it, then he pushed it down the tracks!”

“I asked you nice to pipe down,” Dillon growled, his eyes narrowed, nostrils flaring.“I told you the cops are coming. Now, shut the fuck up or I’m gonna come down and shut you up.”

Cara stood in the open doorway, holding the bottom of her thin white nightgown in one hand, her fearful green eyes wide. She was waiting for Dillon to run down the wrought iron stairs to attack the drunk, knowing they didn’t have the money to get him out of jail if he did. She bent nearly in half, stretching to grab at the over washed boxers, hoping to pull him back into the apartment.

“Dillon, honey, come back. He’ll quiet down in a minute. The cops’ll be here by then. Come on back in.”

Dillon twisted around, glaring at her, the frail overly pampered girl he was stuck with. With her long red hair pulled back and braided tightly, the white sack nightgown matched her ghostly white skin, reminding him of an albino fawn he’d seen abandoned in the woods. She never knew the real world until she married him. Now he had to put up with her timidity. What did she know about angry drunks?

Dillon knew all too well the heart of a drunk. Most of his family were drunks or functional alcoholics, so if he didn't stand his ground, the guy would continue his banging and shouting. He also knew if the guy got to his door, he would break his face for waking up his babies.

"Cara, take your sorry ass back to bed," he ordered, wounding her with his foul words and angry look. Spinning back to the railing, he was ready to lunge at the drunk, but police sirens started converging on the crossing.

The cacophony proved to be too much for the twins' ears. They awoke startled, crying in panic. The drunk heard them. Fearing the enraged look on Dillon's face, he went running towards a fire truck, yelling and waving his arms.

When Dillon turned to go back to the apartment, Cara stood frozen at the doorway. They stood, eyes locked as baby cries turned into screeches. When she made no move to go to them, he pushed past her growling, "What kind of mother are you?"

She turned to watch his back as he went into their bedroom. She had to shut the gaping front door to sit in the beat-up nursing chair by the window. She didn't know what kind of mother she was at four A.M. She had been stunned by everything that was happening. Now Dillon was yelling at her, making her respond in slow motion, driving her into a quagmire of self-doubt.

The neighbors from the apartments were slowly coming out to check out the ruckus, survey the damage, and add their loud voices to the din. Cara finally understood what her mother had meant about the "other" side of the tracks. It was where things were loud and alive until the wee hours of the morning. This was where people argued then made loud love behind paper-thin walls. Where they shared their personal business on phones near open windows for all to hear. Where they honked horns at any time of day or night, blared radios, and sang along without a hint of shame. It was a constant commotion, a brash, annoying, never-ending din.

The babies kept crying, getting louder and more fearful. Whatever Dillon was doing, it wasn't helping. She wanted to go in there, take one in her arms and rock it gently until it stopped the crying, but she didn't dare interfere with Dillon.

If she did something different to one, he would claim she was unbalancing them. He believed they had to have the same treatment, or they would grow up to be serial killers or mental defectives. When he was around she was careful to do the exact same thing with them both, even if she knew it was fruitless. He would claim that she hadn't done it well enough or soon enough. To his mind, it wasn't possible for each baby to have her own personality at this stage of their life. He didn't know anything about raising babies; he knew how to fight her about everything.

He fought her about their names. "Hanna" and "Lorna" it had to be, both ending in "a", both having two syllables, and both being old Irish. She'd wanted Caitlin for her baby. She didn't care what he named his, but by them being twins, he knew that they had to be yoked together in everything. When she was pregnant, she'd been too tired to fight back. Now she was too tired to fight about anything.

She heard the crying, but she sat there, staring out into the side of a coal car. Usually it was pitch dark, with no lights visible for nearly half a mile in front of them. The cemetery was a wide dark expanse stretching to the back end of another dark expanse, the Garfield Ridge Country Club. For Cara, the blackness was comforting, almost hypnotic. She was about to slip into sleep when Dillon shook her. He was fully dressed in jeans, work boots, black tee shirt, and leather jacket. His eyes flashed with anger.

"Cara, get your ass up and go tend to those babies! I thought you were heating formula in the kitchen. What kind of damn mother are you? Falling asleep in a chair!"

"Me? What kind of damn father are you?" she spat out

angrily, seeing that he had taken the time to get dressed but didn't comfort his children. "I bet you didn't even pick up one of those babies or put a pacifier in their mouths!"

"That's your job, you silly bitch. You're supposed to make them happy. If I was supposed to do it, I'd be the one with the tits."

"You got nipples. Does it mean you should do half the work?"

He glared at her, seething. How dare she turn his words against him? He grabbed her by one of her breasts, using it to roughly pull her close. She cried out, leaping out of the chair. She could taste his anger.

"Oh, because you got empty tits, you think you don't have to take care of them, huh?"

He gave it another vicious twist, making tears fly from of her eyes. He released her with a push to her throat, making her fall backwards into the chair.

"Get your lazy ass in there, right now!" he shouted.

Under any other circumstances, the neighbors might have called the police, but this night, everyone was down at the tracks. The mini circus would go on for some time, at least until the truck was towed off the tracks and all the equipment was returned to their places, waiting for the next catastrophe.

Dillon stormed out of the apartment. She could hear him stomp down the stairs, slam his truck door, and pull away. When his tires hit the alley's pavement, he burned rubber, gunning the engine so hard it whined. She didn't care where he was going. She was glad he was gone. She went into the bedroom to gather up her two red-faced babies.

Picking up Hanna first, she tucked her into her side, feeling her kicks pummel the bruised breast. Tears welled in Cara's eyes as she transferred the baby to the double bed with a gentle rocking motion, putting a pacifier in her tiny mouth. Hanna responded immediately, her whimpers slowing to a hiccup. Cara turned to get Lorna from her bassinette. She was a mass of flailing arms and legs, mouth quivering with each yelp. Cara put her in the same crook where she'd put Hanna, letting the pummeling be her punishment for being a bad mother.

With both babies on her bed, and pacifiers in their mouths, she went to get the formula that had warmed on the stove. Hanna started to drift off immediately while Lorna wiped at her face drowsily. Within moments, they were both back to sleep. Cara wondered why Dillon couldn't have done this for her. It was so simple.

She picked up one baby at a time, gently placing each one back in their bassinettes. Looking at the squared digital numbers on the clock radio, she went to make Dillon's lunch. Four fifteen A.M. was only half an hour early for her chores, but better safe than sorry. If he had bruised her for letting the babies cry, God only knew what he would to do if she didn't have his sack lunch ready when he came back. They were out of beer, so she expected he would be back from the all night A&P up on 95th and Pulaski at any moment.

As she made his two baloney sandwiches, Cara sobbed loudly. Moving like a robot, she turned off the burner, screwed on the bottles' nipples, tested the milk on her wrist, and went into the prison of the bedroom, to tend to her charges. Once both tiny mouths were full, the only sound in the room was Cara's continued sniffling. How could she have gotten here?

A few blocks away, Dillon was asking himself a similar question, as he tiptoed through the narrow gangway to the back of the Nabb house. He was sure that the same train wreck had awakened Lee; she only lived a few blocks north, down the same set of tracks. He hoped her mother was at the hospital on third shift. But if she wasn't, he still had a plan. Lee could crawl out the window, and shimmy down the big tree at the side of the house. Then he would take her the few blocks over to the Country Club parking lot off California. Making love in the bed of his truck under the stars would be good. He could drop her off back at her house and still make it back home to pick up his lunch before getting to work on time.

He had a pocket full of pebbles to launch at her window. She was a light sleeper, so he wasn't surprised when the second one made the purple curtain move. He threw another stone, for good measure.

She raised the window slowly. He smiled and blew her a kiss. She caught it with the turn of her head, pretending it landed on her left cheek. Returning the kiss, she signaled, "I'm coming down."

He nodded and headed back to his truck. Mother was home, or else she would have let him in the back door. But this would be better. He didn't have to linger too long.

He put the little pickup in neutral, pushed it out of the parking space and a couple of doors down the street. Old Lady Malloy was deaf as a post, so a truck starting in front of her house would cause no suspicion.

In a twinkle, Lee was slipping into the passenger seat, reaching to kiss Dillon's cheek.

"How'd you sneak out?" she asked as they drove away.

"That stupid bum stuck on the tracks at 111th was out of his truck beating on doors after the train smashed him. Woke up everyone in the building. Then the babies were wailing, and Cara walked around in a trance, so I put my clothes on and left. She probably thinks I'm doing a beer run. I knew all those air breaks and horns would wake you up, so I came down here for some good loving."

Lee smiled, cuddling up under his arm, as they pulled off 103rd Street, bound for the Garfield Ridge Country Club's outdoor motel. They both hoped no one else had the same idea to go to the tiny secluded spot between the clubhouse, the parking lot, and the smart homes that surrounded the island of green.

Saturday, 21 Oct. 1978, 09:56

An Open-and-Shut Case

"Damn it, Rach, this case is about to go stone cold. We're as lost in the woods as that damn sports car was," said Tony, lacing his fingers together behind his head to think. Rachael started listing the facts.

"From the song, she was messing with a married man."

"Which narrows it down to 20 or 30 thousand men in the area, depending on whether we include Oak Lawn, Evergreen Park, and Alsip," retorted Tony without moving.

"We know that the car and the body were separated," Rachael said.

"Yeah, but regardless of the distance, that poor girl never got away from 107th Street, except for her ride to Mount Trashmore," said Tony wistfully.

"From womb to tomb, a 107th Street girl," Rachael sighed.

"I don't think any of those people at the hospital were involved enough in her life to kill her," Tony said as he leaned forward to plant his elbows on the desktop.

"You're right. That's what made me rule them out," Rachael said, tapping her pad with the tip of her pen.

"And those carnival guys," Tony said, shaking his head. "They were a dead end too; excuse the pun. I thought the one living with his mother might be a Norman Bates-type from 'Psycho,' but they were so genuinely loving and almost disgustingly happy."

"They were cute," Rachael remarked, sinking into a thoughtful silence.

"Yo, Culpepper," Detective Cooper barked from across the room. "Ya got a fax coming through from Crime Lab."

Roused from a moment of deep contemplation, she walked over to where he was standing.

"Thanks, Coop," she said stopping next to him.

"Say, Culpepper, where did you get those donuts the other day? They were damn tasty. I was thinking about buying another box for the office—especially since they deliver."

"Good idea, Coop," Rachael smiled as her mind reverted into revenge mode. "Be sure to ask for Blake, the manager. Tell him you don't want the police discount, you want free delivery."

She smiled all the way back to her desk, knowing that Blake would find out how badly his prank had backfired.

The crime lab's full report confirmed what they already knew. Under ordinary circumstances, this information would have been useful, but so late in the case, it was procedural, something to be filed away in the murder book and forgotten.

Rachael adjusted her shoulder harness as she read it, her snub-nosed revolver rubbing her inner arm. Before she could adjust it, she noticed something curious listed among the items found in Lee's car.

She took the report to Tony, who stood by a window.

"There's something odd in this report," she said.

Tony glanced at it, then at Rachael, searching her face for an explanation.

"Take a good look. I need to know if I'm off base. I saw something that stopped me dead in my tracks."

Tony started to read the report aloud. The first part described Leivald Nabb, her injuries, and cause of death. She had been hit in the back of the head—hard enough for a tiny piece of bone fragment to break off her skull and lodge in her brainstem, ceasing all autonomic functions. In laymen's terms, it had stopped her breathing. There were no signs of sexual trauma, but she was pregnant.

"Cassette tapes, typical; tools, not unexpected; used drinking cups, not surprising; last year's calendar book, useless most likely," Tony said.

Rachael nodded in agreement, but said nothing.

"They found a man's handkerchief in her hand, embordered in red thread with TOT above the date March 16, 1973."

"That's weird. Who the hell would put that on a hanky?" Tony asked.

"I think I know what it means, but I want you to look at the rest of the report," she said.

"Okay. I'll play along," he said.

"Miscellaneous clothing items; sweatshirt, bra, underpants…."

He raised his eyebrows at the number of discarded panties, searching Rachael's face to see whether he had discovered what she was talking about. She shook her head.

"Keep reading."

"Makeup bag, two blouses, handkerchief, leggings, shoes. This girl was either trying out to be a model, or she was having a lot of sleepover sex that her mother didn't know about."

"Yeah, she kept everything behind the seat of her sports car. But you still haven't noticed it," Rachael said.

"She had an MG, not a very big car. How much more could there be?" he griped, tiring of the game, but if Rachael needed him to play, he'd go along. His eyes went back to the paper.

"Into the trunk we go. Assorted nuts, bolts and screws, a couple of cans of oil, transmission fluid, antifreeze, windshield scraper and brush, tire iron, spare—okay—we're running out of car here," he sighed. "Miscellaneous is all that's left. A single gold hoop earring, no prints; broken silver bracelet, also no prints; pink plastic hair combs, several buttons, one large black, one small white." Tony locked eyes with her. She tilted her head, raising an eyebrow.

"One brass CFD uniform button with crossed horns. Jeez,

Rachael. A Chicago Fire Department button from a dress uniform? Holy shit! The only one she knew who worked for the Fire Department is…."

"Lieutenant Timothy O'Toole," Rachael stated. "Also known as TOT."

"She was having an affair with Cara's dad?" he asked.

"The way they work their shifts, he's got plenty free time on his hands. He's a silent partner funneling money into the garage. He said it was for Dillon, Cara, and the twins, but who knows? It could be a cover story. Let's pull his personnel jacket and see what day he got is promotion to Lieutenant. If it's the same, he's the father, and we have our motive."

Tony put the report on the desk, shaking his head. "To turn this case on a button and a damned old-fashioned hanky—I'll be damned. He didn't seem the type to go for young girls…."

Rachael phoned City Hall for the personnel records. They promised to fax the information within an hour. She decided to go the bathroom to adjust her shoulder holster. Before she could get into the hall, Detective Dubeck stopped her.

"How you doing, Rachael? How's your slasher case coming along?"

"Pretty good." she said.

"What's it like working with Tony?"

"Good. He's a good guy."

"If you decide to change horses," he said with a sly smile, "you can always work with me. As a matter of fact, anytime you need anything, you can depend on me."

His statement stunned her. If Dubeck was saying what Rachael thought he was saying, she wanted to know what had brought it on. She didn't like the feel of it.

"Thanks, Dubeck," she said, excusing herself to head to the washroom.

Standing in front of the mirror, she adjusted the gun butt, promising that she wouldn't wear it again. The gun's grip was too short, and the leather straps pulled in too deep. The holster was built for a long barrel 32, not a snub nose revolver.

"So, how's the case going?" asked one of the office clerks standing at the mirror. "I saw the prelim crime lab report. Really gruesome."

"We're getting close to an arrest," Rachael replied. "Waiting for a couple of pieces of information, and it'll all fall into place."

"Good. You get the bastard. Downright creepy to have someone that mad walking around."

"Don't you think he had aimed all his anger at the victim?" Rachael asked.

The clerk stopped putting her makeup on and turned towards Rachael with a look of shock.

"Don't care if he did. A sicko like that needs to be in jail. I'm no shrink, but he might get mad at woman and do it all over again. What you bet the poor girl didn't know what she did to piss him off."

"Probably didn't," Rachael replied, adjusting the holster strap, "We probably won't know, either."

"Let me know when you get him, Detective. This one's giving me nightmares."

She tossed her lipstick and mascara into a little careworn pouch. Tugging at her ruffle front blouse, she took a last look in the mirror. Smiling, she headed out the door, with a flick of her hair and a swish of her hips.

When Rachael returned to the office, Tony sat smiling. He broke the news. "I got the fax fresh off the machine, and guess what?"

"Dead end?" Rachael asked.

"Not at all. A classic open-and-shut case."

"We have a match for Timothy O'Toole of the fire house at 76th and Pulaski?" Rachael asked.

"Indeed, we do," Tony said. "Sergeant Burke says with these two pieces—the button and the hanky—the States Attorney says go pick him up for the murder of Leivald Nabb.

Further, according to the fax, he should be there on a 24-hour shift now."

"Right across the street from Daley Junior College," Rachael said. "I guess he was hitting on the young buxom lasses trying to get an education…."

"Bogan High School's a straight shot down Pulaski Road," Tony quipped. "What you bet he's sitting out on the apron of the station right now?"

"Not for long," Rachael said tossing Tony the car keys. She wanted to be the first one out the car, to put the cuffs on Lieutenant O'Toole for trying to make a fool of her over donuts and coffee.

October 1978

A Hidden Pregnancy

"Lee Whelan," called the nurse standing in the doorway leading to the exam rooms.

In a waiting room filled with young women reading and talking, it was to be expected that a name had to be called more than once before the person recognized it to be hers, but this was ridiculous.

"Whelan, Lee." The nurse was on her fourth attempt to get the patient in to see the doctor. Raising her voice, she called out one last time before she went on to the next patient.

"Whelan? Is there a Lee Whelan here?"

A blonde girl jumped up, waving her hand to the nurse.

"Here! I'm coming."

She bolted towards the open door, stumbling over several sets of feet and legs, mumbling apologies.

"I'm so sorry. I worked last night. I think I was napping when you called me the first time."

The nurse frowned as she led her down the hallway. It was so typical. She saw it every day. She didn't for one minute believe this girl had been working because of the way she was dressed. Where would they let her work in flesh-colored leggings, a big flannel shirt, and suede boots? She looked like she had been out dancing and screwing all night. She wore too much chunky jewelry, a tattered lace headband and hair that looked like she'd come straight from a hotel bed. But it wasn't her job to judge. She was there to get her vitals, start the chart, and administer the test.

"Please sit on the edge of the exam table, roll up your

sleeve, and open your mouth."

The thermometer went under the tongue, the blood pressure cuff was slid into place with chilly efficiency, and the numbers noted on the front page of the chart.

"I need a blood sample. It'll hurt a little, but I'll be quick, okay?"

The girl nodded. She was familiar with the medical procedures, but she didn't want to tell the nurse. She went along, saying as little as possible. The nurse took the girl's index finger swabbing it with alcohol and pricked it. The dots of blood went on two different test strips. Everything seemed normal, so she moved to the next stage.

"Did you bring a first-morning urine sample?" the nurse asked curtly.

"Yes, ma'am."

Digging in the big black bag, the girl retrieved a package that might've been mistaken for a lunch. She tore through the small brown paper bag, revealing a large plastic one filled with wadded up toilet paper. Nestled inside was a glass jelly jar, tightly capped to prevent spillage of the amber liquid. Smiling proudly because she hadn't made a mess of herself or her purse, she handed the jar to the nurse.

"Thank you. The doctor will be in with the results in a few minutes."

All that was left was the waiting. She looked out the window. Unlike most exam rooms, here the blinds were left open because the Plaza Professional building was the highest structure in the area. Unless a helicopter hovered outside, there were no prying eyes looking into the room. Being on the eighth floor gave a wonderful view of the tall autumn-colored treetops, generously sprinkled with conical pines which gave Evergreen Park its name. Through the leaves she could see the nearby houses, but most of the view was lush foliage stretching for miles, barely interrupted by the streets, train tracks, and alleys. She tried to find some landmark close to her house, but even as familiar as everything was, she couldn't penetrate the leafy cover. Somewhere under there he was sleeping, getting rested for the afternoon shift. She should be sleeping too, but she had to know, and this was the only appointment the doctor had open this month.

Time had passed with her sitting on the table, swinging her legs gently. The knock on the door made her jump. A tall sandy-haired doctor, who seemed only a couple of years older than she, walked through the door with a broad smile.

"Hello, Mrs. Whelan. I'm Doctor Meis. How're you feeling?"

"I'm okay, just a little tired."

"Good. Let's see what we have here."

He opened the manila folder, checking the stats the nurse recorded. Without looking at her, he began to read them aloud.

"Your blood pressure is normal, no sign of diabetes. For now, your weight is good, but you seem to be at the lower level of your height group, so you might want to start watching what you eat, so you don't slide into the next group weight wise. It's more effective to diet than it is to try to grow at this age. If you're like me, you won't be taller any time soon."

He hesitated for a moment, struggling to interpret the nurse's handwriting. When he got to the remainder of the test results, the ones from the urine sample, he continued, not knowing that the nurse had left it up to him to deliver the news.

"No signs of a urinary tract infection; no venereal disease. Which is very good for your baby. It means you shouldn't have any trouble at delivery time."

He continued to talk about how important rest and a good diet were along with prenatal care. She listened distractedly. When he was finished, she gathered her bag and prepared to leave.

"Any questions?" he asked.

She stopped only long enough to sling the purse over her shoulder.

"No. Thank you so much. I'll be back for my prenatal care."

"Tell the desk that I'd like to see you in six weeks, okay?"

"Yes, six weeks," she repeated.

She walked quickly down the hallway, and through the waiting room without stopping at the desk. Moving swiftly out of the building, she left her fake name behind.

Lee drove fast past the cute Cape Cod houses on Kedzie. She wondered why her dad hadn't bought one of the pretty little brick cottages for her and her mom instead of the wooden shack he chose by the tracks. She knew it was his taste, not her mother's. It was just like him to go for the snug little frame house. It probably reminded him of the tight hand-built dwellings of his rural German youth. If it hadn't been set on a dugout of a basement and facing the tracks, Lee would have thought it was a converted garage intended for a mother-in-law. To her mind, the best things about it were her dormer bedroom where the ceiling slanted in on two sides with one of the windows covered by the big oak tree.

Lee had so wished that Cara was open-minded enough to accept that Dillon loved them both. That way, they'd be a whole family, live together, raise the babies together, and be happy together. She'd have Cara as a sister, the twins as her nieces, Dillon's baby growing up, and Dillon as the head of the family. The rest of the world could kiss her ass. But until Cara came around, she'd have to settle for what she managed to carve out of sneak encounters, surreptitious phone calls, and stolen moments.

At the stoplight, Lee patted her belly, imagining what the fetus looked like. The nurse said that at this stage, they appeared more like seahorses than people. It was hard to understand how something so tiny made her so happy. She had a piece of Dillon all her own. It was a piece no one could take from her, no matter what.

She would raid the trash bins on the maternity floor tonight for some soiled pads to throw in the garbage at home to keep her mother from suspecting her pregnancy. Tomorrow, she was going to go to Marshall's to buy herself a waist cincher to help hide the bulge gathering between her hips. By the time she started to show, it would be too late to have an abortion. When her baby was too big to hide anymore, she'd take off the body shapers and let her belly poke out. She'd keep the identity of the father a mystery, but everyone who knew her would know who he was. Hopefully, Cara would have come around by then.

October 1978

Leivald Nabb's Final Hours

"I'm stoked, Paula!" exclaimed Lee, doing a chair dance across the blemished hospital lunchroom table. "I won a weekend for two at The Playboy Hotel in Lake Geneva!"

"That's bitchin'! They've got suites like the Pocono's Hotel, only way better. When Hugh Hefner puts a mirror on the ceiling, it's the whole ceiling, not only the part over the bed," she declared, her mousey young face belying the knowingness implied in her statement.

Lee shot her a quizzical look. "Pocono's?"

"Yeah, you know, the motel, down on Cicero at 107th."

"I know, but how'd *you* know?" Lee asked, leaning in close, inches of her long white blonde hair falling on the table.

Paula's face flushed bright pink behind her attempt at Farrah Fawcett's hairdo. She whispered, nervously pulling at the collar of her gray housekeeper's uniform.

"I ah, kinda saw some photos, umm, in Dad's magazine," she stuttered. "After my brother stole it."

"Okay," Lee said, "But who'd *you* go to the Pocono's with?"

"Nobody!" Paula huffed. "My aunt works there. I fill in sometimes. And let me tell you, it's not easy to get the shag carpet up on those walls clean."

"I bet," Lee chuckled.

"What contest was it?" Paula pouted. "I wanna enter."

"I put my name in every one of those boxes by the restaurant cashier all the time. Somebody called; left a message with my boss Dana, saying I won. So, um, Paula, do me a favor."

Paula glared across the table, waiting for Lee to drop a bomb. Lee was always asking for something.

"I need to get to the travel agency down on 107th and Western, the one with those hokey plastic palm trees full of dusty coconuts in the window. They're opening this morning to give me the tickets. Please, please, please punch out for me? Pretty please?"

Paula swallowed, scrunched her face, sighing.

"Okay, Lee, but this is the last time. I swear, one of these days you're going to get us both fired. I need this job."

"Paula, I need those tickets. If I miss getting them, they'll give them to someone else. They told Dana they'd been trying to reach me. This is my last chance. Ya know I ain't been out of Chicago since our senior class trip to Indiana Dunes. It'd be like a honeymoon."

As soon as the word "honeymoon" came out Lee's mouth, Paula's expression changed. Using the trip for a tryst was what Lee intended to do; the word "honeymoon" proved it for Paula. She didn't want to be an accessory to one of Lee's crimes of passion. Seeing the change in Paula's expression, Lee tried to cover her white lie.

"The contest people called it a honeymoon package, not me. Come on Paula, I don't have anyone to take except Mama," she pleaded.

Lee grimaced. Of all the lies she'd ever told, none of them had made her feel this queasy. Gulping hard, the sensation to vomit passed.

"I'll do it, but this is the last time, Miss Leivald Nabb! We've gotten away with this too many times; we're bound to get caught."

"This is the last time, cross my heart and hope to die. Thank you, Paula. You're an absolute pal."

Paula smiled weakly as Lee hopped up from table and rushed out of the cafeteria, leaving her tray for Paula to deal with.

6:35 A.M.

On Sundays, both the gas station and car dealership across from the travel agency were closed until noon. In this Indian summer weather, the before-dawn dog walkers and joggers were busy heading for the green strip between the cemetery and golf course, which served as a buffer to stop cars from proceeding west on 107th. Only drivers who lived in the immediate neighborhood, or the occasional stranger, would cross the broad pavement of Western Avenue. Everyone else would turn, heading for either for 111th or 103rd Streets.

Lee pulled around the corner of 107th, slipping into the alley to park near the travel agency's back door. She was early, having left the hospital thirty minutes before punch-out time. It didn't matter because it was her last night to work there ever. She'd left her badge on the boss's desk with a goodbye note before she slipped behind the wheel of "Grasshopper," her hunter green '69 MG convertible.

She fished in her purse for a cigarette. Smoking was a pleasure she'd soon forgo at the end of this pack. It'd be easy. Working in the computer center cut her down to damn near nothing anyway. As she lit up, her favorite song rang out in the familiar falsetto voice. She twisted the radio volume up.

As the last chorus ended, she could see the office lights turn on through the transom. She blew a smoke ring as she checked her makeup in the mirror. She could look like Olivia Newton John, if she wanted to. Stepping out of the car, she flicked her half-smoked cigarette into the middle of the alley, pulled her flannel shirt and wide fake leather belt down over her stretch pants and slung her bag over her left shoulder. Walking up the pavement, the rhythmic click of her new suede boots announced her arrival. Flinging open the front door of the agency with a big grin, she yelled, "H-e-l-l-o."

Brushing past a cardboard replica of the Eiffel Tower, racks of brochures on the walls, and a row of empty desks, it appeared that no one was there. Noticing that the washroom door was closed, she plopped down in a client chair to wait.

Suddenly, Lee's smile melted into a sneer.

"Damn. It's *you*. Why the hell are you here?"

"To talk with ya."

"Well, I don't want to talk to you," grunted Lee, as she hopped up from the chair.

"Ya can have the trip, if ya listen."

"You'll give me a weekend to Lake Geneva for just *listening*?" Lee asked.

"Sure. It's a paid-up voucher. Signed and sealed; no way to cancel."

Lee thought for a moment. Which did she want more: a luxury weekend, or her untarnished pride? She decided she'd polish her pride later.

"I'll listen."

The envelope was pushed under a heavy stapler on the last desk, so Lee couldn't grab it and bolt.

"Lee, I like you. Ye mayn't think so, but I do. But you've gotten sloppy. For instance, my dear, that little car of yours parked at the Miami Motel, way in the back, right next to his truck."

Lee's mouth sprung open.

"Hard to see you from the street, traffic passing so fast and all, but if a body's got a mind to look, you were there to be seen."

Lee always thought she'd be armed with an arsenal of denials if confronted, but she couldn't get a word out.

"Dear heart. There's nothing to say. I've seen it with me own two eyes. More than once, might I add. At the Midway, the Gateway, the Aloha… and the Florida, too. You even snuck to the Saratoga Motel down on 79th Street, parked all cozied up to the dirty bookstore, making it look like you were shopping for smut! You thought it was far enough away, but it wasn't. The first time, I thought it a sweet little fare-thee-well. Once more for old time's sake, but you couldn't keep those legs of yours closed. There you were: green car, red truck 'n all—over 'n over again."

"I won't apologize" Lee huffed triumphantly. "He loves me. He always has."

"Does he now? Risking home and happiness for the likes of *you*?"

"Happiness? Do you think he's happy at home? You are a fool!"

"Fool, no. I'm a fixer. I've got a solution for it all."

Lee felt the heat of hate flash behind her eyes as another wave of nausea swept through her. She gulped it down, straining to focus on the words.

"Here's what ya do. Go, use the voucher. Have fun, live it up, make a memory. Every thing's paid for. Room service, booze...you name it. There's two hundred dollars' credit at the hotel and a hundred-dollar bill in the envelope. Buy yourself something sexy, get your hair done, gas up the car. Then, when you come back, tell him it's all over. Say goodbye. For good. Then every month you stay away, and I'll give you a tidy little sum of cash. What'd ya say?"

"You think you can *pay* me to leave him?"

Lee let out a short laugh. She had never seen such a look of hatred directed towards her. Her reaction to it was instantaneous.

"Fuck you!" she spat out. "You're the reason he's not with me now! You and your snooty overbearing ass full of phony manners and Catholic morals…."

Suddenly, the woman thrust the envelope into her breasts with enough force to push her backward. Lee wanted to lunge, to hit back, but a pain deep down in her gut forced her to double over. Scuttling past her assailant, she dropped her purse. Scooping up a handkerchief lying on the middle of the desk, she held it over her mouth, keeping the vomit at bay until she burst through the restroom door. Flailing to grab the sink to steady her aim, the vomit erupted from her mouth, into the maw of the old toilet. A second wave made her knees hit the floor as she sought the bowl with both hands. Resting her forehead against the toilet seat, she didn't anticipate the blow at the base of her skull that stunned her into insensibility. The blow was so hard that, in a matter of seconds, all she felt was the darkness of death.

Thursday, 26 Oct. 1978, 10:00

A Confession

Tony and Rachael didn't know why Mrs. O'Toole had summoned them back to her house. When they rang the bell, she opened the door herself, without a sign of Mrs. Flynn, her housekeeper.

She was dressed in black pants, a V-neck pullover, and a white turtleneck. She ushered them to the dining room, where she waved them to the side of the table closest to the door. The broad wooden table was bare, making the room feel like a conference room at a law firm. Going to the opposite end, she stood behind the heavily carved chair. When they were settled, she started her litany.

"Thank you for coming. Have ye some time to spend?"

"We have time, Mrs. O'Toole," Tony said. "We haven't been assigned any new cases yet."

"And just how long will it take to get me Timothy out of the hoosegow?"

"I don't know ma'am," Rachael said. "We don't deal with that part of the system."

"After you hear what I've ta say, everything'll be set right," she said, clasping her hands prayerfully.

"We don't deal in absolution Mrs. O'Toole," said Tony, "that's something you'll have to get from the Church."

"Are ye daft man?" she lamented. "I'm telling you I'm confessin' to murder, and you're sending me off to church?"

Tony and Rachael looked at each other, positive that it was a ploy to get her husband out of jail. Rachael decided to play along.

"Let me go to the car and get my tape recorder. You can tell us everything you want, and if it appears to be true, we'll take you to the station for booking and processing."

"Go ye, get the device. I've a tale to tell."

She continued to stand, patiently waiting for Rachael to return. Tony didn't ask her anything, fearful that she might begin to spin her yarn and they might miss something important. Once the machine was placed on the table and the small wheels began to roll, Tony carefully began the interview.

"Mrs. Teagan O'Toole, you have requested this interview with me, Detective Tony Breese and Detective Rachael Culpepper. Today is October 26th, 1978. Is that true?"

"Yes, Detective, it is."

"Before we begin, I want to inform you of your rights. You have the right to remain silent. Anything you say can be used against you in a court of law. You have the right to have an attorney present. If you cannot afford one, one will be appointed to you by the court. With these rights in mind, are you still willing to talk with me and have this conversation recorded?"

"I, Teagan O'Toole, understand these rights, and I am willing to give my statement at this time, without the presence of my lawyer and have it be committed to tape."

"Thank you, Mrs. O'Toole," said Tony, sitting back in the chair. Rachael had her murder book ready. She would need notes to refer to at a later date if this didn't turn out to be a blatant lie.

"What do you know about the Magdalen Houses?" Teagan asked, looking them straight in the eyes.

"I don't think I have ever heard of them," Rachael replied.

"They're workhouses run by nuns, full of unwed mothers."

"Workhouses?" questioned Tony. "Isn't that out of the nineteenth century? They don't have those anymore, do they?"

"They most certainly do, in Ireland. Laundries full of pregnant girls, working like slaves to wash away their sins. It was whispered about far and wide, but no one says how to stay out of them. When I was a girl, people didn't talk about sex. They swept it firmly under the rug and kept it there. If a girl got pregnant without the benefit of a husband, off she'd go.

"As sex education, my mother said one thing to me. I didn't understand what she had told me, but I don't fault her for it. She was as ignorant of the facts as me great grandmother before her."

Rachael knew what she meant. Her mother had been better because she provided pamphlets from the University Clinic.

"D'ya want to hear what she told me?"

"Yes, please tell us," Rachael answered.

"What e'er you do, don't let him come inside you. Can you imagine that? Absurd it was to tell me that. A girl who's got her first period. Back then, with so many children around, we thought men with beer bellies were pregnant too."

Rachael nodded. Tony suppressed a laugh.

"I took the words and filed them away. 'Twas me Mum being her sad self. She lived in depression. I was the oldest girl of her eleven children. There was a gap of nearly five years twixt me and me brother James. He was away at University by me teens, so I wandered unarmed down the road of love. Ignorant, I was. Not a hint of sex education at school. No birth control allowed—even the library was forbidden to have books about human sexuality, but all the animal husbandry ya could imagine.

Blindly, I dated. I went through the nice guys first; then I found Declan. He worked in a shop. Why, he could've passed for Errol Flynn. He had all the right words, talking marriage, and then America."

"He became the cause of me troubles. I thought we were in love, daft girl I was. I decided I was going to live my life with him. So, on me eighteenth birthday, I decided to give him me most precious gift… my virginity."

"He assured me he'd take care of everything. He'd get a raincoat or a Spanish letter or whatever they called condoms back then for safety. We'd go into his brother's cottage where we'd have the finery of a proper bed. I thought we'd roll around, kissing and hugging until we got a faraway look like I'd seen in the movies."

Tony covered his mouth to hide his reaction as he wondered if any of his girlfriends had ever thought sex that mysterious. Mrs. O'Toole paused for a sip of water before continuing her story.

"Well, when we got there, he guided me straight into the bedroom. He kissed me a couple of times, and then started undressing me. His hands under my skirt felt like electric shocks. With me skirt and panties in a puddle at my feet, I must have looked stunned. He laughed. I thought it cruel because I'd never heard any laughing in the love scenes of the movies."

Tony opened his mouth to ask where this was going, but Rachael shook her head. She knew this was something Mrs. O'Toole would never say again.

"I clung to my blouse and bra like they were a plate of armor. He didn't care; he let me have me false security. He pushed me back on the bed. I closed me eyes, tried to relax, but it felt like he was ripping me in two. I howled like a banshee, pushing him off as soon as I could. I'd lost my virginity, but it hadn't been fun. I cried; he cussed because of the bloody sheet. Once we parted company that day, I never saw him again.

"That is how I came to live with the Maggy's. Two skipped periods, a bit of weight gain, a nice dark line down me belly. 'Twas all me mother needed to diagnose. She called the doctor to the house. He told mother I was 'with child' and offered to put things right. The next morning, I was bundled off to the Magdalen's, to be hidden away until the baby was born. It was wretched. They forbade us to talk while we worked. They called us sluts, whores and wantons. We had to work hard as any man in the steam and heat of their commercial laundry as their coffers swelled big as our bellies from the fees they collected. We washed every stitch in Dublin. I give me father credit. He sent me to college as soon as they told him the baby was born. I graduated high in the class; got a job in London. By the time I was twenty-five, I transferred to America. Never looked back. I met Timothy. He was Irish enough to fall in love with, American enough not to give a hang about my past. He never stopped making love to me, even when I was a basket case about sex and the miscarriages I had.

Cara was me greatest miracle. She proved God still loved me, because He let me have her despite the mistakes I made."

Teagan O'Toole looked at the copious notes Rachael was taking in her book. With a deep breath, she pulled out the chair, sat down and started talking to Rachael.

"Detective Culpepper, do you have any idea what it is like? To grow up in a good Catholic family, where the father always takes care of things?"

"Yes, I do Mrs. O'Toole," answered Rachael. "My father was a cop and a Catholic."

"Timothy wanted to send Cara to a place in Michigan, but when I looked it up, can you imagine what I found?"

"That it was an abortion clinic?"

"Heaven's no, he's a good Catholic boy, my Timmy. What he found was a Magdalen House. Here in the States! I couldn't believe they'd spread their tentacles across the ocean. How could I trust your nuns to be any different from mine?

So, I ranted, raved, screamed and cried. Finally, he let me have my way about it. That's me Timothy, he never denies me anything. She married Dillon, left college before she'd even begun and was made to come here for bed rest until she had the babies. It was God's way of torturing us both for our transgressions.

"She thought Dillon was in love with her. Pity is, the love she saw wasn't for her. I guess because there were the three of them, she couldn't see his eyes were for Lee, not her.

"She thinks if they get some money, everything will be all right. They'll get a big house, live happily ever after, like me and her dad. I know better.

"The first time I found Dillon and Lee sneaking around, I was angry, but I didn't say anything. I hoped it was a final fling. A way of getting Lee out of his system once and for all. But, I saw them again and again and again.

"Worse yet, other people began to tell me they'd seen them, too. I wrote down the times and the places. It was too much.

"I called Lee at work, put on me best Australian accent, told her she'd won a weekend getaway. All she had to do was pick up the vouchers at the travel agency at 107th Street and Western. My girlfriend Chris owns it, and I've got her emergency key. I accommodated Little Miss Lee by opening at seven on a Sunday morning."

"So, you lured her there to kill her?" Tony asked.

"'Twasn't my intention," she replied.

"What did you think would happen when you confronted her?" Rachael asked.

"That she would take my offer, have a last fling, and go about her business."

"What was the offer?" asked Tony.

"Luxury weekend at the Playboy Club in Lake Geneva plus a tidy sum every month, enough to pay her rent in Amberly Court down in Midlothian. She'd signed a lease under the name D. Lee Whelan."

"How did you know that?" asked Rachael, looking up from her notes.

"I've a friend in the rental office. She called me to ask if Dillon's brother had recently married. The girl said her husband was working out of state so he couldn't do the application himself. I knew from the first name exactly what she was planning. A love nest."

"Couldn't she be planning on being on her own, away

from her mother?" asked Tony.

"Not by saying her former address was in Hegewisch at 4110 E. 107th Street. There're no houses on the east side of Avenue A. Only powerlines, the Skyway, rabbits, and ducks."

Rachael and Tony were beginning to understand, but they needed more details of the actual act for the confession to be admissible.

"All right, so tell us, what happened when she arrived." Tony said.

"I left the doors unlocked, but I waited in the loo. Ya should've seen her face when I walked out. She curled her lips like a mad cur."

"Why didn't she leave?" asked Rachael.

"Greed kept her there. I offered her the tickets if she would hear me out."

"And did she listen?" asked Tony.

"Aye, she did. At first, she was calm. I told her I'd seen her and Dillon parked at the hotels. I asked her to leave Cara and the babies alone. She laughed."

"Is that when you hit her?" asked Tony, intently.

"No, frankly I was stunned. She went on about how she hated me for making Cara marry Dillon. How I should have kept her and the babies because he loved her, not my Cara. I told her I couldn't agree more. She laughed again. Right in my face. Can you imagine? The cheek of the girl.

"She said there'd be no leaving him alone. I was getting to where I couldn't take one more word from her filthy lying mouth. The more she talked, the madder I got. But I still wasn't thinking murder. I pushed the tickets at her. I wanted her to get out, to run through the front door. I was going to have to think of something else to break them up."

"Did she push back? Strike out at you?" Rachael asked.

"No, she didn't. Her body gave her away. Her anger melted into shock, and she doubled over, clutching her belly. She grabbed me hanky off the desk, covered her mouth and ran to the loo. That's when it all became clear. The two-bedroom apartment, taking his last name, the puking. She was knocked up.

"She'd made a dog's dinner out of everyone's life. I was so angry I couldn't see straight. There she was with her blonde hair, on her knees, head in the toilet. That was when I hit her over her head with the stapler. She hit the floor with a thump. She wasn't breathing. But she still had an imp's grin on her face. I saw a razor lying in the window washer's bucket. I made sure no one would see that crooked tooth grin ever again."

Teagan O'Toole closed her eyes, remembering the moment. Her body relaxed in the chair ever so slightly, the burden of the deed lifted from her. The detectives wondered if she was finished as she began speaking again.

"Ya see, most people have no clue of my strength. They don't know what lugging six-stone bags of dirty laundry as a Maggy does for a girl. I rolled in the empty garbage can, laid it on the floor, and pushed her in. Dumped old newspapers and brochures atop of her, and rolled her out to the alley with the lid on. I wiped up and locked the office. I knew this little soap opera would be finished as soon as I was rid of her pesky car.

"I drove her MG out to the woods—the real thick ones west of the fast byway off 107th Street. I saw a sigh saying McMahon Fen, so I turned in. It was a good Irish place to leave her English car. I drove to the end of the asphalt, around a painted stump and down the gravel path. I tried to get all the way to the slough, but somethin' deep in the mud stopped me. 'Twas good luck that the color blended in so nicely.

"I passed a church walking down the road to Moraine Valley College. They rang their bells from the moment my feet were past the grassy woods 'til I walked up to the door of the college. It felt like absolution.

"I found a phone to call Tim. I said Betty and her daughter stranded me. Said the daughter turned her ankle bad. Knowing how I hate a hospital, quick he came. He's always me rescue. He let you cart him off to jail, knowing all the time that he didn't do it but that I probably did.

"Ya see, I wanted my Cara to have a chance. With Lee dead, if Dillon has one ounce of love for her, it would now have a chance to bloom. And if he doesn't, she'll leave him and come here to live with me and her Dad. She'll make a new life for herself and the twins."

Teagan O'Toole held out her wrists, prepared to be cuffed.

"Shall we get on now? I've a nice lawyer cooling his heels, waiting for me call."

Rachael and Tony moved from their seats, flanking her. Taking a set of cuffs from her belt, Rachael placed them around the extended wrists and closed them gently with a muted snap.

Tony firmly took her elbow as he announced that she was under arrest for the murder of Leivald Nabb. She smiled at him. He nodded sympathetically.

"Detective Breese, did ya e'er think a Welshman such as yourself would be taking a lass such as me down to the county gaol for murder?"

Linking his arm around hers, he patted her arm, resorting to his best brogue to answer her.

"Ne'er in a thousand years, Mrs. O'Toole."

The End

CPSIA information can be obtained
at www.ICGtesting.com
Printed in the USA
LVHW111745190919
631610LV00004B/748/P

9 781732 534803